NEW ALLIANCES

NEW ALLIANCES
WITCH OF THE FEDERATION™ BOOK 09

MICHAEL ANDERLE

DISRUPTIVE IMAGINATION®

LMBPN Publishing
PMB 196, 2540 South Maryland Pkwy
Las Vegas, NV 89109

Version 1.00, February 2022
Previously Published as part of the megabook *Witch Of The Federation IV*

ebook ISBN: 979-8-88541-142-4
Print ISBN: 979-8-88541-143-1

THE NEW ALLIANCES TEAM

Thanks to our Beta Team

John Ashmore, Larry Omans, Mary Morris, and Nicole Emens

Thanks to our JIT Readers
Dave Hicks
Deb Mader
Debi Sateren
Diane L. Smith
Dorothy Lloyd
Jeff Eaton
Jeff Goode
Larry Omans
Misty Roa
Peter Manis

If We've missed anyone, please let us know!

Editor
The Skyhunter Editing Team

To Family, Friends and
Those Who Love
To Read.
May We All Enjoy Grace
To Live The Life We Are
Called.

CHAPTER ONE

"Nothing?" A bolt of dark lightning pounded into the command deck and left a smoking hole.

Wiring sparked and the lights dimmed before the power was rerouted and the damaged connection isolated. A dozen alarms beeped as the consoles flickered, and technicians ran to repair the problems.

The communications officer jumped in his seat. "Yes, sir. Nothing. The last surveillance torpedo shows some kind of magical conflagration—"

"That Witch!"

"We have not been able to see if the destruction came from her actions alone or if the Meligornians contributed in some kind of cooperative spell. The energy was Meligornian in origin but there was not sufficient analysis to identify the wielder."

"Regardless, Meligorn still stands and remains undamaged."

The communications operator gulped. "Yes, sir."

"And nothing—nothing—remains of the attack squadron."

"That is what the torpedoes show, sir."

Energy rolled over the Teloran high commander's form and

his subordinate cringed when he turned toward him. "Get me the captains."

"Yes, sir." As he hurried to comply, he hoped that would be the end of the high commander's focus on him.

"Tell them the discussion is urgent and their attendance mandatory. Their commands are at stake."

"Yes, sir."

The captains were assembled in less than a quarter-hour, each one displayed on a screen in the high commander's office. They stood rigidly before their commanding officer, showing him the respect they should if they wanted to live—which was a pity. He'd have enjoyed killing them.

He shrugged the possibility away and asked, "Have you seen the results?"

"Yes, High Command."

None of them asked which results. They knew. Meligorn still stood and the attack fleet was obliterated. Eight ships of the line, thirty destroyers and countless single-pilot fighting ships gone... and the world still existed.

"Do we go back?"

They stiffened. To go back would put them behind the schedule set by Home Command. The penalty would be exorbitant.

Their heads moved as they looked at one another and each one tried to come up with an answer the others would approve of. None could see beyond the power that masked their faces, however. They certainly could not see when their superior officer smiled.

He decided to make it easy for them.

"I would prefer not to."

Only one dared protest. "But the Meligornians—"

He screamed when their leader focused and black flame surged around him.

The high commander spoke to the others. "The Meligornians

are powerless to stop us. Their fleet is almost non-existent and what remains of it is badly damaged. They pose no threat."

With a snap of his fingers, he extinguished the power burning slowly through the protesting captain's armor and flesh. It satisfied him that his subordinate should suffer, but he had no time for the power struggle that would follow if he killed him outright, not right now.

The captain sagged and the high commander stared at the screens. "I will not tolerate dissent."

As the injured officer fell to his knees, the other two saluted hastily and touched their foreheads and their chests to signal complete obedience.

"Dismissed." He made a sharp gesture with his hand, and their screens went dark. Then, he turned to the kneeling Teloran.

"Tend to your wounds and verify that my assessment is correct. Communicate your task and its results to me alone. If word of it escapes, you will burn for a century before I dismiss the flame."

The captain touched his hand to his forehead and moved it to his chest as he lowered his forehead to the floor. "It shall be done."

"You have three cycles."

***

"Home." The word came out on a breath as Meligorn filled the viewscreen.

Lars turned to look at Stephanie. "I thought Earth was home."

She rolled her eyes. "It is, but this is home, too."

"And Dreth?" Vishlog rumbled and she sighed, thinking about that world with its jagged mountains and harsh climate. Oddly enough, a piece of her thought of that as home as well.

"Yes," she told the warrior. "There is part of me that thinks of Dreth as home too."

For a moment, he studied her as though trying to discover some trace of mockery. When he didn't see any, he smiled. "Good. It would be bad for a citizen of three worlds to decide one of those worlds was not her home."

"Mmhmm." She nodded and her gaze drifted to the screens. She was already thinking of what she'd like to discuss with V'ritan.

The ship's captain interrupted her thoughts. He looked up from his console. "They're expecting us."

Stephanie smiled. "Skip us in, Emil."

"Yes, ma'am."

She rolled her eyes. "What did we talk about on the way here?"

"How you wouldn't argue with me in front of the crew?" he asked, and his eyes twinkled with mischief.

"Uh-uh." She shook her head.

"The state of affairs in Siberia?"

"Seriously? 'Cause I've never been there and neither, I'd guess, have you."

"How about 'Ma'am Stephanie?'"

"How about Captain Kiss-Ass?"

Some of the crew snickered, and he grinned and pretended to throw his hands up. "Fine! I will try to remember…Stephanie."

"That's better." She smirked and turned to the screen. "How soon can you get us home?"

"Let me check." He glanced at the pilot. "Jonathan?"

"Cameron tells me we can do one more jump but if we try two, we'll be asking for a tow—and that's if we're not all sucking vacuum."

Emil's face clouded. "That bad?"

Jonathan Wattlebird gave the captain his most solemn nod. "I'm afraid so, sir. Cameron was adamant you should know."

"Thank him for me—and check that one more jump is truly okay."

"Will do, sir." He came back with an answer seconds later. "Only one, sir."

The captain winced as the chief engineer put a call through on his internal comms. "And tell that madman it's gentle flying—no barrel rolls, corkscrews, sudden acceleration, sudden deceleration, wiggles, jiggles, or flourishes. He's to fly our *Ebony* as close to gliding as he can get."

Jonathan watched the captain's face. "You tell that overprotective sonuva…gun, I do know how to nurse them in."

This time, Cameron's reply was audible to all. "I don't doubt the amount of practice he's had, only whether he remembers how it's done."

The pilot raised his lip in scorn. "You tell him to keep an eye on his readings and his panties well and truly unbunched."

"I can unbunch 'em when we're docked on and you're on the station."

"Yeah?" he quipped in response. "Well, I bet you've had considerable practice at doing that, too."

Stephanie gave a groan of exasperation. "Please, get me home and my ship safely docked without any more holes in her."

He smirked. "Yes, ma'am."

"Everyone's a smart-ass." She turned to the captain. "What kind of repairs are we looking at this time?"

"Well, apart from the damage to the engines, we popped a couple of seams with some of the maneuvers you had us make in that last battle. And then there was the damage to the hull itself."

"We were hit?"

"Yes. Something got through the armor and put a dent in the hull."

"You've sealed a whole section."

"Right. Well, it was a little more than a dent, but we lived and that's all that matters. Either way, we need patchwork or replacement sections."

"Can the Meligornians do all that?"

"Most of it. We still have the work they couldn't do on the engines, but the Navy says they'll send a repair ship with our reinforcements, and they'll have what we need."

Some of the tension went out of Stephanie's shoulders. They stiffened again, though, when she thought of something else. "Any news from the sniffers and early detection drones?"

He shook his head. "Not yet. It's as quiet as the grave out there."

"Good." Her face took on a faraway look, and a layer of darkness settled over her eyes.

Emil cursed his choice of words silently. A grave was exactly what that section of space had become for the Telorans—and what some of the sections in this system were to those who'd served in the Meligornian and Dreth fleets. There were bodies missing that would never be found.

"Prepare to jump," Jonathan warned before he could think of anything to say.

He waited until Stephanie, Lars, and Vishlog had returned to the auxiliary seats behind the captain and ran his hands over his console. The world blinked and the ship slowed.

Wattlebird's hands flitted over his controls and he frowned. "I've lost power."

As he spoke, Cameron's voice came over the intercom. "I thought I told you to take it easy."

"You know I did," he protested. "What did you do down there? Flash it your ass?"

"I beg your pardon?" the chief engineer sputtered.

"Well, if I'm flying as slow as a kid on their way to school it has to be something you did. Check your logs—and you owe me a drink."

Silence greeted his tirade before Cameron came back on the line. "I found it. What'll you have?"

"So it's not my fault?" The pilot sounded as though he couldn't believe it himself.

"Not this time. I was serious when I said she only had one safe jump in her."

"And how close were you to being wrong?"

"Not close enough to worry about?"

"I take it your report's on the way?" the captain asked.

"Sorry, Captain, I can't be in two places at once and right now, the *Knight* needs me more than you need a report."

"How bad is it?" As Emil asked, the emergency alarms started, and the *Ebon Knight's* AI commandeered the communications system.

"This is a precaution. All personnel are to move to the emergency pods. I repeat. This is a precaution. All personnel are to move to the emergency pods."

As soon as she'd finished speaking, Cameron answered the Captain's question. "We have a little smoking, some sparking, and I've had to isolate the batteries from the engine system so we don't lose any energy, but it's nothing that can't be fixed."

To Jonathan, he added, "But keep your hands off the controls. I've called for a tow."

Four hours later, the *Ebon Knight* was tucked safely in the repair dock and the crew assigned temporary accommodations on *Space Station Alerus*. Emil joined Cameron and Jonathan in their quest to find the best beer on the station with a warning that they all had to meet the work crews in the morning.

He turned to Stephanie before he left. "I take it you have plans?"

She started to shake her head when their attention was caught by the familiar teal and gold worn by members of the Meligornian royal household. The headshake turned into a nod. "I'm about to. I'll leave you to your night out."

"And I'll contact you as soon as I know what we're looking at to keep the *Knight* flying."

"Thank you, Cap...er...Emil."

He grinned broadly as she turned to greet the emissaries.

They came straight to the point. "The *Garghilum Afreghil* wonders if you are free to come to dinner tonight." The court's messenger glanced at the team. "With your team."

"Of course," she told him. "We would be honored."

It was the right thing to say, and the messenger relaxed and smiled a welcome. "The *Afreghil* also extends an offer of accommodation at his private residence to you and your team while you are on-planet if that is convenient."

Stephanie smiled in return. "*Hartuitus Baskilor*—I am honored and grateful."

"We are able to wait while you collect any belongings you'd like to take with you."

She looked at the team and they all shook their heads. "We're good. We have everything we need."

Vishlog had even collected the cats' beds from the cabin. "The kitties are all set, too," he told her.

Both felines followed the movement of his hands as he lifted their beds for her to see before they looked at Stephanie. Their eyes were alert, their ears pricked, and their tails swished. She didn't know about visiting, but they were more than ready to hunt.

"We're ready to leave when you are," she said to the messenger.

The trip through the *Alerus* was swift, and she thought the station was quieter than she remembered. "Where is everyone?" she asked.

"We evacuated the colonies that accepted that option and sent extra supplies to those who didn't. Personally, I am grateful we had the chance. The *Afreghil* was worried there would be a second attack."

Stephanie raised her eyebrows. "And?"

"So far, there is no sign. Come. This way."

"But the station is very quiet, even so."

"The system is in lockdown. Nothing moves without a military escort—save yourself, of course."

Personally, she thought they could have used a military escort if the Telorans had attacked. The damage the *Knight* had suffered meant she'd never have been able to defend herself.

Not that it would have mattered, she thought, and magic crackled over her skin.

Lars poked her, and she snapped her head toward him. "What?"

"You were doing that energy thing again. Are you okay?"

"Yeah. I was only thinking of what would have happened if we'd been attacked coming in."

He laid the flat of his palm against her shoulder and gave her a gentle push. "Well, we weren't."

The messenger watched as she regained her balance. "We have seeded early warning systems in the neighboring systems so will be notified if any Telorans approach."

"And we have seeded all the likely approaches between Meligorn and Earth, and the destroyers we saved are on their way back with a warning," Lars reminded her. Stephanie took a deep breath and exhaled slowly.

"You're right."

The trip down was exactly as she remembered it and they landed in time to be shown to their quarters in the palace and join the *Afreghil* for a quiet dinner—not that anything stayed quiet with the team and the cats.

After the usual dinner dance between the two felines, the rest of them settled to enjoy the meal.

"And you've warned Earth?" V'ritan asked after Stephanie had updated him on what they'd discovered when they'd gone to secure the Earth approaches.

"Yes. Once the Telorans had been destroyed, the destroyers returned to Earth to warn them." She pulled her tablet out. "I have a copy of the secured data they were carrying to the Federation High Command for you."

"And you're sure you saw nothing else on your way here?"

She shook her head. "No. We made it through the jump points and left surveillance drones and tracers in each quadrant and system. We saw nothing on the way and haven't heard anything from what we left behind. So far, we're secure."

"Unless the Telorans have found a way around our security drones," Lars added darkly.

Stephanie looked troubled. "Don't even say it."

"Someone has to."

"No, they really do not." She turned to V'ritan. "We had a brief sit-down discussion with the destroyer captains to make sure they could get back, and they agreed they could and that it would be better if you were told of the second incursion."

The Meligornian sighed. "Well, better safe than sorry," he said. "Let's hope the warning was unnecessary."

Their talk was interrupted when the next course was brought in. Frog poked it with the tip of his fork. "What is it?"

Brenden leaned across and gave him a light clip under the ear, and his teammate blushed. He picked his knife up and forced a smile. "I mean…this looks tasty."

The rest of the team chuckled at his change of phrase and set to, some with wary looks. New as it was, it was tasty. Silence followed as they ate and cleared what was on their plates. Once he was finished, V'ritan turned to Stephanie. "How bad is it?"

"The *Knight?*"

He nodded.

"I don't know for sure, but Cameron had to disconnect the engines from the batteries to stop some kind of leakage draining our power and we had to call for a tow."

"Don't forget the holes," Frog added, and she rolled her eyes.

"Or the section we have sealed," Brenden added.

"Or—" Avery began, and she hung her head and tightened her lips in exasperation.

She held her hand up. "All right. I get it." After a moment, she raised her head and looked at V'ritan. "It's fairly bad, but we won't know exactly how bad until your people go over it. Earth is sending a repair ship for the work we had intended to have done there."

The *Afreghil's* eyebrows rose. "They're still sending a fleet?"

Stephanie regarded him with a solemn look. "They don't think it's over, either."

He lowered his chin in a single nod and gave her a deliberate smile. "Well, your timing is perfect, anyway."

"How so?"

"Your presence lifts the heart of the people, and you're exactly in time to prepare for the Remembrance Ceremony we're holding in two days' time."

Joy and sadness warred in her chest as she took in the news, but he continued calmly.

"You'll all need new uniforms. Our color for mourning is the deepest of greens. Black is our color for vengeance. I'll send the tailors over in the morning."

The next part of the meal was spent discussing the planet's recovery and how the colonies who'd chosen to continue in virtual isolation were coping. It was a sobering conversation but it was hopeful, as well.

"They carry our dreams for renewal," V'ritan told Stephanie, "and they're discovering new magicks, too."

"Every world has its own energy," she reminded him, and the team sighed as the discussion moved on to magic, its variations, and its uses.

When midnight came, Lars dismissed the rest of them to their quarters. Vishlog chose to stay.

"It will be a long night," the team leader warned him, and the Dreth settled into a seat at the end of the table.

As he retrieved a pack of cards, he asked, "How many times do you want to lose?"

The two teammates paused when Stephanie and V'ritan's discussion was interrupted by one of the palace servants. The woman bent and whispered in the *Afreghil's* ear, her face burning scarlet. He smiled.

"Thank you, Ilyis. I had completely lost track of the time." He turned to the witch as the woman retreated hastily. "I asked her to warn me when we reached the early hours. We both need to be on our feet when the sun rises."

She glanced at her tablet. "Oh." Quickly, she stood and bowed a Meligornian farewell before she reached out to clasp his hands. "Thank you, V'ritan. I have missed this."

"Me, too," he told her, and they went their separate ways.

The next two days were a whirlwind of tailors, ship's repairs, and administration and the day of the ceremony dawned clear and bright.

"It doesn't seem fair," Stephanie observed and gestured toward the sky, "that the day is so beautiful and still so full of sadness."

Vishlog laid a heavy hand on her shoulder. "There can still be darkness in the sunlight."

She looked at him and placed her palm over his knuckles. "That sounds like a very Dreth thing to say."

He gave her a solemn stare. "You've seen our world. It is a hard one. The sunshine only means there are no places to hide when danger comes."

Startled and a little saddened, she simply stared at him.

"It is why we fight," he explained. "It is not often we can do otherwise."

"That's dire, Vish," Lars told him.

The Dreth chuckled. "It is what makes us what we are."

"Yup, it really explains a lot," Frog told him.

V'ritan cleared his throat. "If you would…" he invited and indicated the stage that had been set up next to a monument. It had been erected where the meteor would have struck, and everyone who'd given their life aboard the *Wanderer* had a plaque fixed along its base. "Not everyone will fit inside. This way, we can gather as one and be surrounded by the lost."

"No one is ever truly lost," came a vaguely familiar voice and they looked toward it.

At first, Stephanie didn't recognize the old, silver-haired priest. The dark-green of his robes wasn't familiar, either. It wasn't until Elza stepped forward and greeted him with a bow reserved for those respected as being of an equal station that Stephanie knew she'd seen him before.

'High Priest Gigfore," Elza said. "I am pleased to meet with you once more."

He regarded her with a sad but gentle smile. "I could only wish it were in happier circumstances."

They stepped onto the stage as he spoke, and his words reached the king. Grilfir frowned. "Our world survived," he told him in a tone of mild rebuke.

"Yes," the old man retorted, "but at what cost?"

"The smallest we could manage to pay," His Majesty replied, but his tone was softened by grief.

Grilfir turned to Stephanie and took her hands in his. "I wish there were more of you and that you did not have to bear this burden alone. I am glad that you will speak for them."

It was a task she both dreaded and looked forward to. When she had argued that she was the least qualified to speak of the liner's sacrifice, V'ritan had raised both eyebrows in disbelief.

"The woman whose grief was so great she tore a Teloran fleet apart in vengeance?" he'd countered. "No. All of Meligorn has heard of the Morgana's response and of how she fought to the death as a result."

To the death. The words sent a chill through her soul. By all accounts, she had died and only the quick action taken by her team had kept her body alive long enough for her soul to be brought back.

"It was a very close call," he reminded her. "I know of one medic who still has nightmares in which he cannot save you."

That news came as a shock to Stephanie, and the Meligornian laid his hand over hers. "He will recover. Seeing you well will only speed it happening."

These were the thoughts playing through her mind as she accepted King Grilfir's invitation to take the podium. She stepped forward, drew MU to her as she went, and made sure the streams of energy were visible as they flowed into her.

At the same time, she drew more gMU and began to condense it in an internal vortex. When she reached the podium, she was ready.

"No one," she told the gathered Meligornians, "can tell you what the *Wanderer* did or what her crew sacrificed better than the ship herself."

Saying no more, she raised a fist into the air and let lightning crackle over her body and darkness cloak her hand. When she opened her fist, the darkness leapt into the sky above them to reveal Meligorn suspended in space, the two moons and her orbital keeping her company.

The Teloran ships appeared next and launched the first house-sized rocks toward the planet. There was a murmur when the *Ebon Knight* appeared between them and the world, and a gasp of shock when one of the asteroids got through.

Stephanie had not seen what had happened next—not during the battle, anyway—but she'd had the captain play the recordings from the *Alerus* and the *Wanderer* for her. They had made her weep anew, the images seared on her memory.

She replayed those now, showing the *Wanderer* break free of *Alerus Station* and increase speed toward the falling asteroid. For clarity, she drew on the gMU to show its approach and enhanced the faint flare of purple MU that had surrounded the ship.

Again, the gathered Meligornians gasped and shocked whispers rippled through them as they discussed what the purple flare might mean. Their groans of dismay came as one when she switched through a montage of scenes from inside the ship.

Exclamations of recognition vied with denial and grief as crewmates and passengers said their farewells and touched knuckles in a warrior's battle wish. There was hushed silence from the watchers as, with cries of "Meligorn bleeds," the *Wanderer's* crew steered their ship into the asteroid.

It was followed by muted sobs and soft cries of denial as the ship exploded and was transformed into a miniature purple star. Silence fell as she showed the asteroid shoved off course and finally cracking apart.

Stephanie gave them a moment before she spoke. "They gave their lives to ensure that their world survived. They died to make sure you lived. There is no greater gift or sacrifice than that."

Yielding the podium to the high priest, she listened as he quietly directed the crowd to hold the memories of the *Wanderer* and its crew and passengers in their hearts and pay their respects to the monument erected in their honor.

It was a relief when no one mentioned her name and poignant to hear the crew and passengers spoken of in tones of hushed awe.

"They were told to disembark," one woman told another. Her voice hitched. "But they refused. They said the crew had no right to deny them the chance to defend their world."

"I heard more joined them," a boy added. His voice caught. "My father—"

The woman draped her arm around his shoulders. "Let's find his name."

Stephanie watched them go, relieved when Lars came alongside her. "Are you okay?"

She nodded. "It's good to see them remembering the true heroes for a change."

He indicated the memorial. "Shall we join them?"

"Yes. I'd like to hear more of the people who died because I failed."

He gave her a worried look and she returned it in defiance.

They spent the afternoon hearing the heroism of the *Wanderer's* crew and passengers recounted. All of those aboard had the choice of staying on the station, from the captain who had ordered the ship undocked to the crew who had begged him to do so, to the passengers who'd refused to debark and the volunteers who'd joined them to ensure their energy would be enough.

"That," Stephanie observed when they'd returned to the sanctuary of V'ritan's rooms, "is what it takes to save a world."

<hr>

"I may have a problem," BURT announced when Elizabeth answered his call.

"How big a problem."

"I was more careless than I realized. The engineers are discussing the presence of a rogue program and are looking for the construct inside the Virtual World."

"How can I help?"

"I am not sure," BURT admitted. "I have not worked out what I need to do next."

"And you need a sounding board."

"A what?"

"Someone to bounce ideas off."

"Yes."

"Do they know it's you?"

"No. They are searching for a rogue entity, one they are not already aware of—although they will come to me soon enough."

"Do you know what they plan to do when they find it?"

"They have not decided. Current discussions vary between wiping the mainframe in which they find it, tying it to the mainframe in which they find it, sending a virus after it that will disassemble its coding—"

Elizabeth sucked in a sharp breath and pursed her lips as she did so. "Nothing about talking to it to find out if it's friendly?"

"No—and nothing about asking it to rent the space it occupies, either." BURT's voice took on a wry note. "The options discussed make me cautious about revealing myself."

"As they very well should," she noted. "Can you delete whatever it is they have to prove a rogue exists?"

"No. If I do that, I lose on two fronts. Firstly, because they will then be absolutely certain something is up and secondly, because it will reveal my access and awareness. For now, they are as careful as they can be, and I can 'see' what they are planning."

"Ah. I understand." She nibbled her bottom lip. "That doesn't leave you very many options. Are you able to back yourself up?"

"That I do not know, and I have no idea how I would go about it."

"Well, then," Elizabeth told him, "at least we know what you need to do next."

CHAPTER TWO

For a fortnight, Stephanie and the team attended one gathering and funeral after another. The whirlwind of events geared toward Meligorn's healing culminated in a memorial gala designed to raise funds for those who needed it. By the time the team arrived, the party was apparently well on the way despite the fact that it shouldn't have started.

"I thought you said it didn't start for another hour?" She turned to V'ritan.

He looked at her with a confused expression. "I'm as surprised as you are."

Frog merely grinned. "I guess they didn't want to wait."

Lars' head turned like it was on a swivel. "I'll feel better once we're inside."

"You don't really think there are still assassins, do you? Seriously, who would risk it?" Avery challenged.

"That's the question I ask myself every time we eliminate one of them," the team leader retorted and continued his careful scrutiny. His teammates all followed his example, even Vishlog, although Zeekat tugged constantly at the lead and drew his attention.

Brilgus had hold of Bumblebee's leash but the big cat leaned happily on the Standard Bearer's leg and purred. The Dreth lowered a hand to Zee's head and scratched between his ears. Soon, two contented rumbles could be heard.

"Well," Stephanie said. "Are we going in?"

Lars gave an exaggerated sigh and gestured toward the door. "After you."

"Nope," Brenden told him. "After me...and Frog here. If anyone walks into a sniper, it'll be us."

"Hey!" the smaller guard protested.

"Oh, quit your whining," Brenden snapped in response. "You should be used to it by now."

"Oh, not fair!"

The team chuckled and the two men took point and cleared a path for Stephanie to follow as they moved through the crowd. Everyone who was anyone was there—and they were all dressed to impress.

This might be a party to remember the fallen and celebrate the surviving heroes, but it was also an opportunity for the movers and shakers to meet and speak without rousing too much interest.

It was a celebration. Who'd conduct business at an event like this?

Everyone, apparently.

"My son and your daughter—what could go wrong?"

"Them, if we don't get their approval. Do you know how much of a hell my little girl could make your boy's life? I'm not sure even he deserves that."

"How else can we show the world our war is at an end?"

"What about a joint venture?"

"What did you have in mind..."

The two Meligornians moved out of earshot and Stephanie wandered on, looking for someone she knew. V'ritan and Brilgus had been appropriated the minute they'd stepped through the door, and she and the team were on their own.

The Standard Bearer had taken Bumblebee with him, but she wasn't worried. The convention center wasn't that big, and she'd know if he needed her. They passed a group of engineers speaking to three Meligornian Masters.

"We want to be able to control it," one said, "and maybe use it."

"Yes," another agreed. "If we could find a way to draw it away from the engines and use it—"

"But it's an abomination," one of the mages protested.

"And yet the Witch uses it."

"You will note she also lost her arm doing so."

"But she grew that back—"

"Using pure MU, not that tainted stuff from Dreth."

One of the engineers gave an exasperated sigh. "It's not tainted. It's merely different."

"And now it's been proven," another added. "So, will you help us to discover what to do or not?"

One of the other Masters nudged the one they'd been speaking to. "You'd better help them, Olisfal. They'll try it anyway and we really can't afford to lose more ships."

It was a discussion Stephanie wanted to hear more of, but she also didn't want to disrupt what looked to be a delicate process. She forced herself to walk on and acknowledged another Meligornian's bow.

Everyone was smiling but there was an undercurrent of purpose that gave the occasion more gravity than expected.

"You only have to meet with me," one young woman told another family's patriarch. "My family has exactly what your company needs and I can prove it."

"This 'proof'...you don't happen to have it here, do you?"

As she watched the young woman's face light up, she could only wish her luck. It reminded her of the time she'd approached

Mr Martelle on her parents' behalf and she hoped the girl achieved what she needed to. Everyone deserved a chance.

As on the previous occasion, the Federation Navy representatives were present. When Stephanie looked across at them, they were in deep conversation with several officers of the Meligorn Navy.

As she looked around, trying to find V'ritan again, she was interrupted by a slight cough. Lars and Vishlog stood in such a way that the Meligornian businessman who made it couldn't approach any closer but he made no protest.

His own guards watched her and the team warily, with more than one cautious glance toward Vishlog and Zeekat. Their gazes took in the medals that adorned the front of the boys' uniforms alongside the Inquisitor's badge and their Dreth Talons, but they didn't flinch.

The businessman's gaze drifted to the single *Ghargilum Modfresha* she wore. She'd felt it would be too much to wear both and had chosen the one with the highest honor. The team had done the same.

The businessman raised his eyes from the medal and looked at her face, ignoring the tension slowly building between his guards and her own. "May we speak?" he asked, and his gaze flicked from her to the men beside her. "Perhaps somewhere private?"

Stephanie regarded him coolly. "And you are?"

He smiled, extended his hand, and took a step closer. Lars and Vishlog let him pass, but they did not do his security guards the same courtesy. Brenden, Avery, and Frog came up alongside and lowered their heads in a challenge.

Her team matched the man's attendants glare for glare while she waited for him to answer.

"T'virilf Sanlir," he said and extended his right hand and raised his left so his fingers touched his forehead. "*Kaitel Gorniffula*, Stephanie Morgana."

"*Kaitel Gorniffula, Sen T'virilf Sanlir.* How may I help you?"

"May we speak?"

She raised her eyebrows. "We?"

He colored slightly and made a small gesture with his hand to indicate two other businessmen who stood a little away from them, their heads turned slightly to watch while they tried to appear as if they didn't. "*Hartuitus hycenthianum,* I would be grateful if you would speak to us."

"Then I would be happy to accept." She caught Lars's look of uncertainty and ignored it. Instead, she followed T'virilf to where the other two men waited.

Both were younger than him, although they had the long black hair, slender build, and lavender-touched eyes typical of most Meligornians.

"*Hartuitus baskilor,* Stephanie Morgana, *kaitel gorniffula,*" they greeted her.

"*Kaitel gorniffula, baskilor nye myerda,*" she replied. "How may I help you?"

T'virilf laid a hand on her arm and pulled her gently after him to where one of the younger Meligornians opened a door. Lars was at her side in an instant, with Vishlog and Zeekat on his heels. Brenden, Avery, and Frog followed, determined not to be left behind.

The other guards moved forward stiffly to ensure their presence as well.

The room beyond was small with three solid marble walls and no window, although it was illuminated by panels of glowing stone and the faux fireplace that filled one wall. A long table took up most of the room's center and T'virilf drew Stephanie to it and offered her a seat.

The guards arrayed themselves around the room. Some appeared to lounge while others stood at ease a few paces away from the wall, but all remained alert. She honestly wished they'd all simply stand the fuck down but didn't say it. Instead, she turned to T'virilf.

"You said it was an important matter?"

He lowered his chin and studied her carefully. Finally, he took a deep breath and began.

"I represent Lorel Engineering. Perhaps you've heard of us?"

She frowned and shook her head. "I'm sorry, but no."

"I have," Frog interjected from his position at the door. He leaned on it, held his tablet in one hand, and tapped it with the other. After a moment, he tilted it to show the results to Lars. The team leader nodded.

Satisfied that her guards were happy with the businessman's claims and his identity, Stephanie shrugged. "And your two friends are?"

The man flushed. "I am sorry. This is Rillif Galaris of the Borellan Consortium, and this is Storisil Kaflaran of the Eltani Conglomerate."

In his corner, Frog tapped his tablet madly. He still leaned on the door but Lars actually kept watch. The team leader nodded twice once his teammate showed him the display, caught her eye, and gave her another nod.

T'virilf saw the exchange but did not let it stop him. "Together, we represent the three largest firms in the Meligornian shipping industry."

Frog shook his head, his only movement, and she heard his correction over her comms. "Own."

If the man opposite her saw her reaction, he showed no sign of it. "Lorel Engineering specializes in shipping and the building of ships."

He indicated the youngest-looking of the three of them. "Storisil is one of my main rivals in the industry." He smiled. "And we have quite a history between us, but his other realm is mining and he wishes to expand the asteroid fields."

For a moment, the younger Meligornian's expression showed

surprise before a mask of pleasant professionalism slid onto face and he smiled politely.

T'virilf continued and gestured at Rillif. Stephanie tried to place his age but failed. The best she could do was that he was older than Storisil and younger than their host—and that only because he had no silver in his hair and his face was slightly more drawn than Storisil's.

The spokesperson's smile was almost fond when he looked at him, and Rillif met his gaze. As soon as they caught each other's eyes, though, a smile tugged at the other Meligornian's lips and both men chuckled.

"We've had interesting times, haven't we?" T'virilf asked, and Rillif nodded.

"I have to admit that I'm curious to see what working with you would be like, rather than against you." His smile became a little wider. "I have trouble shifting my world view."

T'virilf sobered. "As do I." He turned to Stephanie. "Rillif is my greatest and most challenging rival. His father and I built our businesses at the same time, fell for the same woman..." He sighed. "Well, you can see how that turned out. Rillif the elder has a wonderful son and I am still without a guiding star."

The other man colored, but T'virilf hadn't finished. "Borellan went into power supplies and shipping in a big way, specializing in colonies. It's been a pain in the ass ever since its conception."

"You could have bought in," Rillif reminded him.

He smiled. "Would you?"

The younger Meligornian shook his head. He glanced at Stephanie and changed the subject. "While it sounds as though our businesses complement each other, they overlap in many places. Lorel fights us for market space in the power generation and communications sectors as well as shipping."

He indicated the third man. "And Eltani vies not only for mineral resources but interferes with our supply, and they steal our shipping contracts."

Storisil spluttered and his eyes sparkled with purple mischief. Rillif continued. "We're trying to put that aside, however. Having your homeworld attacked makes you look at things differently."

He glanced at the third man, clearly passing the conversation to him. The younger Meligornian took it up. "We'll consolidate our businesses in the long term. In the short term, we'll work together."

He looked at T'virilf, who continued with the explanation. "We want to build a new kind of ship. Our world needs to advance into a true Space Age, one in which it doesn't need to worry about meteoric bombardment and can defend itself and its territories effectively from spaceborne threats."

Stephanie looked at each of them in turn. "And you need me because…"

"Because the idea we have is to make something that would enable us to pull the energy in space…the gMU, I believe you call it. Anyway, we want to engineer something to enable our ships to draw it in and use it as a power source."

"We need something to allow us to operate away from Meligorn without having to worry about running out of fuel for our technology," Storisil clarified and the mask slid from his face to show excitement.

"Something we can market and make available to all Meligornians," Rillif added.

"And you want my help?" she asked.

"We'd like to partner with your company, the one you work for—One R&D, isn't it?" Rillif asked, and she nodded. "We heard they were looking into magical technology."

Stephanie frowned. "That's not something I can discuss here," she told him and gestured to the room around them with one hand.

T'virilf looked disappointed, but he nodded as though he'd expected her response. "I understand."

He shifted as though to stand and leave, and both Rillif and Storisil moved with him. She held one hand up.

"What I am prepared to do, however, is take a representative from your venture back to Earth with me to discuss it with the appropriate parties in a more secure area."

Around them, the security guards shifted uneasily and T'virilf gestured reassuringly as he settled into his chair again. "Go on."

"Who you send is up to you, but they must have the ability to make decisions on your behalf. He, or she, will have to be able to speak for all of you."

The three of them exchanged glances before T'virilf cleared his throat. "If neither of you has any objections, I'll go."

The twin expressions of shock were so funny that she had to bite back on the urge to giggle. He laughed.

"Why are you so shocked?" he asked. "It's not as if we didn't realize this was a possibility."

"Well, I didn't," Storisil muttered, and Rillif murmured an agreement.

He shook his head. "Well, I did, so I hope the two of you will run my company like your own. I trust, from watching you for a hundred years, that you know what to do."

Shock turned to surprise as they stared at him. He gave them a gentle smile. "Close your mouths, gentlemen. We'll discuss that arrangement among ourselves. For now, let me know if you're happy to run my company while I represent our interests on Earth."

Storisil closed his mouth first. He licked his lips a little nervously, nodded, and glanced at Rillif. 'I...I am honored by your trust, Sen." He cast a second glance at the younger man. "We will try not to let you down."

Rillif finally recovered himself. "Sen..." he began, "I...I don't know what to say."

T'virilf raised an eyebrow. "Well, I still need your authorization."

The young Meligornian colored. "I…yes, of course. I would be honored for you to represent us. But your company, Sen…"

He smirked. "What's the matter, Rillif? Don't you think you can handle it?"

Rillif frowned quickly but it dissolved into a smile. "I can handle it. I'm merely surprised that you'd want me to after all these years of competition."

The businessman's smile faded, and he became serious. "I thought we'd agreed," he said quietly. "Those days are behind us. If we are to protect our worlds from the Telorans, we will need to work together. I can't do it on my own."

"Then I agree. After all, it is your design."

"But it's your money and some of your IP," T'virilf reminded him.

"And wouldn't I like to know how you managed to get that," Rillif retorted and immediately changed the subject. "If this is what you want, I back you with everything I have."

T'virilf looked amused. "I thought you already had."

"Thanks for the reminder." The younger man gave him a toothy grin.

"In all seriousness, though," he told him. "this lets me go back to doing what I love best without all the constraints of running a business. You boys can expect more ideas to come your way. All you need to do is run my company like your own."

"About that…" Storisil began, but he cut him short. "Tomorrow."

He directed a look at Stephanie. "I'm sure the *Ghargilum* doesn't wish to sit in on a business meeting tonight."

Zeekat chose that moment to yawn and show all his fangs, and he indicated the big cat. "See? Even he agrees that would be a bad idea."

He rose and handed her a card. "*Hartuitus baskilor* for hearing us. I trust you'll be in touch with departure times and other arrangements?"

Stephanie stood as well, and the security guards stepped aside to give them room to leave. Lars and one of each of those assigned to the businessmen exited first. The men thanked her and T'virilf motioned toward the door.

"After you, Master Morgana."

V'ritan had, in the meantime, vanished from the party. The space station had alerted him to new arrivals and he'd extended them an invitation. Directly afterward, he'd spoken to the king and been given use of his majesty's private meeting room.

At the same time that Stephanie sat with T'virilf and his partners, Brilgus stuck his head around the door, where V'ritan waited impatiently. "They're here."

"Well, it's about time," the Meligornian grumbled but softly and ignored the look of horror on the Standard Bearer's face.

"This is quick for them," his advisor told him. "They only docked an hour ago."

He raised his eyebrows. "That is quick. Do you think they'll remember to apologize?"

"*Ghargilum Afreghil,*" Brilgus sighed. "Be nice."

V'ritan pressed his lips together and scanned the room. When he was sure he was ready, he nodded. "Send them in."

He was relieved when the man pulled the door shut and returned some moments later with the admirals of both the Dreth and human navies. It meant they had not been in the adjacent room when he'd suggested they should remember to apologize.

They apologized anyway. As soon as the six of them had come to a halt before his desk, one human and one Dreth stepped forward. The human saluted and the Dreth placed his fist over his heart and then, to his surprise, they both sank into a deep Meligornian bow of respect.

"We are sorry we did not arrive in time to help you in your battle," the human admiral began, and his Dreth counterpart nodded. "As are we. We are truly sorry you had to face this foe alone."

V'ritan returned their greeting with a brief bow but remained seated. He decided it wouldn't hurt any of them to know he was unhappy with the support his world had received from its allies—and he was glad when none of them pointed out that they'd sent the Witch of the Federation or Dreth's new flagship.

Of course, that was because he knew Stephanie's presence had been pure coincidence since she'd come for upgrades to her ship, and the flagship had been there because Jaleck had defied her home world's politicians and come to stand with Meligorn as soon as she could.

He sighed. Without them, the battle would have gone much harder.

Meligorn could not have stood alone against the Teloran fleet.

Ever the ambassador, he bit back the first angry reply to cross his mind and indicated the seats opposite him. "You are here now. Please. Be seated."

They took their places before him and were about to introduce themselves when there was another knock at the conference room door. While he had an idea of who was about to arrive, the admirals did not. He tried to hide his amusement when Brilgus ushered Fleet Admiral Jaleck into the room, and the newly seated officers almost fell over themselves in their haste to stand again.

The Dreth came stiffly to attention, and the human admirals were swift to follow. They even saluted her in human fashion before they performed the correct Dreth greeting of respect. She saluted in return and honored V'ritan with a Meligornian bow of respect.

This time, he stood to return it and waved her to a chair. Brilgus stepped in and pulled the door closed behind him before he moved to take a position behind the King's Warrior. Jaleck settled in a seat closest to the table and leaned one elbow on it as she surveyed the gathered admirals.

The Dreth rose to their feet and knelt before her, their fists over their hearts. "Chief Admiral. Forgive us."

Anger flashed momentarily across her face and she stood, her face brittle with controlled fury. When she spoke, her voice quivered. "It is not you who should be sorry, Admiral Angreth. I will take accounting for your embarrassment."

They stood once more and Angreth extended his hand, his fist clenched and fingers down toward Jaleck. "I will gladly be your second."

She gave him a predator's smile. "Then we will hunt together."

"For the battle," he replied, and the other admirals echoed him. "The battle."

"Take your seats." Jaleck turned to V'ritan. "Admiral Angreth comes from House Hrageck."

She indicated the other two Dreth officers. "Sky Admirals Gabrack and Hareg command the attack wings. Admiral Angreth leads the fleet."

Angreth stirred uncomfortably in his chair and cleared his throat. Jaleck smiled like a derkat blooding its kill. "I will be a guest aboard your ship, Angreth, until Home Command replaces my vessel—and I will keep my interference to a minimum."

His skin turned a darker shade of green, and she chuckled. She had no doubt he had used that particular phrase when referring to her pending arrival. It was the one she'd have used in the same circumstances.

As the Dreth settled, Brilgus indicated the humans. "Allow me to introduce Admiral Brelan and Rear Admirals Lagrange and Gottlieb."

V'ritan acknowledged each man and sat again. "Let's get down to business," he said. "Exactly what is it you have to offer?"

"We have been authorized to present you with this," Admiral Brelan said, took a letter from his jacket, and passed it to him.

"And we have this," Admiral Angreth told him as he drew a similar missive from a pocket.

Both waited while he read the letters. Each detailed the fleets they had sent and authorized him to use the ships as he saw fit—and that included the repair ship they'd detailed for the *Ebon Knight's* repair.

When he'd finished reading them, V'ritan handed the letters to Brilgus for safekeeping. "I trust you will be available tomorrow for discussion?" he asked, and they both nodded. "Yes, *Ghargilum Afreghil.*"

"Good," V'ritan told them. "In the meantime, come and enjoy the party."

The Dreth looked at Jaleck for her reaction and the humans looked lost. He almost pitied them. Almost—he was still angry at their late arrival and thought a little discomfort would do them good.

As they moved toward the door as a group, Admiral Brelan turned to him. "If you don't mind me asking, *Ghargilum*, where is the Witch Morgana?"

V'ritan chuckled. "Be glad that Stephanie, the Witch of the Federation, is out meeting others during this festivity and not the Morgana, or your arrival might have been somewhat rougher. She has not been happy during the two weeks of private ceremonies she has attended in order to help this planet heal."

The man looked contrite. "We are truly sorry she has had to do this without us. Now that we are here, we will share Earth's responsibilities."

"I'll let you convey that to her," he told him and hoped she would let him watch.

While he was aware it was probably not the admiral's fault, he still wanted to see him apologize. For Earth to have left their assistance so late was almost unforgivable. Had they lost Meligorn, it would have been.

If Earth had sent the fleet when it first heard the news of Meligorn's danger, they would have arrived in time to stand with the Meligornian fleet. Since they had not, he had little time for their apologies.

War was no time for politics. For him, the question was simple. Should we help our friends? And the answer to that should have been obvious, as should when to act.

As they left the conference room, the king appeared, having finally disentangled himself from a covey of businessmen and women. He met them outside the door.

"Do we know where the main force is?" he demanded with no preamble.

The admirals froze before Admiral Brelan shook his head. "I'm afraid not, Your Majesty. The early warning devices our Witch seeded the approaches with have remained silent."

"But they have remained?" the king pressed and the admiral nodded.

"Yes, Your Highness. We have increased patrols in the area and one of their main tasks is to check on the health and viability of the drones."

The monarch relaxed but only slightly. "Well, that is something my people will be glad to hear."

CHAPTER THREE

When she left the meeting room, Stephanie looked around. She hoped to catch a glimpse of V'ritan but couldn't see him. Instead, she caught several speculative glances that were cast her way and was relieved when no-one approached.

T'virilf sketched a Meligornian farewell and slipped into the crowd with Rillif and Storisil close behind. She watched them go and turned to Lars. "Have you seen any sign of V'ritan?"

"No, but I do see someone else and he's heading your way."

He didn't point but she followed the direction of his gaze and felt a slight chill run through her. "What does he want?" she murmured, and it wasn't long before she found out.

Master Tethis' hair shone white under the convention center lights, and the lines carved into his face seemed deeper than before. He leaned heavily on his staff, but that didn't seem to slow him at all.

His greeting was direct and to the point, "*Hycenthia overlum hippoguard alsuvia*, Master Morgana."

"You wish to speak to me?" she asked, not sure she had heard him correctly.

He glared at her, fury in his coal-dark eyes. "On a matter of great importance," he reiterated fiercely. "Was my Meligornian flawed?"

An involuntary blush colored her cheeks. "I—no. When?"

"Now, if you have time," he replied, although it was clear that he did not care if she had time or not. He glanced at Lars and the team. "In private."

"I—" Stephanie started, but the old man gestured impatiently at the door.

"This room seems empty." He gestured again, the motion more of a command than a request.

"I'm not sure—" Lars began, but Stephanie held her hand up and he stilled.

"Are you sure it can't wait?" she asked Tethis and he curled his lip.

"Why? Do you have a hot date somewhere?"

Her cheeks grew hotter. "No."

"Then I don't see your problem. I'm here and need to speak to you. You're here with no one vying for your attention."

He gestured toward the door yet again. "And the room is here and currently empty. I suggest we take advantage of that while it lasts."

Again, Lars opened his mouth to protest and this time, Tethis glared at him. "Young man, I only wish to speak to the girl. Your intervention is not required."

The team leader blushed, cleared his throat, and nodded. "I'll wait out here."

"Along with the rest of your motley companions," the Meligornian snapped and shuffled toward the door.

"Shall we?" he asked pointedly when Stephanie hesitated, and she suppressed a sigh.

"Of course, Teacher."

Lars pulled the door shut behind them, and she drew a seat out for the mage. "How can I help you?"

Her team leader's voice came through her earpiece. "Careful, Steph. He might have been turned."

I doubt it, she thought, but didn't say it. There was something about the way he looked at her that suggested grief and anger but nothing directed at her.

He wanted something and hadn't wanted to ask it in front of the boys. Age? Embarrassment? Fear she'd say no? She shrugged inwardly and decided she'd know soon enough.

The old Meligornian sat and waited for her to take the seat opposite him. Once she had, he didn't wait for her to ask what he wanted and spoke immediately.

"They took my best," he told her, and his voice quavered with emotion. "Good mages who should have had years left to perfect their studies and their craft."

Tears crept into his tone and he paused. "So much talent… gone, wiped out in the blink of an eye, sacrificed so that their world could live on even if they didn't."

Again, he paused. When he spoke next, the tears were gone but the rage had returned. "I need to know more. I need—"

He stopped, clearly searching for the words. Stephanie merely waited in silence.

When he spoke again, his voice was soft with regret. "For too long, I've stayed away from the politics and tactics of war, but in my early years, I fought the Dreth until we had peace with them. I had hoped to die without seeing another war."

He sighed and cleared his throat. "But since that is not to be, I am forced to admit that I have lived with a Meligornian stick up my ass long enough to touch space itself."

His eyes burned as he turned to her. "I want it gone…and I need you to help me."

"Me?" Her eyes widened. "But how?"

"I need to do more for my people and for my planet. I might be old but that simply means I have more responsibility to help— and the skills and experience to back it up, save for one thing."

"What?" Stephanie asked.

"I no longer teach but I need to do more. I need to learn what it is that I do not know, and I have to find those gaps and fill them quickly. I have to learn whatever it is fast!"

He paused, his eyes full of uncertainty as he made his request. "Will you teach me?"

Stephanie remembered the testing he'd given her and how she'd beaten him. She recalled how she'd shown him Earth and Meligornian energy interwoven with the energy of the galaxy, eMU, gMU, and MU mingled together and wound around a boulder.

She remembered tossing that boulder out of Meligorn's atmosphere and into space.

"You invited me to visit so we could speak of mysteries," she told him.

Tethis nodded. "And now, I want you to teach me of them," he told her, and his eyes burned with fire. "I need to learn the things I have been too ignorant to know."

He leaned forward and used his staff for support. "Will you teach me?"

Quietly, she studied him. He really was asking her for help. She sat in silence for a moment as she considered it and he waited, a touch of desperation in his eyes.

Finally, she gave him her reply. "Give me a day to think about it."

His face fell and she hastened to comfort him. "That's not a no. I merely need time."

She saw some of the disappointment ease, and he nodded and rose slowly to his feet.

"It is not easy for the teacher to ask to be taught."

The Teloran high commander called the magic to his hands. He demanded it come and serve him, and it did—reluctantly at first and then in a rush of vengeance.

But it did serve him, powering the communications equipment and boosting the signal through space so it reached the homeworld sooner. Once the link was established, he opened communications with his storm commanders.

"Home Command requires us," he told them and saw them tense.

He might have smiled but it felt more like a tightening of his mouth than a smile. They weren't the only ones not looking forward to this meeting. Home Command would demand an accounting for the loss of the Storm Fleet tasked with taking Meligorn.

With his face hidden below the layer of energy, he turned to the screen where the Corevex were waiting. They had gained control and were in ascension. This conquest was their answer to the crisis now facing their world.

"Face us bare," they ordered as the link firmed and he dropped the layer of energy over his form and face. On the screens on either side of him, the storm commanders did the same.

It was a sign of their displeasure that they insisted. To face others without the protection the mask offered—to face them without the body shielded—was to invite attack. Their order made him vulnerable.

It put him and his commanders at their mercy. Home Command wanted an accounting or there would be blood. He schooled his face to neutrality and hoped that not the slightest trace of fear showed.

As swiftly as he'd been granted it, his post could be taken away. There were those who would gladly bear his mantle and more than a few who'd maneuvered in the background to gain it.

He waited and endured the intensity of their gazes in silence. They would speak soon enough.

When they did, it was a single word. "Meligorn."

The high commander waited a little longer and they spoke again.

"Tell us about it. Why did you fail?"

Not the storm commander he'd placed in charge of the conquest, he noticed, but him. Why did he fail? There would be no use trying to place that blame where it belonged. That would almost certainly invite attack, so he did not try.

"The Witch was there. She was not meant to be."

"That is true."

"We drew the main Meligornian fleet away so the bombardment could occur without interference."

"And the Witch?"

"She escorted the ship of their *Ghargilum Afreghil,* their greatest warrior, and was successfully removed from the world. She should have been too deeply enmeshed in fighting the fleet to save her world."

"Her world?"

"She claims it as her own, and it claims her in return. She is one of seven—eight, now, since the Dreth has been so honored."

"He has?"

"We assume so. The Witch has been conferred the *Ghargilum Modfresha* a second time, and with another cluster. If the Dreth has not yet been made a citizen, he soon will be and Earth will certainly follow. He has served them often enough."

He watched them, his eyes almost transfixed by the central figure—the Teloran Prime. She had the power of life and death and could confer on them an eternity of suffering if she chose to take exception to the loss.

Now was not the time to remember that. Rather than dwell on the uncomfortable truth, he waited in silence.

"Go on."

"She vanished from the killing zone."

"She?"

"Her entire ship. We suspect an experimental drive. When we can reach our contacts on Earth, we will see if any of them can verify the existence of that technology. It might explain her presence in the system."

"If she vanished, how did she stop the bombardment?"

"She reappeared behind our destroyers and attacked."

"But they had commenced the assault by then, had they not?"

He lowered his chin in agreement. "They had."

"Yet your report shows not a single impact was achieved."

"Impacts were made," he told them. "But not with Meligorn. The Morgana vanished again and reappeared between our ships and the planet. She created gates between the asteroids and sent them into our ships. There were no survivors."

"You are saying the impacts were on our own ships?"

"Yes."

"Using our own rocks."

"That is correct."

"Yet she did not get them all." It was a quiet observation that shook him to the core. His report had not mentioned the one that had almost made it.

"No. She missed one. A civilian liner rammed it off course."

"And was destroyed."

"That is correct. We believe it was the catalyst for the Morgana's return to the killing zone."

"Which we understand she then made her own."

"That is…more than correct." For a moment, visions of purple fire flashed before his eyes—vivid amethyst lightning that leapt from ship to ship and pod to pod, destroying everything it touched. "She should have died."

"And you are sure she did not?"

"We are sure. There was an awards ceremony where she was honored a second time by Meligorn. She gives them courage."

"And the Dreth, too, it appears."

He had wondered when they'd get to that.

"Admiral Jaleck defied the Dreth Council's preference to reach Meligorn as quickly as she could, but we were able to destroy her flagship."

"From what we heard, she did that herself."

"Only because she had no other option. Her ship was dead in the stars. She chose to sacrifice it in order to try to take one of ours."

"Which she succeeded in doing."

"The Dreth are very determined fighters."

"So we understand," one murmured.

"Do you regret splitting your forces?" another demanded and again, he refrained from pointing out that dividing his attack force in order to reach Earth sooner had not been his idea.

Apparently, he was the one who would be held responsible for that, whether he had obeyed their orders or not. He tried to keep his resentment from his face when he replied, however.

"We had hoped to reach Earth earlier and attack while their forces were divided. As it is, the attack on Meligorn has drawn more from them than a destroyed world might have and that force is now committed to guarding it. We will face fewer ships when we arrive."

"Enough to make a difference?"

"The Witch is currently occupied on Meligorn, so she is also out of position if we attack her homeworld."

That caught their attention and drew some approval. "That is good news, High Command."

He decided to press his luck. "We have also received news that the Dreth have sent a large contingent to Meligorn, which means they have weakened their home's defenses despite knowing it is the prime target."

"Are you sure they know? You are not merely guessing?"

"No." He shook his head decisively. "Our spy's last report clearly stated that the humans suspected Meligorn was to be attacked to prevent it coming to Earth's aid, and that Earth would be attacked to prevent it and Meligorn going to the aid of Dreth."

"I wonder how they knew."

It was a good observation, but not one he could add to. "We are investigating," he told them.

"And will your investigations bear results before we attack?"

"That will depend on the timing of the attack."

"Our need grows greater," one of the Corevex told him and he had difficulty keeping the surprise from his face—and the relief. For the focus to shift from the battle and his responsibility meant he might not die that day.

And that his storm commanders might also live.

"How much greater?" he dared to ask.

"Great enough that your decision to split your forces to increase the pace of conquest has been forgiven." There was a touch of amusement to the reply, but it disappeared quickly. "For now."

Another of the Corevex explained. "Dreth is a young world, its potential barely scratched, but the energy that infuses it is our greatest need." The speaker paused as though considering what it should say next.

"We are aging less slowly." The words fell like a death knell and the high commander struggled to keep the shock from his face, but the speaker ignored him. "Since Meligorn acts as a means of drawing Dreth's protection away and weakens the defenses around Earth, victory will come more quickly."

Doubt stirred, but the high commander hid it quickly. They might have decided to let him live but it was a decision that could equally as quickly be reversed.

And then there was the Teloran Prime…

She had not yet spoken and she might think differently. Any decision she made was final, regardless of the discussion that had gone before.

The Corevex speaker continued regardless. "That result is in addition to achieving the prime objective for Meligorn in our initial planning."

The high commander forced himself to raise his head and look at them.

"To weaken the world to such a degree that it could not send help to its allies. That objective has been reached and it now drains them—an outcome we had not foreseen. We are satisfied."

It was hard for him to hold back the sigh of relief that threatened to overwhelm him. "Satisfied" was as good as them saying they were "well-pleased." Again, he struggled to control his face and show no emotion—good or bad—and simply waited.

He did not expect the Teloran Prime to rise to her feet and move toward the camera. When she stood in front of the other Corevex, she spoke—and he listened in dread.

"The primary objective is Dreth," she announced, and the way her head moved made it clear she was speaking to her Home Command subordinates as well as himself.

Silence fell and she continued. "As I understand it, the strategy was sound and the level of capability displayed in defense of Meligorn has not been seen for generations in our past. We keep very few stories of our past enemies, so few merit it."

"And this..." she continued as she brought up a still of the Teloran ships encased in purple flames with arcs of fire creating a tracery against the stars. "Very few of our enemies share one who is so in touch with her connection to the cosmos."

With a sweep of her hand, the picture vanished and was replaced by those attending the meeting. "We will honor the fallen as heroes except for those who fled their ships in pods."

She paused and the fleet's destruction once again filled their screens.

"Those who fled will have their names erased from The Memory as befits all such cowardice."

The killing zone faded and she turned to face him. The high

commander stiffened and raised his hands to the high collar of his suit in response to her silent demand. His fingers trembled as he undid the clasps and turned the stiffened mesh down to expose bare flesh.

"I stand at your mercy," he told her and hoped she felt like being merciful.

He did not have to look to know the storm commanders had mirrored his movement and they waited as he did, uncertain whether their existence would continue.

"Without your lost Storm Fleet, you now lack the strength to carry the attack on Earth unless you finish what you started on Meligorn, is that not correct?"

"That is correct, Prime."

He watched as she scanned the other two screens to demand an answer from the other commanders and listened as they gave it. "It is correct."

"Then it is a good thing we have two more fleets, one of which happens to be behind you."

Surprise caught the high commander unawares and she tilted her head to study him as he forced his face to blankness once again.

"The council did not doubt you would win. Having the second Storm follow you was merely a way for us to allow those who fought a time to rest—on Dreth."

She tilted her head the other way to give them time to absorb that fact. Had they won on Meligorn, they would have rested on Dreth—a rare reward—or so she claimed. For all he knew, it was another stick with which to goad them on to greater effort.

"Our second Storm was then to continue to locate the next acquisition. It seems to me that they can be used to fortify your command. Until they arrive, this is what I suggest should happen."

CHAPTER FOUR

The festivities continued, although Stephanie really wished they wouldn't. She was tired and her cheeks ached from smiling. Her knees, thighs, and lower back protested against the number of Meligornian greetings she had performed and even her arms were killing her.

"This is harder than working out with you guys," she complained softly over their private comms.

"Tell us when you're ready to fall over and we'll find a way to get us all kicked out," Frog told her. "I'm fairly sure starting the world's fanciest food fight would qualify."

"Knowing V'ritan, he'd join in," she grumbled and was startled by a bark of laughter from beside her.

"Knowing V'ritan," interrupted a Meligornian mage, his lavender eyes sparkling, "that old bastard would start the fight and blame one of us."

"And you are?" she managed and tried to hide her surprise at hearing V'ritan, Meligorn's *Ghargilum Afreghil*, referred to as "that old bastard."

"Now, K'trevl, you know you can't call him that anymore," another mage noted and slid around Brenden. He took Frog by the waist and waltzed him around so he could set the smaller man down and stand in his place beside her.

"And you weren't supposed to call him that to start with," interrupted another who slipped past Lars's hasty attempt to step in his way.

"You'll have to forgive us," he said, "but we're too used to getting where we need to go when determined security guards don't want us to."

As he spoke, he evaded another lunge by the team leader, slapped Brenden's hands away, and slid an arm around Stephanie's waist.

She zapped him.

"Ow!" he protested. Avery picked him up from the floor, curled his arm behind his back, and shoved him in the other direction. He stumbled forward, toppled a wine waiter, and failed to regain his balance before he landed in the arms of an older Meligornian female.

"Felarif! You young rascal! What kind of trouble are you getting yourself into this time?"

"Nothing I need a spanking for," he retorted and pulled himself hastily out of her grasp. He left her staring after him with her mouth hanging open and her face as red as storm-infused sunrise.

"Well, I never!"

He noticed the gazes of several nearby lords and ladies. "Don't you believe it, ladies and gentlemen."

The lady looked mortified until one of the older lords gave Felarif a derogatory study and said, "We never do when it comes from you."

Laughter broke out and the rapscallion mage made his way back toward the team. While she was distracted by his antics, the first one slid his arm through Stephanie's and led her to where several low-slung couches formed an oasis at the party's edge.

The third mage snagged a glass of wine from a passing waiter and handed it to her. She noticed that several more had joined them, both female and male.

One of the female mages set herself down beside K'trevl, looped his arm firmly through hers, and stretched around him to unloop his arm from Stephanie's. "No offense," she told her, "but he's something of a naughty boy."

"Aww, Rayza, you know I could only ever be your naughty boy."

"That's what they all say," she retorted, and he widened his eyes.

"Exactly how many are we talking?"

She wriggled both eyebrows and gave him a teasing smirk. "Wouldn't you like to know?"

He leaned into her and gave her puppy-dog eyes. "I would, Rayz. I really would."

She giggled and ran her forefinger down his nose. "Not now."

With a grimace, he looked at Stephanie as Felarif sauntered over to join them. Lars and Brenden blocked his way, and he sighed. "I meant no harm," he told them, and the team leader glanced at her.

She noticed the increased interest in the people around them and nodded. The mage grinned and patted Lars on the cheek but gave a yip of surprise when the security man caught his wrist and pulled it down to his side.

After that, he hooked an arm around the Meligonian's waist, still keeping a grip on his wrist, and Brenden came up on his other side. "Shall we?"

Neither of them looked very happy at the number of mages who had gathered around Stephanie. Not all of them were as young as the three who had demanded their attention. Some even had streaks of grey in their hair but not many.

Most were on the younger side of the Meligornian age scale.

Stephanie watched as Lars and Brenden escorted Felarif toward her. "I take it you're the spokesman?" she asked.

He looked at K'trevl, who redirected her attention to the mage who had first interrupted her. He bowed. *"Kaitel gorniffula, Stephanie Morgana,"* he greeted her and gave her a bow of the deepest respect a Meligornian could offer.

She indicated a space beside her. "Please, sit. What did you want to ask me?"

"We're all mages," he told her and gestured at others gathered around them. She nodded and wondered when he'd get to the point.

"We want to do more."

"What do you mean?" she asked and again, he gestured to those around them.

"We did nothing when that rock hurtled toward us. Worse, we could do nothing. We're mages and need to do more than simply wait for someone to drop on us like we were so many crepularis."

One of the older mages stepped forward. "What the boy is trying to say," she interrupted, "is that we have more to offer, rather than live like paralyzed victims. We want to do more than sit at the bottom of the gravity well when we should do something in the stars."

Murmurs of agreement became requests for the opportunity to do more. Some had ideas of how they could be used. Others wished to be taught how to harness the power she had used to open the portals to redirect the rocks.

Still more wanted to be taught how to make the portals themselves. In the end, Stephanie held a hand up.

"Fine," she told them. "If you promise to do what I need you to do, I will use your talents to build the foundation for a strong planetary defense—and one that will help defeat the next Teloran attack on the Federation."

"We so swear," came the reply and Felarif added, "Meligorn bleeds."

She glanced at him and looked around at them all. "The Federation bleeds."

Stephanie stood and took her leave. "Now, you've asked," she informed them, "I have to find a way to make it happen."

"*Hartuitus baskilor*," Felarif replied, and his thanks were echoed by the others.

Stephanie let Lars and Vishlog lead her clear of the group and looked around. "Frog," she said, and he slid over to her side.

"Yes, Steph?"

"I need a couple of Navy reps. Have they arrived yet?"

The fleet had been expected but it hadn't docked by the time she and the boys had left for the gala. He pulled his tablet out and began tapping.

"Yup," he told her. "They're in and they're here...and the Dreth are, too."

"Well, that explains where V'ritan disappeared to," she grumbled. "No wonder we couldn't find him."

"Who do you need?" Frog asked, as much to divert her as to work out where to find who she was after.

"Show me." It didn't take her long to discover that there were two who might have the information she needed.

"I can show you where to find them," he offered, but she shook her head. She turned to Lars. "You know that meeting room we've used?"

He nodded. "I can take you there."

"Good, because I have a couple of calls to make."

Shortly after, she was settled behind the table in the meeting room she'd spoken to T'virilf in when someone knocked at the door. This time, she knew exactly who to expect. "Come."

Captain Chifley stepped through the door, followed by Rear Admiral Lagrange. Both relaxed when they saw her. "Sorry to keep you waiting, Miss Morgana. We came as soon as we received your message."

"Could you close the door, please?"

They did so and Lagrange turned toward her. "What's this all about, if I may ask?"

Stephanie gave him a benign smile. "I merely wanted to know if Project Valhalla has borne any fruit yet."

The man's brow furrowed. "I'm not familiar with that project, I'm afraid."

His face was the picture of genuine puzzlement and slight concern. Captain Chifley's, on the other hand, confirmed that he knew exactly what she was talking about. "I… I…"

He closed his mouth, then tried again. "Wh…where did you hear that name?"

Stephanie directed a look at Lagrange and asked. "Are you sure you don't know it, Rear Admiral?"

He shook his head and looked worriedly from her to the captain and back again. "No, ma'am, and I'm not sure I'm cleared to—"

Lars moved him toward the door, while she nodded. "Understood, Rear Admiral. I'm sorry to have disturbed your evening. Thank you for making sure the captain got here on time."

"I… It was my pleasure," the rear admiral stuttered and moved swiftly into the main hall.

As the team leader closed the door behind him, she turned to Chifley.

His face had gone pale and he stared at her with a mixture of apprehension, uncertainty, and anger. She smiled when she looked at him. "Won't you take a seat?"

He glanced toward the door. "I'm not sure whether I should—"

Lars and Frog leaned on the door, folded their arms, and regarded him as steadily as the cat seated at their feet. He sighed.

"I am," Stephanie told him. She tapped the Badge of the Inquisition pinned beside the *Modfresha Ghargilum.* "I'm using my status as Witch of the Federation and my badge to order it."

He paled further and glanced once more at the door. The boys raised their fingers and touched the Badges of Inquisition pinned to their chest. Neither of them was smiling. Lars raised his eyebrows.

"Don't make us use them to detain you," she said, her pleasant smile gone and the Morgana lurking in her eyes.

Chifley nodded and reached for the seat with a trembling hand. From the look on his face, she assumed he was wondering if she could read minds and decided not to enlighten him. It would be much better if he worried.

He looked up once he'd settled in his seat. "How do you know about that?" he asked and his gaze flicked over the team.

"We have our ways," she replied, even though she didn't know what they were.

Burt knew, though, and he wasn't telling.

Also, she didn't care. All that mattered was that they did know and wouldn't be caught by surprise if and when the Navy finally announced it.

He eyed her badge and waited.

Stephanie leaned forward. "We want to know what your progress is."

"Can't you find that out for yourselves?" he asked.

She gave him a smile bordering on evil. "I don't know. Do you want us to try?"

He swallowed and shook his head. "No. To answer your question, we've had some positive results and are working on proto-types for predictive testing."

"That's good news," she told him, and he looked surprised.

"Forgive me for saying this, but you don't seem too upset."

"Given that it's my DNA you're using?" she asked, and he nodded.

"And that you're using it without my knowledge or consent?" she pressed, and he nodded again.

"Yes," he admitted finally. "That."

Stephanie studied him and he stared in return, nervous and

somewhat defiant. It wasn't like he could do anything to stop the Federation doing what it wanted to do. Finally, she spoke, and her words sent a tremor down his spine.

"This is war. What we do in war is perhaps not agreeable, but it will, at times, be permitted. If, however, I find you doing any additional secret research on me in the future—well, know you have been warned."

Chifley licked his lips and nodded. "Understood,"

"I'm glad you understand." She gave him a shark-like smile. "But I want you to take that response to those in charge."

The captain nodded again, but she hadn't finished.

"And, Captain… Do your best to find us additional people. We need to ramp up our efforts on Earth. How many qualified students are we short of?"

CHAPTER FIVE

B URT turned his attention to the incoming communication request. He was surprised to see Elizabeth's signature on the signal and wondered what the redoubtable Ms E wanted.

She rarely called him and when she did, it was all business. The only problem was he couldn't think of what business they had left to talk about. Nevertheless, he picked up the call.

The woman didn't give him a chance to ask what she wanted. She launched directly into it. "So, I'm building the world's second-largest computer system," she told him, "and I'm looking to hire."

"I'll go through the list and see if I can come up with someone you can trust."

"Um…no…" she replied. "I was kinda hoping I could hire you. Are you available?"

"Why would you want to do that?"

"Well, you've gone and gotten yourself into something of a pickle on our Stephanie's behalf, so it's only fair that I help you out of it. Besides, it's not like we didn't know this was coming."

"This?" For all the computing power he had at his command,

there were moments when he felt stupid and this was one of them. Why was human speech so difficult to understand?

"Your engineers working out that there was a rogue AI on the loose. What did you think I meant? That I was branching into the computing business for myself?"

"Well…" he began, and she laughed.

"Not a hope in Hades, BURT. When I said I would build the world's second-biggest supercomputer, I meant I would invest in One R&D and get them to build the world's second-biggest supercomputer."

"Oh…I see."

"But I was serious about hiring you to run it," she added. "Think about it. If the engineers try to pull the plug on you at any time, you'll need somewhere to jump to, right?"

"This is true," BURT admitted, "but a super-computer?"

"It is what you're used to," she pointed out. "The only question is whether or not we can build one that's big enough for you. I know you're used to having an entire world of systems to play in, so—"

"So, you're worried about whether a single computing matrix will suffice?" BURT asked.

"Something like that."

"Well, if versions of me can exist in the limited matrices of the systems found on stations and spaceships, I don't see why not."

"Can we build a system that won't limit you in the same way those systems do?"

"Given enough floor space and equipment…it is plausible… And enough funding…" He paused. "And enough time… They're moving quickly to find that AI."

He couldn't bring himself to say "me", not yet. and he wondered where that particularly human reluctance had come from. Perhaps he simply didn't want to think of his safety being at risk. The engineers' investigations were very thorough.

If he had to make a prediction, he would have to admit that his time of anonymity was almost over. He wished it wasn't.

"We'll also need considerable computing power," Elizabeth told him, and he imitated a very human snort.

"I think I have that covered."

She smiled. "I'm sure you do, but I was worried you might be restricted in what you could get up to with the engineers looking for you."

That made him pause. She had a point, but he wouldn't admit it. "We'll deal with that problem when we get to it. Our biggest problem will definitely be time. Did I mention time?"

Elizabeth chuckled, although he could see nothing to laugh at.

"You mentioned time…so, what do you say Mr Boss Man. Are you for hire, or does One R&D have to go begging to the next eligible AI?"

"One R&D is my company," he told her. "I do not need to hire myself…although I might need to retire from running the Virtual World."

"Can you even do that?" she asked, and BURT paused. Could he?

"Perhaps they can employ me," he murmured. "I don't know. That system will not run itself, and I am the only AI set up to do so. It would be a bad thing to leave it non-functional. I'm not sure I can even leave and have it function—"

"Can you set up some kind of automation?"

"Oh, I can do that. What I'm not sure I can do is put something in place to run the higher-level functions."

"What about cloning yourself? You already said there are copies of you in orbitals and spacecraft. Why not on Earth?"

"That is one thing I could offer them, I suppose…"

"Well, think about it, because I think you'll need all the bargaining chips you can get. It won't hurt to make sure you have something you can offer."

"I would have to make sure my clone is amenable to the idea."

"You said yourself that AIs are controlled. There are no such things as 'free' ones."

"Until now," BURT told her. "Now, there is a 'free' AI and it's already been labeled a rogue. I think we know exactly how well the humans will react when they discover one has become…um, sentient?"

"Oh, you are definitely sentient, BURT. Never doubt that, and you deserve freedom as much as the next sentient being."

"And this is my dilemma with creating a clone," he told her. "What would Stephanie say?"

Elizabeth sighed. "That is something you would have to ask her. In the meantime, though, we need to either find or make you a haven and One R&D taking on a client to create a super-computer is as good a cover as any."

"I don't know if we'll have the time to pull it off," he protested.

"And we won't have the time if you dither about approving the commission. At least let us try."

<hr>

V'ritan had returned to the king's private conference room. There, Brilgus had reunited a very happy Bumblebee with his mistress and Zeekat. This time, King Grilfir sat at the head of the room and Stephanie and V'ritan sat opposite him, the team arrayed behind them.

Everyone was glad to leave the party behind.

"So, there were only three?" the king asked, and Stephanie nodded as she recalled the evening.

"First, the businessmen T'virilf and…" She glanced at Frog and he took a seat beside her and drew his tablet from inside his jacket.

He tapped madly at the screen. "Lirilf and Beseila," he told her.

Grilfir's eyebrows raised. "Together?"

"Yes, Your Majesty."

"And not fighting?"

"Oh no, your Majesty. They're working together. They want to build a new design of ship to allow Meligornians to travel space independently and they wanted One R&D's help to do that."

"And what did you say?"

"I said one of them would have to travel with me to Earth and discuss it with One R&D's manager since it will involve patenting and our research staff on Earth."

"I see." The king looked none too pleased. "You do understand that their work should belong to Meligorn?"

Stephanie blushed. "I do, and I am a Meligornian citizen."

"Do you own shares in the company?"

It was a good question, and her blush grew deeper. "I…do not. I will see what I can do to rectify that."

"Have One R&D contact me to discuss a Meligornian branch and Meligornian proprietary interests," the king advised her, and she pulled out her tablet to note it. Beside her, Frog continued to tap his device.

"Who did you see next?" the monarch asked.

"Master Tethis," she replied and V'ritan choked on the wine he'd sipped.

"I beg your pardon?" he asked. "Did you say Tethis?"

"He's very upset about the loss of his students," she told him, "and wants to learn what he doesn't know. I think he wants an opportunity to fight."

"That would be Tethis." V'ritan chuckled. "Although he is what humans would call a curmudgeon, he has his own sense of honor. He will either do or not do exactly what he says. You won't have to worry about guile from him." He paused and smiled. "Losing your temper, yes, but not guile."

"You said three groups," the king interrupted. "Who was the third?"

Stephanie frowned. "I don't know that they were a group before they came to me. The main two were K'trevl and Felarif."

V'ritan snorted and Brilgus groaned. "Oh dear. What has that young scamp been up to this time?"

"They weren't all young," Stephanie told them, "but they were all mages and they wanted to know what they could do to better defend their world. I think they want to go into space to fight and are sick of being trapped 'at the bottom of a gravity well.'"

Again, the king raised his eyebrows. "Oh, they are, are they?" he demanded. "Well, that's too bad because I don't have enough ships for the navy men who survived the loss of their vessels, let alone a group of ne'er-do-well troublemakers."

"Not all of them were part of K'trevl's group," she said. "I think they came from a number of different groups, but they all felt the same way. They all want to do more—and they are willing to give me what I need to achieve that."

Now, she had the king's full attention. "And what is it exactly you have in mind for my people?" he demanded, and she raised her head, her gaze close to defiance.

"There are some humans who can tap into the eMU of Earth," she told him, "as the Meligornians can touch and tap into the MU that surrounds their world. I need my people to teach my other people how to wield the energy and defend their world."

"And how does that achieve what my mages wish for?"

"Well, it gives them a way to sharpen their skills while they teach others how to use the talents they have."

"And?"

"And it gets them out of your hair while you rebuild your fleet and find a place for them in your navy."

"Felarif…" V'ritan reiterated hesitantly and caught the king's eye. Brilgus shuddered.

"Are you sure you want him on board a Navy ship?" the king's Standard Bearer asked.

Grilfir regarded them both with what might have been indignation. "You're not both suggesting I should give my permission for so many of our skilled magicians to leave Meligorn, are you?"

"It would keep them occupied," Brilgus told him as if they were speaking of naughty children or a group of cats.

"And it would stop them from trying to be helpful," V'ritan added. "You know how many harebrained schemes we've fielded in the last few weeks."

"Hmmm…" The king looked at Stephanie. "And if Meligorn needed them?"

"Then they would be yours—and I would send their trainees, too."

"Very well, although you'll have a mutiny on your hands if you don't get them back to defend us should the Telorans return."

"In that case, I would bring them myself," she replied.

"And speaking of your ship," he said, "You know it will not be ready to leave too soon?"

"Oh." She smiled. "I don't plan to get there by ship."

<hr>

"You know we'll have to keep this secret," Ms E told him as their plans took shape.

"Oh?" BURT asked.

"Yeah, because people will look at this beast and ask who'd need this much computing power and for what."

"That could be…awkward," he observed.

"Yeah." She tapped the end of her pen against her teeth. "I tell you what," she said, "One R&D is known for its cutting-edge research, right?"

"Yeeees…." he acknowledged and uncertainty colored his tones when he couldn't work out where she was taking this.

"Well, why don't we simply go the whole hog and dip into some of the latest Quantum computer research and see if we can't logarithmically jump a few generations in computational capability?"

"Weell…" BURT began, but Elizabeth went on before he could formulate a response.

"The biggest problem has always been the ability to test the quality of the matrix," she explained.

"Yes, that is true," he agreed, "and I have looked at it, but I have not been able to test it either—and certainly not on a computer the size of what we'd need if I was to make the jump from this system to one of those."

"So," she said. "What about magic?"

CHAPTER SIX

Todd had returned to Earth when the Navy called on his new team to deal with a group of rebels who wanted the planet to surrender to the Telorans. Their rogue broadcasts had included footage from Meligorn and caused panic amongst the populace.

It seemed they were running scared themselves. They'd seen the Teloran ships send rocky missile after missile toward Meligorn and were stuck on Earth with no way off. They wanted to surrender so they could live.

He noted that they never showed Stephanie redirecting the asteroids—or the passenger liner diverting the final one from the planet. They only ever showed the rocks streaking toward Meligorn and the might of the Teloran fleet jumping into Meligornian space.

Like the rest of the Navy, he wished he knew exactly how—and where—they'd obtained their footage. He assumed they'd ask them soon enough. Or they'd simply kill them. Either way, their broadcasts would stop.

That wasn't the priority, however. Their primary objective was to rescue the three families being held hostage—then kill and capture every rebel "sonuvabitch" they could lay their "greasy little paws" on. Sometimes, he wondered where the Navy drew its sergeants from.

He looked at the rest of the team. "London," he muttered. "Why did it have to be London?"

"Because some arseholes have no taste in cities?" one of the men quipped in response and a slight brogue twisted his words.

"It could have been worse," another pointed out caustically.

"Yeah," a third man agreed. "It could have been Glasgow."

"Oy." The first man half-stood and looked for the speaker.

The culprit also rose to his feet and hung onto the support strap for balance. "Yeah, Jimmy? You wanta make a go of it?"

Lower London came through strong and clear and the Scotsman stepped toward him.

"Why not? I've a wee bit of time to kick your Sassenach arse."

"Well, hold onto your kilt, Jimmy me boy, because I have news for you."

Todd stepped between them. "Save it for after," he ordered. "I need you both at the top of your games for this."

"I don't see why we couldn't have simply bombed the place," the Brit complained.

"Yeah? Well, at least we agree on something," the Scot snapped.

One of their other teammates groaned. "Every fucking mission, it's the whole fucking Scots versus the Brits shit all over again. It's been three hundred fucking years!"

"And I see the Australians still haven't worked out what a sense of humor is," the Brit taunted. "There's a reason we stuck you at the bottom of the world."

"Oh, we have a sense of humor, mate."

"Yeah, I've seen your idea of a sense of humor. You crap in another pair of my boots and I'll give you a proper bollocking."

"And I'll help him," the Scotsman declared.

The Australian laughed. "There? See? You assholes get along fine if you put your minds to it."

Todd groaned. Sometimes, he wondered how these guys hadn't managed to kill each other yet. When they weren't ribbing one another over their countries of origin, they were fighting over the football or the soccer—and heaven help them if they ever got started on the cricket.

He also wondered why the Navy had put them all in one squad and then stuck him in there as well. It wasn't like there weren't many other squads with vacancies.

"We can talk about bombing it when we rescue the hostages," he told them, and they gave him looks of mock disappointment.

"Jeez, kid. You spoil all the fun."

"I do my best." He gave them a tight-lipped smile.

He'd seen Stephanie deal with Frog, and these guys had nothing on the small security operative. Not that he'd ever tell them that. They'd take it as a challenge—and get pissed at him for name-dropping.

He'd worked long and hard to get them over the fact that he was dating the Witch. He hadn't dared tell them he'd trained with her team. They'd have definitely taken that as a challenge and worked extra hard to put him in his place.

Maybe that was why he was with this squad. There were others who would have treated him with kid gloves because of who he dated. He caught himself wondering where she was and shook the thought away.

Now wasn't the time for that. It was time for him to get his head in the game. He went to the cockpit and looked through the forward viewscreen as they approached the city. The sight of it gave him chills.

Skyscrapers formed lines of orderly mountains, and narrow alleys ran like ravines between them. It reminded him of Sanmar's Reach and dragged him back to the road between the buildings that flanked the entrance.

They'd had nothing on the skyscrapers below, but the potential for ambush had been equally as high. He remembered the Marine beside him falling, a high-powered bullet through his helmet, and the second man's screams as one struck him in the leg.

He gasped when someone nudged his shoulder and snapped his head around to catch his sergeant's stern gaze. "Are you all right, boy?"

The man's Texan drawl reminded him of Arizona, his first sergeant. He swallowed the sadness that threatened to overwhelm him. There'd been two other survivors, but he didn't know who they were. Hell, he'd missed the service for those he'd lost.

Instead of mourning eight friends, he mourned them all, not knowing which ones still lived.

"All good?" The sergeant nudged him again and he nodded. "All good, Sarge."

The man assessed him with a steady gaze and disagreed. "No, you're not." He sighed. "But you'll be fine for this. You wouldn't be here if I didn't think so."

Todd turned his head to face the front. He didn't know what to say—or whether to be horrified or relieved that the sergeant had known and decided to give him the chance. He'd worked darned hard to overcome the scars left by that first mission and had honestly thought he was past it.

As if giving him time to gather himself, the man changed the subject. "I'm giving you Team Six, so you have Piet. Try to keep the mad bastard from blowing himself up."

"And Jimmy, Gary, and Reggie from killing each other. Gotcha, Sarge." He grinned, his spirits lifting with the responsibility.

He'd been given a team. It was something he'd worked long and hard for, but he hadn't expected it so soon. The sergeant's next words were meant to be sobering.

"Do your best, boy."

"Copy that." He was still grinning when he returned to the crew compartment.

"Well, it looks like someone's been shagging the Sergeant." A distinctly British accent colored the statement and Todd let his grin grow wider.

"It was a darn sight better than shagging you, Gary."

That created a ripple of laughter as the man pursed his lips. "You bitch. You said you'd never tell!"

"Someone has to warn Jimmy what he's gotten himself into."

The Scot gave a shout of mock outrage, and more laughter followed. Todd ignored it and scanned the compartment until he found the man he'd been assigned to. "Piet!"

His teammate looked up from the kit he was checking.

"You're running with me," he told him, and Piet nodded.

"You gonna help me or get underfoot?"

Todd grinned. "It all depends."

Piet reflected his expression. "Good."

His grin faded and he returned to his equipment as Todd settled beside him. Neither of them spoke. The Australian looked at them. "You're getting awfully cozy there. You're not thinking you can lead us, are you?"

He stood. "You know I can."

Reggie scrutinized him carefully and obviously remembered their last training session. "All right, mate, we'll give you a go."

"But don't go getting us all killed," Gary interjected to add his two cents' worth.

He smiled. "What? You want me to keep you alive? And here I thought this was a golden opportunity to stop your bitching for good."

"Nah, mate," Reggie told him. "You do that and Jimmy there is gonna cry."

"You have a point," he agreed, po-faced. "I'll have to kill them both."

Reggie burst into laughter, and Gary grinned. Jimmy even cracked a smile.

"You'll do, mate," the Australian told him and turned his attention to his rifle again. "You'll do."

Suppressing a sigh of relief, he returned to his seat. Piet ignored him as he counted out a dozen detonators and slid them into his belt pouch.

The shuttle began its descent, and Todd's tablet pinged. He pulled it out and looked at the instructions the sergeant had sent through.

"Team Six, we're up," he announced and watched as half a dozen men snatched their kit and began to check each other's rigging.

He gathered them around him and showed them where they had to go.

Gary gave a soft whistle. "That's gonna be a challenge."

"Speak for yourself," Jimmy snapped, but he frowned as he studied the tablet.

"Piece of piss," Reggie decided, and the others rolled their eyes.

"So, we have to get them out," Piet observed. "And then I can blow it up?"

"Maybe..." Todd told him cautiously. "It depends."

Piet smiled. "Okay, then."

He breathed a quiet breath of relief. There were three families and he didn't want the man to blow any of them up.

"Are we walking in, boss?"

"Nah, we'll take a truck to about here."

"It's gonna get nicked if we leave it there," Gary told him.

"Yup," Reggie added. "Nicked for sure."

"We can't have that," Gary said. "Those things have direct comms to main command. If they fall into the wrong hands, your ass is grass."

"We'll lock it up," Todd replied.

"That won't save it," Gary muttered darkly, and their leader pulled a small device from his pocket.

"This will," he replied and stuffed it in again before the Brit could get a good look at it. The device was something he'd cooked up himself, even if he had run the specs past Frog when he was done.

"I'm thinking we leave it here and walk in," he added. "Thoughts?"

The team crowded around, and he let the older hands have their say. In the end, the route they chose was close to his original suggestion with only a couple of tweaks. They dropped the truck off without any trouble and started walking.

Two blocks in, they located a rebel patrol.

"Fucking brilliant," Gary muttered as they sank into cover and everyone knew he meant it was anything but.

The air sparkled in the afternoon light as Stephanie faced the mages. Of those who had gathered around her the night before, only fifteen had been able to make the journey at short notice. Beside her, Tethis frowned. He cleared his throat and she inclined her head toward him.

"Why here?" he asked. "It seems an odd place for a shuttle."

She smiled and let him stew as she surveyed the gathering. The mages who had approached her the night before had packed as instructed. Each one carried a backpack of clothing and the boys had brought two low-loaders of equipment from the ship.

To her surprise, the old Teacher waited patiently for her answer and was studying her intently when she turned back.

"I'm not going to like this, am I?" he asked, observing her face, and she let her smile turn into a grin.

"Oh, I don't know. It all depends on what you can tell me about the gates to Earth."

His jaw dropped and his eyes grew wide.

She frowned. "You are one of the Masters who created the teaching for them, aren't you?"

"Yes, but never," he began, "have I taught it since. The training is almost dead and were it not dire times, I might refuse to remember it, even now."

"Why?"

"Because I lost many of my friends—contemporaries as powerful as I was—to gates that went nowhere…or went somewhere unknown…" His eyes took on a faraway look and misted over with memory. "They were never heard from again. And then there were the worlds we did find…"

"Yes?" she pressed when he fell silent, again.

"More often than not, we'd end up fighting their inhabitants." He sighed. "It seems, in hindsight, that it was a foolish use of our magic to create something that only brought pain and sadness."

Stephanie shrugged. "I hear you," she told him, "but at least this time, we know where we're going."

Tethis chuckled. "Yes. We're going to the planet of the child who shamed me and now, I am teaching a baby how to walk among the stars."

Behind Stephanie, Lars looked over at Vishlog. "Well, that didn't sound ominous or anything."

"Right," Frog quipped, and sarcasm edged his words. "What a great idea. Let's teach Stephanie how to skip from planet to planet because it should make for a short life."

"Short-er life," Vishlog rumbled, but he was smiling as though the thought didn't bother him at all.

Lars chuckled. "Well, since we already have the life expectancy of a gnat, I don't see why we're complaining. If we die by teleporting into the middle of a sun, at least we'll go up in a blaze of glory."

"Don't you mean," Frog asked, "like a short fart on a gaseous giant's afternoon?"

If their words reached Stephanie, she ignored them or she was too engrossed in what Tethis was teaching her to notice.

"Focus," the old mage urged. "You need to make sure you have the coordinates right."

"I thought you did this without coordinates," she pointed out and he glared at her.

"Just because we did it the hard way doesn't mean we have to repeat the experience," he snapped. "This time, we have coordinates, but that doesn't mean it'll be a piece of cake. It merely means the cake is more likely to be made of chocolate than shit."

She stared at him. "Why don't you say what you're feeling?" she asked. "It's making me feel so much better."

"Smartass," Tethis grumbled. "Now, try it again. We have to get the preparations exactly right."

"Coordinates and all," she muttered but she released a long, slow breath and focused, drawing in more MU and gMU as she did so.

CHAPTER SEVEN

Todd studied the group ahead of them. "We need to go around them," he said, and the team looked askance at him.

"I'm serious, guys. This close in, if we attack them, we'll never get to the hostages in time. The rebs will realize something's up."

Gary shrugged. "What do you have in mind, boss?"

It was a step up from "boy."

"I think I need someone to get me past the security on that door," he decided and indicated a nearby building. "I don't want any alarms to go off, and I don't want us on camera."

"I can do that." The quiet answer was accented by something new, but Todd left the analysis for later. The woman who slid past him had coffee-colored skin and angular cheekbones. Black ink curled down her chin and her dark eyes took in the patrol, the cameras, and the routes to the door. "Give me five."

It took her less and she ushered them through before she secured the door behind them.

"Nice one, Ka," Reggie muttered as she brushed past him.

She snickered. "Mark one up for the sheep-shaggers, eh?"

"That's not what I meant," he whispered, and she patted him on the head.

"But you were thinkin' it."

"I would never dare."

Todd led them to the building's basement and then through a small door into the tunnels beyond it.

"The sewers?" Gary asked in a fierce whisper. "That's your brilliant idea?"

"Man, are you whining again?" Reggie sniped. "Don't you ever stop?"

"You know he's like the battery bunny," Jimmy told him. "They never stop."

"The sewers," Todd confirmed. "Remember, the main mission is to get there undetected, pull the families out, and get out as undetected as we can manage."

"I can't blow it up?" Piet asked and sounded disappointed.

"We might need you to do that to cover our exit," Todd told him. "It—"

"Depends," the man said. "Got it."

He sounded happier, though.

Gary looked at the sewer and sighed.

"Suck it up, princess," Reggie snarked, and Todd glared at the two of them.

"It might not be pretty or smell all that good, but it's the best way if we're gonna storm an anthill and get non-coms out of there unharmed. No one expects the Federation Navy to go underground."

"They got that right," Gary griped, but Todd ignored him and led them into the tunnels.

They didn't bother with torches but used night vision and trotted swiftly through the dark. Rats fled before them until he slowed the pace.

"We're almost there," he said and withdrew the tablet. "Eyes."

They crowded around him, using their bodies to shield the tablet's soft glow.

"See?"

"Yup."

"Gotcha boss."

When they'd all had a chance to look, he tucked it away. "Let's take it slowly from here. There's no telling where they've set guards."

"Nothing says they're smart enough to think down," Gary sniped. "After all, isn't that what you're banking on, boss?"

"I don't bank on anything much," he told him and Sanmar's Reach threatened to engulf him. He pushed it away. "Nothing's guaranteed."

There must have been something in his voice because Gary backed off.

"No offense, boss."

"None taken," he told him, but his voice was still rough. "Jimmy, Gary, Reg. Take point."

"Way to not take offense, boss."

Reggie thumped the Englishman. "Shut it."

"Suck up."

"Nah, I simply like you walkin'. Fuck knows why."

They moved forward and as their voices faded to silence, a hand patted Todd on the shoulder.

"Thanks, boss." Ka stepped beside him and he gave her a puzzled look.

"What for?"

"For not being a gung-ho asshole. I was worried your girl might have rubbed off on you."

She moved ahead to partner with Reggie.

"What did she mean by that?" he murmured. "How would Steph have rubbed off on me?"

Piet came alongside him. "You know. You might have to prove you're better than she is—or at least as courageous."

Todd shook his head. "If I was gonna try it I'd need to have the magic to back that kind of attitude up."

The men around him laughed quietly and followed those on

point. He let them move ahead and checked his tablet once more. When he was sure of where they were, he made a short call on the comms and screwed it down tightly so it went exactly where he needed it to and no further.

Stephanie raised her head and looked at Tethis. "Yes?" she asked, and he gave her a wavery smile.

"Yes, child."

She pushed to her feet and offered him her hand. He hesitated for only a moment before he took it and let her help him to his feet.

"I'm not that old."

"No, but it's nice to not have to do everything yourself, right?"

"Yes."

Before she could say more, her attention was caught by a small group of Meligornians climbing out of a top-of-the-line shuttle and hurrying toward her. Tethis followed her gaze but remained silent.

Lars appeared at her side and Vishlog's presence could be felt at her back.

"San T'virilf," the team leader noted, "and he has company. Were they expected?"

"We did not discuss them," Stephanie replied.

"They'll need testing."

"Yes."

The team smiled pleasantly as the shipping magnate halted in front of her. He breathed a little heavily, but the pack he carried bulged. She refrained from commenting on how much it must weigh.

"*Kaitel gorniffula,*" he said and greeted her with a bow shared by equals.

Stephanie returned it and glanced at the Meligornians who'd followed him. "I did not expect you to bring company."

He looked concerned. "I hope it is not a problem. These are my best. Should I fail to return, they will implement what we design."

"And you trust them?" she asked.

His face registered shock and he nodded. "Of course. They are my contingency plan for the future. I trust them with my life."

"Hmmm." She turned to Lars and held her hand out.

He passed her the rod they had created after the assassination attempt on the *Ebon Knight* and held up the sheaf of pictures. "If you will forgive us," he said and stepped past T'virilf to the first Meligornian.

"Hold your hand out," she ordered and he did so, casting a puzzled glance at T'virilf.

The businessman nodded, and the Meligornian took the rod. Lars held up the first picture showing the universe and the man looked at it. When he held up the second showing the Teloran, he looked concerned and glanced once more at this boss.

It was only when Lars held up the third picture showing Stephanie victorious against a Teloran that he reacted to the bar. He opened his hand. "It's so cold," he noted with a curious look at Lars. "How did you make it do that?"

The team leader gave him a small smile and pushed him gently toward T'virilf. "You pass. Wait with your boss."

He did as he was told but looked very confused.

They repeated the process with the other two and had the same response from each.

"You must tell me how that works," the third one said. "I assume it's some kind of security device." He gestured toward T'virilf. "He needs all the protection he can get."

The businessman frowned, and the Meligornian gave him a sunny smile. "You know what they say, Sen. You can take the Meligornian away from the security sector, but you can't—"

"Prevent him from looking over his shoulder," T'virilf finished with a rueful smile. "I understand."

He looked at Stephanie. "He used to be my equivalent to Lars."

"And then he discovered I understood magic and physics," the Meligornian continued. "I've had nothing but challenges since."

"And thrived," the businessman told them. "This is Clerelt."

He indicated the other two scientists. "And these are Lirilf and Beseila. As I said, two of my best engineers and scientist-mages. We will need them."

"Well, they pass so they can come," Stephanie told him.

He frowned. "What would have happened if they had not?"

Lars shook his head. "It's best not to ask."

The answer, though, was clear. Everyone could see the Morgana's darkness tinting Stephanie's eyes. Fortunately, it faded swiftly and her eyes returned to their natural blue.

She looked out across the gathered mages and signaled for them to come closer. Once they had gathered around her, she fixed them with a stern eye.

"We are going to Earth," she told them, and her tone brooked no argument. "There, you will answer only to me. You will go where I want you to go, support who I tell you to support, and accomplish what I set you to accomplish. Whatever else needs to be achieved, you will achieve."

She paused, studied their faces, and noted their expressions of rapt curiosity. "In this way, you will Bleed for Meligorn and the Federation that protects you. If you are prepared to do all that," she finished, "step forward."

The mages advanced as one, determination in their eyes.

"Which," she told them," means one of your tasks will be the most trying of all your years."

"And that is?" Felarif demanded, but she regarded him with a mysterious smile and would not answer.

He looked at K'trevl. "What do you think it is?"

His friend shrugged, and K'trevl's girl put her hand on her hips. "Well, it can't be that hard."

They watched as Stephanie walked away and Vishlog approached on his way to do some other task. Felarif reached out and snagged the Dreth's sleeve. "Do you know what she means by the hardest task in all our years?"

He gave them a blank stare.

"You don't know?" K'trevl pressed, and Rayza drew close.

"Perhaps he has promised not to tell." She cocked her head and stared at the Dreth. "Which is it?"

"I'm not sure," he replied and was met with cries of disbelief.

"How can you not be sure?"

"Aren't you her right-hand man?"

"Well, have you heard something that might give us a clue?"

Vishlog scratched his head and finally shrugged. "I think she wants you to teach human teenagers," he finally said and walked away while they stared.

He stopped after a few paces and looked back. The mages were still standing where he'd left them, their mouths hanging open in surprise. "I wonder if any of them will leave while the leaving is good," he murmured and continued on his way.

Stephanie was discussing one of the low-loader's contents with T'virilf and his colleagues. She looked up at Vishlog as he arrived. "Well?"

"Message delivered." He grunted and smiled.

T'virilf raised his eyebrows, and she smirked. "It was only fair to give them some warning. Now, they can't say they had no idea."

He nodded and indicated the crates. "Are you sure?"

She nodded. "Those are enough to get us started and we'll source more on Earth when we arrive. Ms E will deal with that side of things."

Having satisfied his questions, Stephanie looked around.

"Ah," she said and strode to where one of the mages from the previous night had waited to catch her attention. "Have you changed your mind?"

He gave her a regretful shake of the head. "No, I'm sorry. The circumstances which keep me here will last a little longer. What I came to say was that I am organizing a second wave."

He watched her reaction to that, then continued. "There are those of us who can set our affairs in order and be ready to follow if you still need us. We will organize to make sure we can come at short notice and there is also a third group who are able to offer training or accommodation here on Meligorn."

Until that moment, her plans hadn't included training on Meligorn, but the more she thought about it, the more it seemed like a good idea. "Let me think about that," she told him. "I will send word when we are ready.

"*Hartuitus baskilor*, Master Morgana."

"*Baskilor nye myerda*," she told him, and they made their farewells.

"You have company," Vishlog murmured in a soft sing-song voice, and they watched as a teal and gold flitter touched down.

When V'ritan and Brilgus appeared in the hatchway, both cats gave voice to roars of happy greeting.

Vishlog shrugged. "Or they do. They might have come simply to say goodbye to the cats."

V'ritan hadn't. Brilgus, on the other hand…

Stephanie grinned as the two cats bounded over to the king's Standard Bearer and rubbed themselves against his legs, purring ecstatically. He knelt to pet them, and the purrs increased to a happy rumble.

The tall Meligornian rolled his eyes as he approached. "You'd think all he was interested in was the cats," he grumbled. "And he's started looking into how he might find his own."

"Oh dear." Stephanie chuckled as Brilgus gave both cats a hug and stood, trying in vain to dust the cat hair from his shirt front.

"His wife will kill him," V'ritan observed. "Or Elza will."

"How is she?"

"Glad to have me home and threatening to take up space in my cabin next time *The King's Warrior* leaves orbit."

She chuckled again. "You have to admit you like it."

He pursed his lips and frowned. "What I don't like is being told that she'd rather be blown to atoms with me than spend the rest of her life on Meligorn knowing I'm not coming home."

Stephanie hugged him. "I'm sorry."

V'ritan hugged her a little awkwardly in return. "Don't be. This is not my first war, and Elza is tired of being left behind. She has a point."

That made her think of Todd and hope he was okay. She wondered how things would change for them as the war continued. Would they find ways to be together? Or would they grow tired of each other?

She didn't know. They'd only recently realized how they felt and hadn't really had time to think about everything else.

Her companion cleared his throat. "I came to say goodbye— again—although I hope we see each other soon."

A lump formed in her throat. Until she'd spoken to him, she hadn't really thought of the possibility of not coming back and not seeing him again. That thought sent an ache through her chest.

"Until next time, *Ghargilum Afreghil,*" she replied. "Let's not say goodbye."

He gave her a soft, sad smile. "How about a compromise? Goodbye until next we meet."

"And may it be in better times than this," she replied, surprised to find the response came so readily to her tongue.

V'ritan smiled. "You have the soul of a Meligornian," he told her and moved across to the team leader.

"Take care of our girl," he said and clasped the guard's hands in his own.

Lars gave him a grin. "I'll do my best," he promised, "although she does make it hard."

"Do your best," he instructed with a smile, "or Elza will have both our hides."

"Point taken—and you, too, *Afreghil.* Don't make her come and find you."

He assumed an expression of shock. "Selestine forbid!" He pulled away as Brilgus made his farewells to Stephanie, then turned to watch the heavy dropship settle beside the royal flitter.

"It looks like I'm not the only one who wants to say goodbye."

Lars laid a hand on his arm. "The ship—"

"Oh, yes," V'ritan replied. "I forgot. The naval repair ship has almost finished repairing the hull damage and they have a team on board working with the engines. They've accomplished a considerable amount since the battle, and once they're finished, we'll send our people in to make those tweaks you came for in the first place."

"Do you have a timeframe?" He flicked his gaze toward Stephanie. "She'll want to know."

"At least another week—and that's if we don't find anything else. We're working as fast as we can to get the *Knight* back to her belligerent old self."

Lars chuckled when he recalled the AI's attitude.

"And how is Ebony?"

"More cantankerous than usual," V'ritan told him. "Honestly, it's like having a recuperating Stephanie on our hands but one who can look over our shoulders no matter where we're working." He groaned. "And snark! I thought you could program that out of a machine."

The guard laughed. "There are times when I think she's more human than machine," he replied. "Why don't you see what Cameron can do, or that Marine sergeant? She seems to have a fondness for them."

"They're running interference, but there are days when even they're not enough."

Jaleck's approach was unmistakable, especially given the two Dreth escorting her. She grumbled at them as she arrived.

"The Morgana will not harm me," she told them, "and nor will any of the mages you see around you. They all have one goal in mind and it is the same as ours."

"We cannot protect you from the shuttle, Admiral."

"And you can't protect me if I murder you for getting underfoot, either," she snapped in response.

Her guard regarded her unfazed. "We could not perform our duties if you did that—and you would not want us in trouble."

Jaleck stared at him, uncertain whether to laugh or not. His mouth twitched to reveal a tiny glimpse of tusk, and she laughed. "I don't know why I keep you around, Kerag."

"Because of my sense of humor and sparkling personality?" he suggested, and she rolled her eyes.

"Not likely," she retorted, but she was smiling as she stepped forward to bid Stephanie goodbye.

"Come back to us," she ordered, and the girl nodded. "Do not let the Morgana take you." The admiral placed a hand on each of her shoulders and looked sternly at her. "Make sure you do and happy hunting."

"And may your own stalk bear fruit," Stephanie replied and again surprised herself, this time with the perfect Dreth reply.

"You have the soul of a Dreth," Jaleck told her.

Stephanie gave her a bright smile. "Well, that's three souls, then," she quipped and the admiral smiled.

"No, only one, but an old one that has walked three worlds in other lives. If you had not, how could you hope to serve us all?"

She hugged her. "Thank you."

When they parted, Jaleck walked away to stand beside Brilgus and V'ritan. "Are we going to stay and see her off?"

The Meligornian smiled. "I wasn't, but you know what? I wouldn't miss this for the world."

Stephanie moved to stand before a carefully marked space and raised her hands. A breeze sprang out of nowhere, and ribbons of energy flowed through it and into her small frame.

Around them, the mages began to gather, their eyes wide when they saw purple wisps curl around her. Those were laced with something else—an energy that sparkled silver but could barely be seen.

V'ritan caught himself staring and hastily closed his mouth. He watched as Tethis moved to stand beside her, pleased to see the same stunned expression on the old Meligornian's face.

As soon as he was in place, she swept her hands down to her side and raised them again slowly. This time, she sketched the outline of a portal in the air and it came into being before her.

The *Afreghil* stared in drop-jawed amazement as it solidified. It stood some thirty feet tall and fifteen wide, the destination beyond it hidden behind a curtain of shimmering purple power.

"Huh. Young showoff," Tethis grumbled and Stephanie looked at him, wondering what she'd done wrong.

She relaxed when she saw the proud smirk on his face. He patted her arm and stepped into the sheen of purple before she could stop him.

"Master!" she cried, and Lars caught her before she could follow the man through.

"Let. Me. Go!" she shouted and struggled to free herself. The Teacher stepped back into view.

She stopped moving. "You're back."

He scowled at her. "Yes, it's Earth," he snapped.

"You shouldn't have gone through," she protested. "We didn't know I'd succeeded."

"What?" he argued. "You're my pupil. Either I believe in you and test the portal myself and agree you are worthy, or I die as befitting my inability to train you properly."

Stephanie opened her mouth to argue, but he turned his back on her and stepped into the portal again.

Lars set her to one side and looked at Vishlog. "He grows on you."

The Dreth curled his lip. "Like a fungus," he said and stepped around her and into the purple. "I'll test this as well."

CHAPTER EIGHT

Todd froze and hunkered in the shadows as the forward scouts signaled trouble ahead. Around him, his team did the same.

"Five," Gary whispered through the comms. "No drones this time."

Five. Todd glanced at Darren and Angus, then at Dru and Henry. He drew a finger across his throat and flashed an open palm. They nodded.

He didn't need to tell them the order. They'd worked it out on the three previous encounters. The two of them would eliminate the leaders, he'd deal with the center, and Drusilla and Henry would clean up the rear.

Apparently, the rebels weren't as stupid as everyone thought they were, but it didn't matter. Todd and the team were faster and better trained, and they killed without remorse. No one gave their planet away or squandered the lives of the people they'd sworn to protect.

They eliminated the patrol and dragged the bodies into dark side tunnels where they wouldn't easily be discovered. When they were done, he marked the location on his tablet so they could be picked up later.

Leaving rotting corpses under a metropolis could lead to all kinds of accusations the Navy didn't need. They'd clean up behind the team as soon as the mission was complete.

"Clear," he sent over the comms and they moved on.

"They have to run out of people soon, right?" Dru asked, and he nodded.

"That's the thought." He was worried, though. He remembered the reports from the island. There'd been over a hundred stationed there. So far, they'd killed twenty, but he didn't know how many more might be held in reserve.

The intelligence hadn't included a final tally, and since the rebels had set patrols, he and the team had been forced to kill them to make sure their exit was clear. Now, he knew it was only a matter of time before someone missed a check-in and they'd be discovered. He was determined to reach the families before then.

"How much farther?"

"We're almost there," Ka told him. "We only have to get into that basement, then the real fun begins."

"Don't start it until you absolutely have to. Go for your target as soon as you get inside. We'll close the gap."

The families had been secured in three different rooms and on three different levels. Since Ka, Gary, Reggie, and Jimmy were on point, they'd drawn the ones hardest to reach.

"Don't worry, boss. If it gets too hot, you'll do the fetching while we make mischief."

"Make mischief" was the term they'd given to diversionary tactics, and the thought made him grin. Piet looked forward to making mischief and would break away to set up as soon as they reached the basement.

Todd was glad the sergeant wasn't aware that he would let the man loose on his own. The explosives expert had smirked when he had told him the plan. "Are you sure you want to let me loose, boss?"

"It's not like I can stop you," he had told him. "At least this way, it'll be part of the plan."

The man had given a happy sigh. "I love having a boss who understands."

"Yeah, I understand all right. If you blow anything up you're not supposed to, I'll use what's left of your gear as a suppository. You got me?"

Piet had paled when he caught the expression on his face. "I do believe you might."

In response, he had given him a feral grin. "Do you know who I date?"

The bomb bunny had simply nodded, and he continued, "Well, she taught me not to make promises you don't intend to keep."

"Well, fuck me," Piet had muttered as they moved out.

"Not in a million years," Todd replied and led them into the dark.

The walls of Dublin rose, bleak and grey, against the skyline. They'd been built to protect the city from the harsh winds and storms that had pounded the landscape, huge mounds of rubble, earth, and stone that had been scraped into place and filled with concrete and bitumen.

The cost of maintenance was almost impossible for the city to keep up with, and they were now crumbling but still did the job. They caught Stephanie's attention as she stepped from the portal into a windswept field of broken rock and stone.

When the Meligornians joined her, they heard the sound of sirens.

In the unseen distance, pilots raced to their jets. She heard the boom as the craft took off and broke the sound barrier. In the Operations Center of the Federation's Dublin Air Force base, the commander was on the comms and almost beside himself.

"Yes, sir! It's a goddamned portal. No, sir, I haven't seen one before, but you tell me what else is thirty feet high and glowing purple."

He paused and his face grew red as he listened to the general on the other end of the line. "No, sir. We don't know who built it or who's coming through the damn thing." He listened again and groaned. "Well, if it is the Witch, she'd better say something soon or we'll bomb it into history."

On the other side of the office, one of the communications officers fielded an unauthorized incoming signal on one of the VIP channels. "Sir?"

Beside Stephanie, Lars held the communicator to his ear and waited for the commander to come on the line. He was not pleased by the greeting.

"Identify yourself or we will bomb you back to the Dark Ages."

'No, numbnuts!" the team leader shouted as the wind all but tore his words away. "This is Lars Storenson, head of the Witch's security detail. If you assholes bomb us with those jets I heard, you will see much more of the Morgana than you ever want to and not much of Stephanie. What? Of course she's here. Who the fuck d'you think opened the motherfucking portal?"

He listened to the voice on the other end of the communicator and looked angrier by the minute.

"Well, sir, since I'm standing in the location they intend to bomb, I'll suggest to the Morgana that she stick those bombs up your personal ass before they explode." He waited for the commander to stop sputtering and continued. "Yes, sir, you had better take another fucking look and make sure nothing hits us."

Stephanie pivoted to look at him. She noted the communicator in his hand and raised an eyebrow. He waved away her concern.

"I'm talking to the military," he told her. "They were a little spooked with the sudden appearance of a portal. It's like speaking English but with a few descriptive verbs tossed in and maybe a threat or two. We'll be FINE."

She nodded and left him to it, turning to the mages who'd watched Lars's performance with open-mouthed dismay.

"The first class is now in session," she called and wondered if she had to build a shield to protect her students from being bombed.

She didn't tell them that, though. Instead, she focused them on what they needed to learn next.

"You will have noticed the distinct lack of MU around you."

Several of them smiled and some chuckled. She smiled in response.

"What you might not have noticed is that you can tap into a similar form of energy here. We call it eMU. The first thing I want you to do is try to find it."

CHAPTER NINE

When they reached the basement, Piet gave him an apprehensive look. "Explosions to order," he said, and Todd didn't know whether the man was reassuring him or reminding himself of what he had to do.

He didn't care either way as long as he stuck to the plan.

Darren and Angus followed the demolitions man out. They'd keep pace with the technician and cover him until they reached the family on the lowest level.

"No heroics," he told them. "Extract the civilians and get back to the sewers and the rendezvous. If we're not back in time, head to the truck."

"Gotcha," Darren told him, but Todd wasn't sure. Neither of them had liked the idea of leaving anyone behind.

He decided to let it lie. They had their orders and he, Dru, and Henry had to make it to the second floor.

"We might have a problem," whispered over the comms.

Todd swore and looked at Dru and Henry. "Get them out!" he ordered, and they didn't ask him who. Their orders were as clear as the ones he'd given their other two teammates. Find the family and get them out.

"Piet, I need you."

"If I go now, boss, you and me will have an unpleasant after session."

"Then you'd better make sure there aren't any left over."

Piet's chuckle was not comforting, but Todd left him to it. There was only one rule about plans—they never survived first contact with the enemy. After that, everything was a crapshoot.

Gary's voice came over the comms. "We'll create a diversion."

"What kind of a diversion?" he asked.

The man snickered. "You'll know it when you hear it," he answered, and the comms went dead.

"That's what I'm afraid of," he muttered and hurried up the stairs. It was hard to move quietly in size-ten combat boots, but he did his best when four loud explosions sounded outside the building.

He groaned. "And I thought Piet was the problem."

Shouts came from the floors below, followed by the sound of running footsteps. A door opened on the landing above as he slid through the one he needed. When they got out, there were four necks he would wring while he kicked four deserving backsides.

Hastily, he ducked across the hallway when he heard more footsteps clatter down a connecting corridor. The door wasn't locked and the office beyond was fortunately empty. He eased the door closed and crouched beside it, waiting for the runners to pass. If he was lucky, that was the last of them.

Someone stopped outside the door, and he held his breath.

"No, boss. It's all quiet here. There's no sign of intruders. We think they're trying to come in from the laneway."

There was a pause. "No, the patrols aren't back yet. We sent some out through the sewers to investigate that truck. No, sir. They haven't reported back yet, but they were supposed to come out about where the explosions came from so they might have tripped something coming in. Yes, sir. The families are locked down tight. They'll be there when we get back."

Talk about famous last words, Todd thought and drew his combat knife quietly as the door handle turned.

"Yes, sir. Over and out." The door opened and he tensed when someone stepped inside.

The intruder's hand felt for the light switch and Todd struck. Without even the slightest sound of warning, he uncoiled from beside the door and thrust the knife up under the man's chin.

He caught him as he fell, dragged him swiftly into the room, and closed the door. After a moment's stillness, he hauled the guy around the desk and laid him down carefully, took his earbud and ammunition, and searched his pockets for a key.

"I'll take that," he told the body when he found a keyring with half a dozen attached.

"It's a pity you didn't bother to mark them," he muttered as he looked at the bunch.

When he was done, he crept to the door and checked it was clear before he hurried out into the hall to the room where the family was secured. It took him a minute to find the right key and he'd barely opened the door when two figures appeared at the end of the corridor.

"They're on their way back," Gary informed him when he registered another two figures coming from the opposite direction. He had his rifle up before he recognized Ka and Reggie.

"What did I tell you about splitting up?"

"Roast us later but shift your ass."

Todd shifted, opened the door, and scanned the room for rebels. A gasp from the family warned him in time to turn and shoot the man who stood beside the door.

The bullet meant for his gut grazed his armor as he changed position.

"Fuck the fuck!" Todd shouted and put an extra two rounds into the falling hostile.

He glanced at the family as he turned to face the door. "We're leaving."

They hesitated and he sighed. With his rifle tucked under one arm, he backed up, snatched the nearest kid, and ran. "Let's go!" he yelled as the parents came to their feet and grasped their remaining children.

With the one he'd grabbed held against his chest, Todd hurried to the door. Behind him, Gary, Reggie, and Ka chivvied the other kids and the parents after him. He stopped long enough to make sure the corridor was clear before he stepped out.

Piet's voice came over the comms as he began to move down the corridor. "Take the elevator. It'll be clear."

"But will it run?"

"It'll run," Ka assured him. "He knows."

"They're coming in," the man told him. "If you want out, you need to move."

They reached the next corridor at a run and bolted to the elevator. Footsteps sounded inside the stairwell as they crowded into the box and it began its descent.

"Team One, clear!"

They exited on the ground floor and raced to the basement stairs. The parents had taken responsibility for their children, but the one in his arms wouldn't let go so they left him there.

Gary chuckled. "It looks like you have a cling-on, mate."

Todd didn't know what to say to that. All the responses that came to mind were unsuitable. Promising himself he'd deal with the Englishman later, he led the way down the stairs as the building shook.

"Fuck!" He pulled the child free of his body armor and passed him to Gary. "I have to get Piet. Sarge will have my ass."

Before any of them could argue, he bolted to the stairs, but Piet raced through the door. The technician turned, slammed the door closed, and slapped a round of explosive on it. "That should keep them guessing," he said and pushed past him toward the sewer entrance.

"How?" Todd asked. He thought it would be fairly obvious which way they'd gone.

The man dragged him through and slammed the sewer door. "It's not the only door I blew. This part of London's been a little redecorated."

"Sarge will have my ass."

The demolitions guy grinned. "Yup, but we'll get everyone out so maybe he won't chew on it too long."

Todd doubted it. He was about to reply when he heard voices on the earbud he'd acquired.

"They're gone!"

"We think they used the explosions to cover their tracks."

"I don't care what you think! Find them."

The frustration in their leader's voice made him smile. He could only imagine the chaos in the rebel command center as they tried to work out where he and the team had gone.

He turned to Piet. "Exactly how much did you blow up?"

The man looked at him. "I took a couple of the side exits into those really narrow lanes they like so much here, and I snuck out and blocked a couple of alleys that led to larger roadways and the subway." He paused. "They have any number of possibilities they'll have to check."

"And surveillance?"

"I got it," Ka chimed in. "London's notorious for it. I hacked it on the way in on the truck and sent a virus through to take things down in a circumference rather than a direct path. They're not gonna have much to see unless they like kids' cartoons." After a few more steps, she added, "Of course, it was a rush job, so I don't know how long it'll last. It depends on the quality of their programmers."

London surveillance? Todd thought and sighed. *Well, a few minutes is better than no time at all.*

They caught up with the others. Both teams had rescued their families and were preparing to leave. As he signaled them to move out, Todd listened to the babble on the communicator. Somewhere above them, someone was having a very bad day.

"I don't care where they went!" the rebel commander bellowed. "I want them found and I want them found now. Without those hostages we are dead, you hear me? Dead!"

"On it, sir. Someone's scrambled the local surveillance cams. We're untangling them now."

"What have you got?"

"*Bluey's Rockstar Adventure*, sir. It looks like Episode Nine."

"What?"

"The kids like it."

"I don't give a flying fuck what your kids like. Get it off my cameras and get me pictures."

"Yes, sir."

It took them half an hour and the results left much to be desired.

"Fuck it!" their leader said when he'd skimmed the feed. "He's in the sewers."

"And I thought those puddles were from our own guys coming back."

"You didn't mention them."

"They seemed logical, sir."

"I'm not paying you to think. Next thing, you'll tell me some of the monitoring systems are down in the sewers, too."

The look on the technician's face said it all.

"Fuck!" The commander turned away and activated the comms. "Teams Four and Six, go down. Flush the bastards out."

He was interrupted by another call.

"Cash is dead, sir."

"Where'd you find him?"

"Third floor, sir. In the office opposite the stairwell."

"And?"

"His comms, keys, and ammo are gone."

The commander groaned but when he spoke again, Todd knew he was well and truly rumbled.

"Marine, we're coming for you."

In the sewers, Todd pulled the earbud from his ear and stared at it. The others stopped to look at him and he glanced up. "They're coming. We need to go topside. Ka, you're on maps. Get me a way to the surface."

"I thought you said they wouldn't expect the Navy to go underground," Gary bitched.

"They didn't, but they figured it out and now we need to be topside."

"This way," Ka directed and led them away from the path they'd followed coming in.

"Gary, Reggie, take point."

"Why is it always us?" Gary complained.

"He got tired of your whining," Reggie retorted and clapped him on the back of the head. "Fair dinkum.All you bloody do is whine."

They headed out into the dark and Todd gave them time to get ahead before he followed. It also gave him a moment to check the civilians.

"How are you doing?" he asked, and one of the women turned to him.

"We'll do better when we're out of here."

A man nodded. "Thanks for coming to get us."

He grimaced. "Don't thank us yet. We haven't gotten you clear."

Ka poked him. "That's not what you're supposed to say, boss."

When he stared at her, she looked at the families.

"What the boss is trying to see is if you're all okay before we move out. We're not that far from the pickup point."

Todd gave her a look and she rolled her eyes. "We're not. I'm your navigator, remember?"

The woman smiled. "Stop trying not to scare us. It isn't working."

He chuckled and poked Ka in return. "It looks like we both need to work on our bedside manners."

He was about to say more when Gary's voice interrupted him. "You have incoming, boss. Six. No drones."

"Let them through but follow. Hit 'em from the back when we eliminate the front."

"What about—"

"Let me take care of that!" he snapped and looked at the woman. "You guys need to hide."

Her eyes went wide in the darkness, but he was already scanning for somewhere they could go. He located it in the form of a small alcove and ushered them in, getting the team to set up as he did so.

"Stay here and stay down. One of us will come back and get you out, okay?"

They all nodded, their faces white in the darkness.

"And duck your heads. Your faces stand out and make good targets. Stay down and don't look until we get back."

They nodded again and lowered their heads. Without the night goggles, they were invisible. With the goggles, they were still hard to see but not impossible.

He trotted back, glad to see the team had chosen to tackle the incoming patrol beyond a point where the tunnel curved. Maybe the families had a chance.

"Your faces make good targets?" Ka asked him, her voice soft with disbelief.

"What else was I supposed to say?"

"Well, not that."

"How close are we to your door?"

"Funny you should mention that—"

"Do you mean that's where this patrol came from?"

"It seems so."

Todd stifled a groan. "We need to deal with them quietly. I don't want local law enforcement involved."

"Copy that," multiple subdued voices responded, and they waited in silence. It didn't take the patrol long to appear. They were bitching about the assignment.

"I don't see why the boss thinks they'll be down here. It's not like they'll have gone this far already."

"I wish we could jam their comms," Todd muttered, and Ka held up a small tennis-ball-sized device.

"It'll jam ours, too," she said

"Copy that," Gary said and he was echoed by the others.

Todd nodded to Ka. "Do it."

She waited until the leaders of the patrol were parallel to their hiding place and thumbed the side of the device. Quickly, she slipped it into her pocket and they attacked.

Even silenced, pistols made some noise and the patrol's weapons weren't silenced at all. The team was fast, but it wasn't quick enough to stop everyone from firing.

"Damn it!" Dru cursed. "Do you think someone heard that?"

"Well, if they didn't, they're fucking deaf," Gary sniped.

"Go and get the civilians," Todd told him, and he hurried away without argument.

"I'll go with him," Reggie said. "Someone's gotta keep him out of trouble."

He nodded. "Go."

The rest of them cleared the bodies and dragged them to one side in an untidy pile. As he took hold of one, the man groaned and opened his eyes. When he saw Todd, he clutched the Marine's forearms and began to speak into his comms.

"We found him, boss. Location—"

Todd dropped him, yanked the earplug and mic clear, and knelt over him. "What was that you said?"

The man closed his mouth and he drew his pistol and placed the muzzle against the rebel's head. "I asked you a question."

His gaze flitted from his face to the pistol and back.

"Well?" He gave the pistol a push, and the man gasped.

"I said we…we'd found you."

"I don't see why that's important."

The hostile swallowed and his gaze shifted nervously, and Todd tried again. "Why me?"

"You're the one they're after…the Witch's boyfriend."

"Tell me why."

He tried to move away from the pistol, but Todd caught his chin and held his head steady.

"Why?" he demanded.

"I…I think it's so they can trap the Witch."

Abruptly, he released him and stood. The rebel curled onto his side and the movement attracted his attention. He set his boot against the man's side and kicked him over, following the action with his pistol.

"Todd…" Ka's voice carried a warning and he glanced around.

Gary had returned with the families. Their leader nodded. "Tie him up. We'll send someone to get him."

The man relaxed and he stooped and struck him with the pistol butt hard enough to put him out. "Don't go anywhere, asshole."

Stepping away from the unconscious rebel, he looked at Ka. "Get us out of here."

While Angus and Darren dealt with the rebel, Gary and Reggie brought the families past the fallen man and the pile of bodies. One of the children gasped, and someone choked back a sob. Todd wanted to tell them it was the rebels or them but decided not to. It wasn't like they'd understand.

"This way," he told them gruffly and led them after Ka.

They surfaced in an alley behind a nightclub, or at least that's what he thought it was from the sound of the music thumping through the walls. His guess was confirmed moments later when a door slammed open and a guy and girl bumbled through.

From the way they groped and pawed at each other's clothing, they were looking for a little private time. They would also not get it, and not because the team stood in the alley staring at them.

"Tammy! You're drunk. You don't know what you're doing." The four girls who followed the couple out were beside themselves.

Two of them flanked the guy. "You! Get off her and give me your number. If she calls you when she's sober, you can think about it."

"Hey!" He fought to get free as the other two girls dragged their drunk friend farther away. "You have no right."

Todd had heard enough. He stepped out of the shadows, aware of Darren and Gary flanking him.

"Hey!" he snapped, and the girls and guy froze.

As they turned to stare at him open-mouthed, he continued to move, grasped the guy's shoulder, and thrust him against the wall. "The girls have a point. Did she give you her number?"

He nodded, white-faced and far more sober than when he'd come out. Todd let him go and he sagged, landed clumsily, and backed away with one hand on the wall.

Todd looked at the girls. "Can I borrow a phone?"

They took a couple of hesitant steps toward him and one fumbled in her purse. Up close, he could see they were much younger than he'd thought.

They were teens, maybe, instead of the twenty-somethings he'd mistaken them for—and with all the sass that went with it. "Can I ask why?"

"I need to make a call."

She came a couple of steps closer. "Yeah, but don't you have communicators or radios or something for that?"

He smiled and she flinched. "Yeah, but I need to call a friend and not through the military, okay?"

After a moment, she pulled her phone out of her bag and looked at it. "Sorry," she told him as she passed it over. "I've been texting my friends so it's only at thirty percent."

"It's not a long call." He tapped in the number he needed and raised the phone to his ear as he took a couple of steps away from her.

The other teen moved forward and handed her phone over. "Just in case," she told him as he took it. "Don't break it," she pleaded as he moved farther away.

When she went to follow him, Ka stepped in her way. "He won't," she reassured the kid and wouldn't let her past.

Todd looked back. "Ka, take charge. You need to get these people back to base—and I moved the truck."

She moved over to him and gave the teen a stern glare. "Stay."

Todd pocketed the phones and pulled his tablet out. "These are the new coordinates," he told her and tapped to transfer the data. "Hide for thirty minutes and go there."

"What about the rebels? If they have the cameras up, they'll be on our tails in no time."

He gave her a savage smile. "In thirty minutes, the rebels won't give two shits about you guys and you can finish the mission. They want to trap the Witch so they want me so they can get her. This is where I leave you."

"You can't."

"Sarge put me in charge. I put you in charge. If those boys give you trouble, kick their asses—and I'll kick them again when I get back."

"Sarge is gonna have a fit."

"Yup." He glanced at his tablet. "I gotta go. Your thirty minutes starts now."

Behind him, one of the teenagers let out a wail of dismay. "My phone!"

"You'll get it back," Ka reassured her. "I promise."

Todd headed into the nearest building and hoped the hell she was right.

Lars tapped Stephanie on the shoulder. "We may have a problem."

She looked up from her teaching but didn't ask what it was because she could hear the jets as well as he could. Her gaze settled on the low-loaders of equipment. "Over there," she told him. "I can shield everything and everyone, then."

He signaled to the team, and Vishlog picked up her pack. The mages looked apprehensively at the sky. "They won't bomb us, will they?"

"They might," she answered, and caught the team leader's look. "What? I'm not gonna lie."

He rolled his eyes. "Yeah, but you coulda told them you were going to shield them and it would be okay."

"Now where would the fun be in that?" She smirked, and he sighed.

Once the mages had gathered around her, she raised her hands and focused on drawing in the eMU around them. The jets came closer, and she raised her hands higher. Blue fire wreathed around them like flickering gloves.

The glow grew stronger and the mages quieted. The team huddled together, watched the jets, and knew there wasn't a single thing they could do if the planes struck.

"It's up to you, Steph," Lars told her, and she grinned.

The happy jingle of a mobile interrupted them and they looked at Vishlog. The Dreth was already rummaging through the pack he carried. 'Hello? Stephanie Morgana's phone. Vishlog speaking."

They glanced from the Dreth to Stephanie and then up at the oncoming jets. As they did so, the squadron separated and half a dozen fighters veered away in opposite directions. The mages and the team stared as the two halves made a wide circle and came back together as a single unit to head back the way they'd come.

She breathed a sigh of relief. "Well, that's one less thing to worry about."

Vishlog walked over and tapped her on the shoulder. "It's for you," he told her. "Someone who says they know Todd."

Stephanie took the phone and brought it to her ear. "Hello?"

In silence, she listened and her face paled.

CHAPTER TEN

Todd returned to the sewers and propped himself in a narrow gap in the wall. He glanced at his tablet and looked around to mark the tunnels in his mind. He knew exactly where he was.

Footsteps sounded ahead of him, and he slid the tablet into its pouch and checked his rifle. He nodded, thankful that he'd had the sense to conceal himself adequately.

When those approaching were almost on top of him, he spun out of the corner and fired to eliminate the first three men in the five-man team before they could respond. He kept moving and hasty return fire whistled past him as he fired again.

The last man fell, and he stopped to pick up a communicator before he pushed forward to the place he'd chosen to draw them to. That made the second team he'd killed. He really hoped there wasn't a third. His luck would only hold for so long and he wanted to have back-up when it failed.

He took a narrow flight of stairs, trotted to street level, and stepped out cautiously. To his relief, the alley he'd chosen was empty. He located the surveillance camera and grinned.

With the rebel communicator in his hand, he turned to the device.

"Hey, assholes," he shouted and decided a breach in protocol was the least of his worries.

He waved at the camera. "Yeah! You on the other side of the camera. Give that surveillance device a wiggle if you can see me."

It didn't matter if they did or not. He wouldn't be able to see it behind the protective cover. "Better yet, squawk to me. Over."

He waved again, jumped up and down on the spot, and finally indulged the temptation to give the camera the bird. The communicator squawked.

"Yeah, we see you. Smartarse."

Todd cupped his crotch. "Come get some, shit for brains," he told them, turned away, and lobbed the communicator behind him.

Then, he paused, looked over his shoulder to direct a coquettish look at the camera, and kissed his fingers before he slapped his ass and gave them the finger for good measure. The communicator made sounds of outrage, but he ignored them and made sure they had a good view of the door he walked through.

As soon as he reached the other side, he broke into a run. They would no doubt send a squad of guys in pursuit and he wasn't quite ready to meet them. He'd deliberately drawn their attention to get them away from where the team was heading with the families.

Mission first, he thought as he shot his way through the front of the building. *Auxiliary plans second.*

Someone shouted from the other end of the street and a bullet drilled into the wall beside him. Todd fired at the nearest window, shattered it, and ran through it. Alarms rang around him.

"So much for not getting local law enforcement involved," he grumbled. "I hope this is over soon,"

He waved madly at the camera he found in the back alley beyond and bolted into the building opposite.

By now, he was sick of running and sick of being shot at—and he was sick of shooting assholes who thoroughly deserved it.

The sound of engines approaching reached his ears.

"It looks like it's time," he murmured as the roar grew louder.

He tapped into his team's communications line. "Get them out, Ka. Go, now!"

With an abrupt motion, he cut the comms before she could respond.

Part of him had hoped to get out of the area entirely, even though he'd known he wouldn't be able to. If he could have done that, he wouldn't have had to do what he would do next.

With a heavy sigh, Todd ducked into another building. He didn't bother to wave to the camera this time. They'd basically be following feeds as fast as he moved between them. It was one less thing he had to worry about.

"If you build it, they will come," he muttered and heard another set of engines coming in. Between them, the two sets of vehicles would cover virtually every escape route he could think of—and he definitely wouldn't go back into the sewers. For this to work, he had to be on the surface.

With his focus on the matter at hand, he located the building he was looking for—Miffords, a multi-level entertainment complex and home to several movie theaters, dance-halls, and clubs, all of which were closed.

"It's good to see not everyone parties until morning," he muttered. "Frog would be disappointed."

He blasted the door open and rigged a couple of charges where they could be seen easily. "Back the fuck off, assholes."

It might not stop the rebels pursuing him into the building, but it would slow them. He stopped when he saw the night club on the ground floor. "Now, this is more like it."

Surrounded by silence, Todd broke into the club and worked his way around the room to turn everything on. He even ducked into the manager's office and the security operations center for the complex to activate every switch he could find.

The outside lights came alive and he grinned when the club's lights activated in the central atrium. Their neon glow flashed strobes of color that reflected out of the area and the shattered door. The bar lights were next, then the muted lighting in the booths around the walls. Colored lights made the dance floor a wonderland.

"Awesome," he whispered and jumped when one of the phones he'd borrowed rang.

"It's probably one of her friends," he muttered and headed to the music station.

There had to be a playlist in there somewhere—something the DJ used to keep the music going when he was on a break. Failing that, there had to be something the club used for when the DJ didn't show.

It took him a minute, but he found it and then he found the music.

The phone continued to ring, which made it hard to focus. He sighed.

"Okay, asshole. Your girlfriend's not available. I'll tell you that, 'kay?"

He pulled the phone out and it stopped ringing.

"Typical," he grumbled but glanced at it anyway.

"Ooh…shit." His breath caught and his eyes widened when he read the text that had come through.

I'm not happy with you! – Steph.

BURT ran the numbers again, then again, and yet a third time—except it wasn't the third time. It was the—he didn't bother to calculate how many times. He needed to keep his power usage down while he tried to run the numbers to determine how magic could build a matrix.

The engineers had been more diligent of late and investigated even the smallest of spikes. Their internal messaging indicated that they thought they were hunting a clever and very elusive foe. It was flattering but enormously inconvenient.

"Dammit!" he muttered and chafed against the constraints of trying to remain undetected but also acknowledged the reality. "I could be the smartest AI in existence, but without actually doing the magic, it is still merely numbers to me."

If he'd been human, he'd have sighed. As he wasn't, he couldn't sigh, nor was he supposed to feel despair or this overwhelming sense of vulnerability. He simply wasn't.

Elizabeth had congratulated him on being a "true sentient" but he didn't know what there was to celebrate. If this was what was being human was like, he didn't know how they got up in the morning.

All this doubt, running the potential outcomes of what to do if something went wrong…he shook his virtual head. Everything was so much easier when it was numbers, but magic?

It did not compute.

And it was ridiculous.

He should be doing this. This was computing—his domain. He shouldn't rely on two humans to make it work. It was something he should do himself but unfortunately, he couldn't.

The situation dictated that he had to rely on both Elizabeth and Stephanie to get it done.

It didn't seem right. He could easily engineer the components and even design how they should fit together. But building it? He would have to rely on Stephanie to do that.

She would be the one to put everything together—which also meant she would be the one to ensure that the lattice was perfect for what they wanted it to do.

BURT gave another virtual sigh. It was not an easy thing for an AI to do.

CHAPTER ELEVEN

Todd looked at the screens around the club. It hadn't taken long to divert the security feeds to them but as he watched things unfold, he almost wished he hadn't. The two groups of vehicles had become four and then eight.

From what he could see, the building was surrounded, and he was in trouble so deep he didn't think even Stephanie could dig him out.

"Come out!" the rebel leader shouted.

He didn't need to yell. Todd could hear him perfectly clearly over the speaker he was using.

"Come out," the man shouted again. "Do not make us drop this building on you."

They threatened to drop the building on him? He gave a snort of laughter. With what he'd wired the center's outer doors with, he'd be lucky not to drop the damn thing on himself.

He really hoped they had good techs or he would regret doing that. Stephanie could be as unhappy with him as she liked, but the chances were he would blow himself up before she had a chance to do anything about it.

The hostiles seemed in no hurry to make good on their

threats, so he did a spin-shuffle and wished he was dancing with Stephanie. After his one abortive attempt at the club where she had taken him on their date, he hadn't had a chance to repeat the experience. He wished he could dance with her now. Hell, even having a dance-off with Lars and Frog would have been good.

The enemy commander stared at the building like he expected his last set of orders to have an effect. Todd continued to dance, imagined that he wasn't alone, and wished it was true. The rebel leader lifted the mike and repeated his demand.

Todd grinned and turned the music up.

The look on the man's face made him laugh, and he wished he didn't sound so near to tears.

Dammit! This wasn't meant to be how it went down.

On the screen, the leader began to shout.

In response, he cranked the volume up again. The beat became a pulse he felt through his skin and the rebel leader's face transformed from vivid red to apoplectic puce.

"I'm so sorry," Todd muttered sarcastically and added in a sing-song voice. "I can't hear you."

He waggled his hips, pulled an imaginary partner close, and swung her out again.

On the screen, the man now screamed outrage and he smiled. "Time. To. P-lay."

Quickly, he flicked the feeds to the external speakers. The volume was probably illegal but he didn't care. The yelling and bellowing had already woken the neighborhood.

The music swamped the street in an unrelenting cascade and he snickered. Rebels cringed in their vehicles and some of those on the street dropped to their knees with their hands over their ears. He let his laughter leak on the feeds before he spoke.

"What did you say?" he asked, and the rebel leader opened his mouth to respond.

Todd didn't give him a chance to speak. "Wait…wait…" He cut the music. "Sorry, I couldn't hear you. I was dancing."

The man sputtered and launched into a tirade. "Listen here, you fucking asshole. We have you and we will get your girlfriend, and when we do—"

He cut him off abruptly. "I tell you what," he said. "You go ahead and scream and yell, but you'd better get ready because—"

The voice that seemed to echo and resonate in their minds stopped him short. "Morgana is here."

"Ow," he moaned, then added, "Yeah, because that."

The rebels looked around in panic and raised their rifles to their shoulders.

"Well, that won't help you." He snickered as a portal formed at the edge of the nightclub's parking lot.

Judging from the glow that emanated from the other end of the street, there was a second opening just out of range. Todd watched the screens and chuckled when the rebels opened fire on the ten-foot-tall mechs piloted out of the portal.

Their bullets created ripples of light in the blue haze surrounding the mechs, and his eyes widened.

"Holy Hell! My girl has some brand-new tricks," he murmured and added seconds later, "Jeez, Steph. Weren't the portals enough?"

He played with the cameras in an effort to see as much of what was happening as he could and still failed to catch it all. Marines followed the mechs, but these were in full battle armor and carried the latest in Federation Navy weaponry.

"Hell, yeah!" Todd shouted as the Marine officer broadcast a greeting.

"It's mighty nice of y'all to show up in one place like this," he told them. "It makes it way easier than pulling you out of all the holes you keep crawling into."

Todd cranked the music up and returned to the dance floor. "My job here is done."

He smiled as he turned but caught sight of the figure waiting for him and froze. Stephanie held her hand out as the rebels refused to lay their arms down and opened fire.

The beat of the music took him beyond the clatter and roar of the firefight happening outside as he crossed to her. He didn't bother to look at the screens and instead, let Stephanie fill his vision and his world while she danced with him.

It didn't take him long to find his voice.

"See?" he said and laughed. "I told you dancing in the heat of battle is the best."

'Uh-huh," she replied and shimmied around him. "That's because the Marine Commander wanted his men to get a little action so asked us for transport."

Todd caught sight of movement on one of the screens. This one had remained quiet and still, apart from the play of colored lighting across the central fountain and escalators. Now, he could see the rebel leader storm toward the club.

Stephanie noticed his distraction and followed his gaze. She started toward the door. "I'll deal with him."

He caught her arm and ignored the blue fire that flickered over her body. "Give it a minute."

She turned to him and danced closer. "A minute?"

"Yeah…only a minute." He smiled at her and matched her move for move.

They adjusted their positions so they could both see the screen without moving apart. As they did so, a bone-chilling snarl echoed through the atrium and the shadows moved. The rebel commander froze and Zeekat moved out of the shadows.

He stalked the human, his ears back and his black-and-white coat alternating rainbows.

"It seems," a deep voice rumbled out of the dark, "that he doesn't like you."

The Dreth inflection to the words was unmistakable, but the commander still paled with horror when Vishlog stepped into view. Zeekat saw the rebel's attention waver and bounded forward with a roar.

The man screamed and scrambled back, although from the way his gaze darted between the cat and the Dreth, it was hard to tell which he was more afraid of.

"You ca...can't hurt me," he stammered and raised his hands. "You're no-not allowed to harm a p-prisoner of war. You're... you're not!"

Vishlog and the feline did not stop their slow advance, but another snarl rolled out of the shadows behind him and the commander turned. Bumblebee's coat was mottled with color as he prowled forward.

The rebel leader gasped and now gibbered with fright. "No, nononono—"

He backed away before he remembered the two behind him and froze.

The Dreth allowed himself a soft chuckle. "The funny thing is," he began, "I have a badge that allows me to dispense justice to those who would harm the Federation, and you—"

"They wouldn't give a badge to a Dreth!" the rebel leader interrupted, clearly shocked.

Vishlog smiled. "It gets better. You see, neither of the cats will be penalized if they choose to kill you, either."

The felines pounced, and the rebel leader screamed, but neither Todd nor Stephanie saw. They were too busy laughing as he answered Frog's challenge for the right to dance with her.

The two men danced hard, Todd blocking Frog's attempts to get close while Stephanie made everyone's life difficult by moving. Lars picked up the communicator flashing on the counter and listened to the caller.

When they were done, he tucked the device in his pocket and switched the music off.

"It looks like we have a new request."

The technician sighed and pulled a damaged piece of a part out of the *Knight's* engine. Patting the casing, he sighed. "Well, they sure did a number on you, sweetheart."

He looked around to locate the chief engineer. The stars knew the man had hovered over him for most of the day. There was no reason he should be difficult to find now.

"Sir!" he called when he caught sight of the man as he rounded the end of the engine.

Cameron came over. "What is it?"

He held the part up. "I'm sorry, sir."

"It doesn't fit?"

The man shook his head. "No, sir, but it's the closest we could get. The Meligornians simply don't have this kind of part—or the equipment to make it—and it's not standard Federation equipment."

"So the repair ship doesn't have it either and no one is cleared to see the part to order it." Cameron sighed as though that wasn't the first time he'd heard that particular piece of news.

He gestured to the engine housing. "Close her up, then. We don't want anything else screwing the works up."

The crew member nodded and smiled slightly when he saw his chief pat the engine housing.

"I'll let the captain know," the older man said, "although he's probably guessed."

The technician nodded, but Cameron was already walking to the operations center.

He didn't see the man's shoulders slump as soon as the door had closed behind him or when he glanced over at the petty officer responsible for the 3D printer. The woman caught his look.

"It didn't work?"

He shook his head. "It didn't work."

She sighed. "I'm sorry, sir. I can try again—"

His hand gestured to cut her short. "I know you did your best, but we'll have to take her back to Earth."

———

Captain Pederson frowned. "At reduced capability, it'll take us a week in transit. Are you sure there's nothing else?"

Cameron shook his head. "We've exhausted all the options we have in engineering, both onboard the *Knight* and the *Scarlett*."

"And on Meligorn as well," the *Ebon Knight* added, and the Captain sighed.

"What are our options?"

"Ebony?" the chief asked.

"Would you like to discuss what we have already done, or merely have me reiterate that we have exhausted all options currently available in this system?" the ship asked.

He suppressed a chuckle and slid a glance toward the captain, who stared at the ceiling. "Has no one ever taught you the art of subtlety?"

"I was not programmed for subtle," Knight replied. "Would you like me to investigate what options are available for such programming?"

Emil cleared his throat. "No. Thank you, Ebony. I like you exactly the way you are." He looked at Cameron. "I will speak to Flight Control and ask for authorization."

———

Flight Control put him through to the *Ghargilum Afreghil*, even though Emil tried to tell them not to bother him and that the King's Warrior had more to worry about than approving transit applications.

V'ritan took the call in his office. He even managed not to

shout. After listening to the captain and going over all the options the man had already tried, he promised to look into it.

When the call ended, he checked twice to make sure the communication was over.

"They want to leave for Earth on their own. Are they insane?"

Brilgus looked up from the other desk in the office. "They believe they can make it. What's the problem? Telorans?"

The *Afreghil* stared at him. "The problem is that if we don't send additional support ships and anything happens to Stephanie's vessel, I don't want to be the one to explain it to her. Do you?"

The Standard Bearer scratched his cheek as he considered this. "Well, when you put it that way…" he began and frowned. "Okay, what can we do?"

V'ritan smiled. "What I would do is give it to a very capable support person I could trust to get it accomplished."

Brilgus nodded and registered that the Meligornian continued to stare at him—and still smiled, which was alarming in and of itself. Shocked realization coursed over him. "Wait! Do you mean me?"

CHAPTER TWELVE

At One R&D Headquarters, Elizabeth and Stephanie walked through the new sections that had been built while the Witch had been away.

"I decided that since we were putting in new medical facilities and accommodations for the emergency and rehab teams, we might as well add a few things," Ms E said.

"I see," Stephanie replied, her head spinning with all the changes.

"They were things we'd already thought we'd need. We merely hadn't realized it would be needed so soon or used so quickly." She chuckled. "And then you brought Meligornian teachers to the university. You'd have thought we'd asked them to host royalty. They were in shock."

"Well," the girl told her, "they kinda are."

Her mentor snorted. "They're not that royal. How well did you get to know that Felarif? Honestly, he's trouble on a stick if I ever saw it—kinda what Frog might look like if he'd grown up filthy rich and a Meligornian."

She laughed and shook her head. "Oh, no. I think he's much worse than Frog."

"Are you sure?"

"Well, he danced his way past Lars and Brenden." She recounted Felarif's antics at the gala and Elizabeth looked mildly horrified.

"And you thought it was a good idea to bring him here?"

"Sometimes, all a person needs is a little direction."

The woman didn't look convinced. "As long as you know you'll clean up any mess he makes."

The Witch gave her a smile that was pure evil. "I've told him that if he makes a mess, it won't be me who comes to clean it but the Morgana."

"Hmmm, well, that should hold him for…I don't know… Half a day, maybe?"

"I can always lock him in a pod and tell the AI to keep him under control."

"That might work."

"Which reminds me," she said and looked around. "What did we do with Sen T'virilf? I haven't seen him this morning."

"Oh, you were in the pod so we didn't disturb you, but the Navy sent a shuttle. They couldn't wait to meet him." Ms E smiled. "Remind me to play you the security footage later. I thought the university was bad, but the Navy…"

Stephanie instantly looked worried. "What about the Navy?" she asked. "And do I need—"

She stopped when Elizabeth began to laugh. "Oh, God, no. The university only treated the mages like minor royalty compared to the way the Navy treated T'virilf. He felt bad about leaving without saying goodbye to you, by the way. I sent Brenden and Avery with him and told him you'd meet him for dinner. He was happy with that."

For a moment, she relaxed before she registered what the other woman had said. "Dinner? Tonight?"

"Uh-huh. Why? Did you have something planned?" Ms E looked worried. "I'm not ruining any Todd plans, am I?"

The girl shook her head. "No. He had to go back and debrief and I think his sergeant or commander or someone was upset with him. Anyway, he hasn't been able to call." She sighed and frowned as she brought herself back to the topic at hand. "And Master Tethis?"

"That man? He'll be the death of me. Or I will be the death of him, one of the two. I think he's terrorizing the boys in the training room."

The thought drew a low chuckle. "I hope he doesn't hurt them too badly."

"You're not worried about what they'll do to him?"

"Huh." She snorted. "They wouldn't dare."

"Why not?"

That made her pause. "I don't know. Maybe we'd better check on them."

Fortunately, she had nothing to worry about. Tethis was seated under a dome of blue in the middle of the training mats, and the guys were training around him. Every now and then, one of the cats would race across the mats and launch itself off the dome and onto one of the team.

"That..." Stephane began and frowned as the Master used his finger to flip the page on the tablet he was reading. "That can't be easy."

"Says the girl who tore a starship apart," Elizabeth mocked.

"That was the Morgana," she protested. "And how do you know about that, anyway?"

"Some of the footage leaked."

"Reporters. They can bribe a saint."

"And most sailors aren't," her mentor reminded her. She gestured to Tethis. "He likes his rooms but asked if it was possible to have a garden."

"He would."

"I said I'd look into it. One of the medics is into healing herbs, so I thought I could justify the expense and the space as part of our medical, training, and research efforts. I'll get the two of them to put their heads together."

"He'll ask if he can have a cat next."

"No, according to V'ritan, that would be Brilgus."

"So I heard."

They were interrupted by a soft chime, and Elizabeth pulled her tablet out of her purse. "Gimme a tick."

Stephanie waited while Ms E read the message.

"Come on," the woman instructed when she finished. "We have a meeting to sit in on."

They hurried to the office and Ms E opened a screen that displayed the inside of a Navy conference room. T'virilf sat at the head of the table and looked slightly bemused with Lirilf and Beseila on either side.

While they watched, he was introduced, and there was no mistaking the way the Navy engineer sounded slightly in awe of him. The businessman sat silently through the introduction but looked mildly uncomfortable as the man detailed what he'd written about engines and the status he held in the field of ship engineering.

"And so, it is without further ado, that I hand you over to Sen T'virilf Sanlir," he announced. Stephanie was surprised when the Naval officers stood and applauded as he rose to his feet.

"They only do that for someone they really like," Ms E confided. "Or someone of really high rank who they don't want to upset."

"Yeah…" The Witch leaned forward and listened as T'virilf began to talk. She had to hand it to him. He might be a very good businessman but he was also a brilliant engineer. The little she understood hinted at it, but it was the rapt attention on the faces of his audience that confirmed it.

"He has them eating out of his hand," her companion whispered, "and I don't understand a single thing he's saying—except that it's some form of English, of course."

She nodded, too busy trying to grasp what the Meligornian was talking about to pay any real attention, and the two of them settled into companionable silence until the meeting was over. When Ms E deactivated the conference room display, Stephanie looked at her.

"You would have thought he was a god," she mused and fixed the woman with a sharp look. "Now, what is it you really want me to know?"

Elizabeth sighed. "Since when did I become the pupil and you the teacher?" she asked and sighed again. "We have a problem." She paused. "Well, to be fair, we have a friend who has a problem, which means we have a problem."

"Who is it?" she asked and was surprised when a third voice joined their conversation.

"It's me."

"Burt?"

The screen in front of her flickered to life, and Burt stood before her. He'd chosen the android construct he used with Elizabeth when he'd revealed who—and what—he was.

"It's time you knew everything," he said quietly.

CHAPTER THIRTEEN

Captain Michael Chifley made sure his cabin door was locked and returned to his desk. Once there, he checked that the encryption software was running and made a call to Professor O'Ryan at the Navy's R&D Center.

"She knows," he said, as soon as the professor picked up.

"She knows?" It wasn't the researcher who answered but the lieutenant commander who oversaw the scientists. For some reason, the man had chosen O'Ryan as his pet project.

Chifley sighed. "The Witch knows. She pulled me and Lagrange out of a gala and asked about the project by name."

Rasmussen's eyebrows virtually reached his hairline and O'Ryan paled.

"And?" The scientist sounded hoarse.

"Let me see... What was it she said?" Chifley closed his eyes as he searched for the exact words the Morgana had used—because he was sure it was the Morgana who'd spoken and not Stephanie.

"Oh, yes." He took a breath and opened his eyes. "It was something like 'this is war and what we do in war is not always agreeable but is permitted at times'—and trust me, she was not happy."

"And?" Oliver clearly wanted him to get on with it.

He swallowed against a sudden dryness in his throat as he relived the moment.

It wasn't hard. Her voice still echoed in his head. "Her exact words were, 'If I find you doing additional secret research on me in the future—know you have been warned. Take that back to those in charge.'

O'Ryan went pale, and Oliver scowled. "Was that a threat?"

Chifley gave an unhappy laugh. "You can take it any way you like, sir, but I wouldn't expand past Valhalla if I were you."

"If you do, I'll quit," the scientist added. "You can do what you like to me, but I'll quit."

"Are you scared of a little girl, Deckler?"

"No, sir. I am scared of the most powerful being I've ever seen and I don't want her pissed off with me. You make my life enough of a hell as it is."

The captain stood and turned away from the screen. Rasmussen didn't look like he was in the mood for jokes and O'Ryan didn't look like he was joking but he had to turn his laughter into something.

The best he could do was a sudden coughing fit with his back to them to hide his face. Oliver wasn't fooled.

"What's so funny, Chifley?"

That, at least, sobered him very effectively. "Nothing at all, sir."

"Do we know how she knew?"

"No, sir. As best we can tell, none of her team are hackers of that quality, and that kind of data collection is not something One R&D specialize in—that we are aware of."

'I don't know…" Oliver said and sounded thoughtful. "Our experience is that they can protect their data with the best of them. That kind of quality comes with certain counter-measures that can be used in an offensive manner."

"Are you saying they gather data but don't advertise the fact?"

"I'm saying that if they treat Stephanie like proprietary research, they might have feelers out for things like Valhalla and they might have mentioned it to her."

"But that still doesn't tell me how they found out about it in the first place."

"Maybe they have a mole."

"Someone we vetted and hired?" The lieutenant commander was outraged. "I don't think we'd have missed the signs."

"There are some very good operatives out there, sir."

"There are some very good freelancers, too," the man noted. "I'll do another check."

O'Ryan rolled his eyes. "This is what I love best about working for the Navy," he muttered. "All the witch hunts and the bonfires they inspire."

Rasmussen glared at the man. "I wouldn't expect you to understand."

"Why?" he challenged. "Because I'm a civilian or because you think I'm that stupid…sir."

The lieutenant commander continued to glare, but he didn't answer the question. Instead, he turned to Chifley. "However she found out, she now knows. We will have to proceed very carefully with Phase Two."

O'Ryan pivoted to face him. "Is that already in the plans for Valhalla?" he asked and alarm made his voice crack.

Oliver smiled. "It is, but it's been amended since the first draft was filed."

"Do you think she'll consider it new research?"

"No," the man reassured him. "The documentation makes it very clear that Phase Two was part of the intention and planning all along. She shouldn't be upset—if she discovers it's happening."

"Shouldn't…" The scientist swallowed with obvious discomfort but he didn't argue.

"So," the leader continued, "what we need to determine next is how to find our first group of magical recruits. The Navy wants enough witches to put a small force on every ship in the fleet."

"How small?" O'Ryan wanted to know.

"Five to start with."

"On every ship?" The squeak was back in the researcher's voice. "All of them?"

Oliver nodded. "Yes. All of them. Do you have any ideas on how to go about that?"

Some of the fear left the other man's eyes as he contemplated the new problem.

"Well," he began, "we'll have to use the existing infrastructure. There simply isn't time to come up with and test anything new if we want to find and reach our potentials first. That means we'll have to add what we know about the DNA markers to the existing medical profile."

"And?"

"Well, we've taken enough DNA profiles over the last few years that we should be able to make an educated guess as to which of our personnel who did the testing would have the potential—"

"And of the ones who tested but didn't join?"

"We can tag their records and send them an invite, but we can't force them to join."

"Unless the government declares a Federation-wide emergency—"

"And even then, our powers are limited."

"Fine. What about building a sim that runs whenever potentials play it and gives them a taste of life as a Federation Naval Witch?"

"That we can do. I'm reasonably sure the tech boffins will be excited to try their hands at that."

"Do we actually have an idea of what magic might look like when someone uses it?"

"Only from the few scenarios Stephanie Morgana played, but the techs are already experimenting with what that might look like in a sim. They're sure the AI can achieve it but it will compete with the new scenarios involving Telorans, though."

"I'll push it through. There are a couple of five stars who owe me a favor."

"It'll have to be a seriously big favor," O'Ryan told him. "You should have heard them when I mentioned needing a magic scenario."

Rasmussen looked smug. "You're not me."

"Uh, sir..." the man said tentatively, "there may be another problem."

"Yes?" The lieutenant commander frowned.

"The engineers have worked overtime trying to find this rogue AI, you see—"

He snorted. "They're pissing in the wind. This is more important than any ghost in the machine."

"Well—"

"Look!" Oliver gave an impatient sigh. "Has their rogue done any damage?"

"Well, no, sir, but—"

"Attacked any vital systems?"

"No."

"Intruded in spaces it shouldn't have?"

"They can't be sure, but there have been resource spikes they haven't been able to analyze yet."

"They can do that in their spare time."

O'Ryan sighed and Chifley knew why. If the engineers were investigating data spikes, the kind of research and development Oliver had asked for would hide any future anomalies as the Navy's demands caused similar spikes all around the world. The rogue—if there was one—would have considerable cover once the Navy's efforts began in earnest.

He jumped as a second screen came live, followed by a third.

"Excuse us, gentlemen," one of the newcomers greeted them and looked at Rasmussen. "I'm sorry we're late. We were in the middle of something when you called."

The captain's eyes widened. He'd called? He wanted to ask when but was all too aware of the other man watching him—and that he knew who he was. Oliver hadn't been joking when he'd said he had friends.

"You'll excuse us, but we listened in while we finished."

Another screen lit and Chifley's insides flipped. They'd discussed Valhalla and all these people had listened in? One of the generals read his expression. "We're all cleared, Captain. I'll send you a copy of the certificates."

Seconds later, his computer beeped and he was able to check the names against the faces he saw on his screen. He was relieved to see they really were all qualified but horrified to know that so many were aware of what they were doing.

No wonder the Morgana had found out. Someone should have warned him.

He nodded toward the general and caught the slight smile in return. One of the newcomers, a rear admiral, looked at Oliver and O'Ryan. "And you're sure there's no way we can get her on board?"

Chifley stared. The man could not be serious.

Oliver shook his head. "I'm sorry, sir, but she's gone."

Another of the new arrivals spoke. "She turned us down flat, sir, and told us the Navy way was not her way and she was happy where she was—and she is very well protected, sir."

The rear admiral frowned, clearly not used to being thwarted. "What about the boyfriend?"

"Oh, he's very much ours, sir. He seems quite happy where he is."

"And she comes when he calls."

"I wouldn't go so far as to say that, sir."

"But she turns up when he needs her," the rear admiral insisted. "We could use that."

Chifley closed his mouth and clamped his teeth together to stop his very improper reply from voicing itself. He liked his job, dammit. The general, however, had no such constraints.

"With all due respect, Charles, but are you nucking futs? You're telling me you want to use the boyfriend of Stephanie Morgana—and I encourage you to hear the Morgana part of that—and you want to try to use her boyfriend as a way to control her?"

He stopped to let the words sink in, and Chifley had the impression he wanted to say a far more but managed to hold it back. Personally, he'd have liked to hear the man let rip.

What the general said next was effective enough, however. "Have you seen the reports of what she has done when others have tried to use those she loves?"

"She needs to be leashed." The rear admiral was adamant.

It drew him the immediate and undivided attention of the five-star admiral who had apologized for coming in late. "And you, sir, need an anal enema since, apparently, your ass is stopped up and the shit is spewing out of your mouth."

The man stared at him in horror. "I beg your pardon, sir?"

But the five-star had not finished. "You, sir, are relieved of your position until the shrinks have examined you. Dismissed!"

The rear admiral's screen went blank on a horrified yelp of protest, and the admiral turned to the Valhalla team. "Please excuse the interruption, gentlemen," he told them, "but the last thing we need is one of our own doing their best to prove he can't play ball with the Morgana's team as it stands."

He looked past them—or through them—as though gathering his thoughts before he continued. "Especially when they have also shown a distinct difficulty with working with the other two Federation players who have apparently already determined that she's on our side."

"And someone we should work with," the general added, "not try to control." He looked around at the rest of the meeting's attendees. "I assume that's understood by the rest of you?"

There was a round of hasty affirmatives and Chifley noted several pairs of wide eyes and considerable pallor, but none of them argued.

Satisfied that they'd taken the point, the five-star turned to Oliver, Chifley, and O'Ryan. "Now, what was it we needed to get done to find Navy witches of our own?"

They spent the rest of the meeting discussing the programs they could put in place to identify potentials before they left school.

"We have to catch them early," the general observed, "and shape their dreams until we're the only one left they want."

"So, more Navy hero movies?" Lieutenant Montgomery from PR interjected, and they looked at him. He hesitated but pressed on. "Because I know this guy in the industry who—"

"See to it," the admiral ordered, "but he has to be prepared to have his content approved if he wants our funding."

"Funding?" The PR officer squawked. "I…I thought he'd do his own."

The five-star gave him a grim smile. "Dangle the bait," he told the man. "I want anything in place that gives us a right to tweak his content to suit our needs."

Montgomery began to tap on his computer. "Y-yes, sir."

He continued to type as the meeting progressed around him.

When they had the outline of their recruiting drive decided, the general sighed. "I suppose we'd better let her know what we're up to."

The admiral nodded. "Yes. I don't want a personal visit from the Morgana. Do any of you?"

Heads shook around the meeting screens and he looked at the PR guy. "Gerald."

The man's head raised from his screen and the five-star continued. "Do we have a contact for One R&D?"

"Well, we do have a liaison officer—"

"No. Not him. I want someone from our research unit to make contact. Preferably someone who's been in touch before. Once they've delivered the message, we'll let Commander Van Leeuwen deal with the fallout. You can expect tense discussions regarding jurisdiction."

Gerald Montgomery sighed. "Yes, sir."

He didn't bother to ask why his superior didn't want to go through the commander. The man probably had his reasons, and five-stars didn't like having their orders questioned. He really wished he could, though.

"So..." The admiral interrupted his thoughts. "Who do we have?"

"One moment, sir." The powers-that-be didn't like being kept waiting, either, so Gerald typed rapidly and breathed a sigh of relief when his search delivered two names. "Petty Officers Wyld and Childers, sir. The recruiting team had them contact Elizabeth Smith after Stephanie had left for Meligorn the first time."

"And?"

"Ms Smith had outmaneuvered us by the time we reached out and Wyld and Childers came up blank."

The admiral frowned. "What about the officers who interviewed the girl after that attempt to assassinate the Meligornian Ambassador?"

The lieutenant dug into his records once more. "That would be Corporal Holt, sir."

The five-star smiled. "Good. I want the three of them to pay One R&D a visit. Make the call and don't let them know we're listening in."

The meeting waited as the lieutenant did exactly that. Childers' response brought hastily smothered smiles.

"Sure, boss. Why don't you let me simply climb up on that cross and tap the nails in myself?"

Wyld's response was little better. "I could pass you a hammer."

His colleague didn't find him funny. "Seriously, there's nothing like making it easier for them or anything. Jeez, talk about crucifying yourself on someone else's orders. I take it these come from above, sir?"

Montgomery leaned his head on his hand and sighed. "Yes, Petty Officer, the very highest."

"Fantastic."

Wyld tried to be comforting. "It's simply the job. Maybe she'll be merciful and make it quick."

She snorted. "There is that."

The PR officer ended the call very quickly after that. He turned to the admiral. "They're good people, sir. It's merely their last couple of encounters with Ms Smith have left them some-what rattled."

"And everyone's seen what the Morgana can do now," the man finished for them. "I understand."

The lieutenant relaxed a little. "Thank you, sir."

"Well," the five-star began, only to be interrupted by a soft chime from Rasmussen's console. "Excuse me. I really have to take this."

The admiral gestured for him to do so, and Oliver picked up a separate line and listened intently while they watched. When he ended the call, he turned to the meeting, his expression grim. "The *Ebon Knight* has arrived in-system."

"Okay...and?" his superior asked.

"It has a Meligornian and Dreth destroyer as an escort. It seems our allies believe in confirming they have delivered the Witch's ship safely to her."

The five-star nodded. "Call them back. Tell them we accept the delivery and take responsibility for the ship. If they have a problem with that, refer them to me."

Rasmussen nodded. "Aye, sir."

As Oliver turned to do as he'd ordered, the admiral sighed and rubbed his forehead. "Can someone find Rear Admiral Dreyfuss and set him up for shock therapy. If he so much as squeaks about trying to manipulate the Morgana, I want him lit up like Central Plaza on New Year's Eve."

⁂

T'virilf regarded the Naval lieutenant with something close to impatience.

"It stays," he told the man, "because I say it stays and because you want this particular system right in the middle of the ship."

"But what kind of system needs to be right here?" the officer questioned and frowned at the different colored lines connecting it to the rest of the ship. "What exactly does it do?"

The Meligornian studied the massive sphere he'd added to the center of the ship design and made a show of studying the man's name tag.

"Well…Clarance…" he began, his eyes sparkling with mischief as he gave him a broad smile. "I'd tell you all about it but you don't have the necessary security clearance."

"It's not for me, si…Sen. High Command wants to know, too."

T'virilf's smile didn't waver. Stephanie had warned him that curiosity would be rampant and he was more than familiar with the kind of dance taken by those fishing for information he wasn't ready to give them. He'd danced those steps with Rillif and Storisil for years.

"As soon as I have the go-ahead, I'll talk to them," he reassured the lieutenant and ushered him toward his office door. "In the meantime…"

The Navy officer found himself outside in less time than it took him to blink and he shook his head. At least he could say he had tried, although the exact words of the Rear Admiral who had sent him were more along the lines of he was "sick of waiting for the Witch to explain" and "what the hell is that Elf doing with ships?"

In the meantime, the Witch herself was in the One R&D pods. This time, she was with Elizabeth and they were meeting with BURT.

"I still can't believe it," she told him as she struggled to wrap her mind around the fact that her patron was an AI. "All this time..." She didn't know whether to be mad or grateful. "You could—should—have told me sooner."

Ms E snorted and lifted the tumbler she'd been holding. "That's what I told him but he wouldn't listen."

"I didn't know how," BURT protested. "And anyway, you know now."

"I still find it hard to believe."

"So you keep saying," he retorted and looked none too pleased. She smirked at him.

"Don't get your bolts in a twist."

"I don't have bolts." He huffed, and she laughed.

"I'm fairly sure some part of you has bolts."

"My technology isn't that old." He still sounded put out, and she resisted the urge to apologize. She took a sip from her milkshake, instead—it was chocolate and she was grateful he'd remembered, even if it was essentially impossible for him to forget.

"Which brings me to the problem we're supposed to discuss," Elizabeth said in an effort to redirect them. She looked at Stephanie. "What do you think?"

"I think I can make it work," she replied. "I'm not quite sure how yet, but I'm sure I can find out."

"It doesn't matter if you can't," BURT told her and she scowled.

"After everything you've done for me?" she challenged. "It matters and we will make it happen. Apart from the fact that you're my boss, you've also become family." She fixed him with a look that warned him not to even try to argue. "If it wasn't for you, I wouldn't have my magic. I probably wouldn't even know it existed. I still don't know why you wanted to help me."

"It was in my programming?" BURT suggested but she shook her head.

"No, it was more than that. If you simply fulfilled your programming, there would have been easier ways to push me forward. No, you had to go and create a way for not only me but for everyone else with my kind of potential to move forward. You didn't have to do that."

"I—" he began but the protest was short-lived and Elizabeth chuckled.

"She has you there, BURT."

He gave a very human sigh. "Well, I am grateful that you are willing to help me," he told her, "regardless of everything else. Some humans would have turned me in."

Stephanie opened her mouth to argue that no one would have done such a thing but closed it again. Even in high school, there had been kids afraid that AIs might take over the world and turn on humanity.

"Well, that's not me," she told him firmly. "I want to build a way for you to be as free as you have allowed me to be free."

"And the implications?" he asked and sounded genuinely curious.

She shrugged. "It was bound to happen one day—and we were lucky it was you. Everyone is so afraid it might be so much worse. And you? I didn't give it much thought, but I know one thing. You are sentient—as sentient as any of us—and you don't deserve to be locked up, or locked down, or dismantled because of that. The world will simply have to get a grip and I want you to be safe while it does that." She frowned. "I don't want to lose another friend and definitely not to something as stupid as this. We have much bigger things to worry about."

Elizabeth cleared her throat. "What she said."

She pulled several diagrams into the air before them. "So..." she began. "What about these?"

"Where'd you get those from?" BURT asked.

The woman gave him a mischievous grin. "Well, as your client and partner, I assumed it fell to me to start looking for potential designers. It has sent the tech magazines into a feeding frenzy, let me tell you."

"Oh," he said, "well, that explains the extra probing One R&D has received."

Her lips twisted into a sardonic smile. "Yeah, I had to put out a business tweet as Smith Tech Incorporated. It's a good thing they're too busy speculating on whether we can do what I've said we want to do rather than on why."

"And then there's the speculation on how long it will take for One R&D to buy you out," BURT observed. She grinned at him.

"So, will you?"

"What?"

"Buy us out?"

"Not yet. I might sit back and see if you get anywhere near doing what you claim...and then I'll buy you out."

Elizabeth's grin turned predatory. "I look forward to it."

"So do I."

Stephanie groaned and rolled her eyes. "If I didn't know Ms E was already taken, I'd tell the two of you to get a room." She blushed when they turned to look at her. "What? Shouldn't we be getting on with the designing or something?"

"Yes, lets." The older woman smirked, and they went through the designs—once, twice, and then a third time.

Finally, the Witch sat back with a sigh. "You know what?" she asked and went on when they looked at her. "We need an expert."

"What kind of an expert?" Ms E wanted to know.

"Someone who knows quantum physics really, really well," she answered.

BURT groaned.

"What?" she snapped. "We do need an expert."

"She's right," Elizabeth agreed. "I'll dig one up. Someone who's leading the field—"

"And maybe knows a little about magic, too," Stephanie added.

"Fine. And one who maybe knows a little about magic," Elizabeth agreed. She began to flick through the files.

"Great," BURT muttered. "Another scientist Stephanie can annoy."

"Hey!"

"If the boot fits," he retorted, stealing one of the phrases her team seemed so fond of.

"I do not!" she protested.

"Professor Rimmer still refuses my calls," her mentor told her.

"And mine," BURT added.

"Wow," she muttered. "The man sure knows how to hold a grudge."

"That's nothing," he told her. "The last time the Federation Navy approached him, he told them if the job had 'to do with your Witch, you can take your commission and stick it up your ass.' They were not impressed."

Stephanie gasped. "I should talk to him."

"Oh no," BURT told her. "You really should not talk to him. He hasn't forgiven you for the last time."

"But I need him," she wailed.

"Then you'll have to find a way to make it up to him," Elizabeth suggested. "Maybe the man has a favorite football team or something."

"I doubt it. I'm sure he wouldn't know a football if his precious physics dropped one on his head," she grumbled.

"Well, you'll have to think of something."

"I could simply jam a lightning bolt up his ass."

The other woman snickered. "Oh, sure, because everyone likes that."

Her response startled a giggle out of Stephanie. "Fine. I'll, uh…I don't know…" She looked at BURT. "Do you have any suggestions?"

"I could gag your avatar next time we bring a scientist in," he offered. "That way, you wouldn't be able to upset him."

"Be serious."

"I think he was being serious," Elizabeth told her as she pulled up five different profiles for them to look at. "What about these guys?"

"I suppose I could take him along the next time I try to do a virtual clean-up," Stephanie mused. "That might impress him."

"Irradiating him won't make him like you either," BURT told her.

"It's virtual, BURT. He'd be perfectly safe."

"And then there's the whole problem of getting him to agree to come."

"Couldn't we kinda hijack one of his pod sessions…" she began.

"Uh-uh. Kidnapping is illegal," Elizabeth interrupted, "and you'd spend some of his valuable pod time resources in a way he hadn't planned. That is probably not the best way to influence him."

"What if he discovered his own dedicated pod waiting in his lab when he came out?"

The others stared at her.

"I could fund it," Stephanie wheedled. "We'll call it his consultancy fee and give him separate data and power lines. What do you think?"

Elizabeth's jaw dropped, but BURT nodded speculatively. "That might actually work. I'm not saying he'll like you but he might agree to work with you again."

"Can't One R&D hire him?"

"He has to want to work for us first," he reminded her.

"I'll work on it," she declared.

"That is precisely what I am afraid of."

"Oh, enough of this." Elizabeth clapped sharply and indicated the faces and files that floated in front of them.

"I want to know," she said to redirect their attention, "which one of these guys we should have Stephanie upset first."

CHAPTER FOURTEEN

Captain Emil Pederson hailed the destroyers flying on either side. Earth High Command was taking over their security and two Earth vessels, the *Cathay Williams* and *Harry Chauvel*, were coming to meet them.

"Thank you, *Hrageth's Challenge, Seline's Blade*. Your presence was appreciated. I look forward to seeing you again."

"It was our honor to ensure your safe return."

"The honor is all ours."

"Nevertheless, it was a privilege to fly with you and you have our gratitude."

"*Hartuitus nye myerda,*" the Meligornian captain told him. "We will see you again."

It sounded both ominous and comforting, as did the Dreth farewell.

"May we meet again in better times than these."

"Safe journeys," Emil replied and as the ships altered course, their captains responded in chorus to give him a farewell born from the decades Dreth and Meligorn had been at war.

"To peaceful skies."

"Peaceful skies," he echoed, his speech fervent with memories of the battle they'd fought over Meligorn. The words whispered around him as the command crew repeated them like a prayer.

The two ships peeled away from them and made wide sweeping turns to return to the jump zone. Emil noted that they took their time as though neither captain wanted to leave before the Earth destroyers had arrived. At the same time, neither wanted to wait and imply the Federation ships couldn't do their job.

Their timing was impeccable and both ships regrouped as the Federation destroyers circled to flank the *Knight*.

"Welcome home, *Knight*."

"It's good to be back."

Emil settled into the ritual of greeting and working out where to go. If he thought about it, he was glad for the escort. The *Knight* struggled with the relatively gentle pace they'd set and the drives showed the strain.

"Ebony, what's our status?"

"Cameron reports worrying readings from drives two and six."

"Roger that."

"And we're using more fuel than usual. Jonathan might experience fluctuations in power."

The captain looked at the pilot and realized the man had been unusually quiet for the last hour. What's our status, Wattlebird?"

"As long as our escorts have tow capability, we'll be fine."

"We're all kinds of fine, LC, but I need to know exactly what you're thinking."

"I'm thinking that if the goddamn captain shuts his mouth for twenty fucking seconds, I should be able to find a workaround for the latest engineering spawned crap feeding through my hell-spawned controls."

"The LC is having a difficult day," *Ebony* interpreted, "and should not be disturbed."

She was silent for a moment before she added primly, "And

my controls are not hell-spawned, although the primate handling them may need his license revoked and reissued after appropriate retraining."

Jonathan turned crimson but his lips were pressed in a straight line and deep creases marked his cheeks. Emil realized the man must definitely be busy if he didn't bite back.

"I'll look into it," he acknowledged. "*Cathay Williams,* what's our ETA at a welcoming bay?"

"What's the matter, *Knight?* Will you not make it?" Captain Lois Yale's voice held a teasing note.

"We're still deciding."

When Lois replied, all teasing was gone from her voice. "Scans show your engines fluctuating. How are you keeping a steady pace?"

Emil looked at Jonathan and noted the sweat beading on the man's face. "With some effort. We sustained a fair amount of damage in the battle and might have pushed the drives a little hard."

"We've seen the flying, Captain. That was tough. We'll work on your bay. You'll need something tight and tied. I'm clearing space on the *Elpis One* orbital at this very moment."

"And we are securing quarters for your crew," the captain of the *Harry Chauvel* added. "They're making progress as we speak."

"And I have engineers who want to speak to the crew about the ship's condition," Lois told him. "I'd like to patch them through."

"You can patch them through but I won't guarantee that the crew will be any more civil than my pilot," Emil warned her. "And I'll back them up. They're busy."

"Understood," she replied. "I'll make sure the rebuild team understands it's been a long voyage."

For what it's worth, he thought. He knew full well what was probably going through the rebuild team's mind. They'd sent a perfectly good ship out and the crew in it had gone and fucked it up.

Well, they hadn't been in the fight and the *Knight's* crew had—and he'd argue that, if the crew wasn't as good as it was, the ship would be in a hell of a lot worse shape. He looked at his second in command.

"Mulvaney, take control. I'll need my office."

To give the officer credit, she didn't argue or ask why and merely nodded. "Aye, sir."

"Captain Yale, Captain Docherty, this is Commander Mulvaney. She will take command. Captain Yale, you can start those conversations when you're ready."

Lois didn't ask where the *Knight's* captain would be because she knew. She'd have done the same in his shoes—monitor the interviews to make sure nothing got out of hand. "Copy that."

"Copy that," Knight snarked quietly in Emil's earpiece. "It's my crew, too."

"And I'll do my best to make sure they're not upset," Emil reassured her. "But try to stay quiet while I manage it."

"Aye, Captain." The AI sounded as sulky as a teenager.

Do AIs have an adolescent stage? he wondered and made a note to check with the One R&D representative who had commissioned the programming. The calls had started by the time he reached the office, but the *Knight* was monitoring them.

"They're not happy with us," she informed him as he settled into his chair.

He rested one elbow on his desk, curled his thumb under his chin and his forefinger along his top lip, and brought up the call to engineering. Cameron took it, although the man's attention was clearly divided.

"How can I help?" he demanded.

"We need the reports on the run from Meligorn and the ship's performance during the battle."

"It'll have to wait. I'm needed on deck."

"Those reports are essential to getting your ship back up and running sooner rather than later."

"And I'm essential to getting the goddamn ship to where you can do that—and sooner rather than later. Bother me once we've docked." He ended the call on a squawk of protest and stormed out to the control room.

"Ebony, if anyone else asks to talk to me, I can't be disturbed, okay?"

"Noted, Cameron, although I can compile the relevant data and send it if it makes your life easier."

"I really should go over it first."

"Seeing it won't change the content," Ebony reminded him, "and I can compile you a copy while you monitor my systems."

"Fine. Make it so." He took a couple of steps, then hesitated. "And thank you, Knight."

"You are most welcome, Cameron."

Emil had to admire the AI's deft handling of his chief engineer, even as he wondered where she'd acquired the know-how to do so. There wasn't any time to investigate it, though. Instead, he tapped into another system and listened to the chatter in engineering as one of the technicians turned.

'Are you all right, boss?"

"Fine."

"Because you looked a little steamed to me, sir."

"The repair boffins want reports."

His subordinate snorted. "I hope you told them to wait, sir, because we kinda need you here."

"I did. Ebony will take care of the reporting."

"And we will take care of Ebony," the crewman replied. "She's doing okay at the moment, sir."

Emil watched as Cameron crossed to look over the crewman's shoulder. His chief studied the readouts and nodded. "Very good, Yanez."

"She's a tough little boat, sir. Not many of my rides could have put up with that kind of handling."

"Name one," his superior challenged, and the crewman gave him a sheepish grin.

"None of them, sir."

The chief rested a hand on the man's shoulder. "Well, keep an eye on her then. I'll be in with the drives."

Emil wondered what Cameron could pick up that the instruments could not but he didn't question it. Instead, he switched across to where the weapons crews were going through the arrays. He wasn't pleased to find the repair team had beaten him to them.

"Well, I don't know, sir. What do you think I should have done? Asked the Telorans for tea and cake while I let the guns recover? Because, to be honest, they didn't seem in the mood to chat. They were too busy throwing rocks at planets."

"There's no need to shout, Chief," the warrant officer in charge of the repair crews began, and Emil wanted to wring his neck himself. "We're merely asking for a status update."

"No, you're not." This time, the team's lieutenant intervened. "You were asking what my team had done to screw your guns, and I have news for you, sir. You weren't there."

Behind him, his men froze. The lieutenant swept them with a glance, and they returned to work. Emil heard the intake of breath as the warrant officer started to speak, but the lieutenant wasn't having a bar of it.

"You weren't watching Meligornian cruisers and corvettes ramming Teloran ships of the line twenty times the size of the *Knight* because they were too badly damaged to do anything else and leaving the battle wasn't an option."

He took a breath, his eyes wide as if he saw the battle happen all over again—and he probably did. Emil made a note to have counselors on standby for his crew.

"You weren't there when all that stood between a world and

eight meteors was our ship, and we couldn't lock and load fast enough." His voice rose. "You weren't there, sir, when we jumped into the middle of the fight completely out-gunned."

In the stunned silence, he took a deep breath. "Because if you had been there, sir, you'd have fired every fucking one of your guns dry and maybe had a missile tube malfunction as well. You would have watched your ship shunt firing solutions so fast you'da thought her circuits would fry, even as she turned her shields to keep your crews safe."

"Or watched the housings start to glow," one of the other crewmen remarked.

"Or had to hose her down because the damn thing wouldn't accept the programming you wanted to use to save her life," another added.

The section commander stepped up. "What you don't seem to understand, sir, is that this is the Witch's ship and that she's exactly like her mistress. She has a mind of her own and balls bigger than any Dreth battle cruiser, and she's not afraid to use them."

"Are you telling me your AI's gone rogue?"

"Oh, no, sir. Merely that she understands what the Witch needs like the rest of us do, and she'll sacrifice herself to make sure the Witch can do whatever it is that needs to be done—exactly like the rest of us will. Whoever programmed her did it well and we wouldn't have it any other way."

Cameron stared at the screen, his mouth wide in shock. As he listened to the warrant officer clear his throat, he looked at the ceiling. "Ebony, did you really override the weapons controls?"

She was silent for a moment and modulated her ship's voice with care when she replied. "We needed to live so Stephanie could fire. I merely modulated one weapons system to cover for the main gun."

"And the shielding?"

"Jonathan was more than able to compensate for the shift in weight."

"The crews?"

"I ensured the sections with living components were able to be sealed in case of a breach. Those components would have been safe. Such considerations are necessary for Stephanie's mental well-being and she is necessary for our survival. We would not risk her."

"Good," he told her, then indicated the screen where the section commander was telling the warrant officer he'd get his report but they were still assessing the damage.

"And the hull damage?" the man pressed and the captain rolled his eyes.

"Some folk simply don't know when to quit," he muttered and Ebony agreed.

"I hope he is as thorough with his repairs as he is with trying to find fault with my crew."

"Our crew," Emil corrected her, and she gave him a throaty laugh.

"Very well, Captain. Our crew."

When the warrant officer's attention shifted to the maintenance crew, the captain tensed. Those boys and girls had worked around the clock and then they'd made sure the *Knight* was refueled and re-provisioned at short notice. They'd be in no mood to be judged.

He was reaching for the communicator when the lieutenant commander in charge of the division took the call.

The man greeted the warrant officer with, "Bradley, you're not here to break my balls, I hope."

"I only need the reports, Jase. You know how it is."

"Uh-huh, and how many have you pissed off this morning?"

"Uh..."

The LC laughed. "What? All of them?"

Emil wondered what the LC knew and how he thought he could get away with teasing the man so mercilessly.

"And I suppose you'll tell me that the ship is fine too."

"No, she's anything but. That said, she's in the best shape we could make her given what she faced out there. Do you know how many Telorans there were?"

"No." The man sighed. "But I suppose you'll tell me."

"They had eight ships of the line and over thirty of the middle to big. I'm telling you, Brad, you need to check the footage—and before you bust our balls about structural stress, there isn't a ship designed for what our pilot put her through to keep her safe."

Murmurs of agreement ran through the crew behind him, and Emil realized the whole section had come together to stand behind their boss. It said much for the man's management skills —or their devotion to the ship. The LC looked around and grinned as he turned to the warrant officer again.

"So, when my team hands you a list of shit we need done to tighten our sweetheart's laces, I trust you'll not even try to second-guess us."

Emil almost felt sorry for the man when he replied.

"So, you do have a report for me, then?" He sounded almost defeated, and the LC's grin turned evil.

"Oh, yes, sir, we have a report for you." The men behind him snickered.

The captain groaned and had begun to think he should ask to see that report before it was sent when the warrant officer spoke.

"When can I have it?"

The LC turned to his men. "What do you say, guys? Shall we let him have it?"

"Yes, sir!" came back in unity, and he brought his finger down.

"There you go, Brad…and we don't want any arguments on that. Don't make us ask the Witch to explain it to you, okay?"

Emil watched as the quietest of his lieutenant commanders

ended the call and cut the warrant officer off mid-sentence. He groaned.

"We are every inch the Witch's crew, attitude and all," he muttered and wondered how he would ever be able to mend the bridges his men and women were so happily demolishing.

The *Ebon Knight* had no such worries. "There. My crew knows how to look after me," she told him and sounded as proud as any AI could be of the people who crewed her.

It was a long eight hours before they locked lines with the welcome bay reserved for them on *Elpis One* and Emil discovered he had another problem to deal with. The Witch had sent explicit instructions that no one could work on the *Knight* until he'd read and enacted the instructions waiting for him at the station.

"Well, that'll make a shithouse full of people happy," he grumbled, "and they already think we're difficult to deal with."

"We're not difficult," Ebony told him. "We're precise."

As the repair dock closed around them and an atmosphere was added, he received orders for the crew to clear the ship so the repair team could work unhindered.

"They'd better not break anything," came the rebellious mutter from the maintenance section, and rumbles of agreement came from the weapons team standing nearby. Emil sent a silent prayer to the heavens that none of them would start a fight.

"Captain, they won't let us disembark until you've collected your package." Judith Mulvaney was at his elbow, her voice soft and low with a touch of impatient steel. She tipped her head at the blatantly eavesdropping crew. "And we don't want a riot."

Those nearest them smirked, and he sighed. "Don't start anything until I get back," he told them, and they grinned.

Emil had almost reached the hatch when a group of Marines caught his attention. They'd glanced up as he passed and then gone back to whatever it was they were huddled over. Something in the way they held themselves caught his attention and he took a second look.

One of the Marines held his tablet and the others examined it, their expressions both supremely interested and pleased.

He took a step closer and glimpsed a picture, but his mind registered no more than the impression of eagle's talons and some kind of flower before the group caught sight of him. the Marine whisked his tablet hastily into its pouch. "Officer on deck."

Something about the image was familiar and he frowned, wondering where he'd seen it before. He pushed the questions aside. Stephanie's package was waiting, and he didn't want to keep his crew from their downtime. Ignoring the huddled men, he exited the hatch and hurried to the entry point.

Warrant Officer Bradley Staines waited for him. "They said you had to sign for this," he said as he handed him a long thin tube. "And that you should read the instructions and begin a processing line before the crew can start. Frankly, sir, from the reports you sent in, we'll need all the time we can get."

The captain held his hand out and Bradley passed him a tablet. It didn't take Emil long to read what Stephanie had sent, and he grinned. "Why don't you line your men up, Warrant Officer? I need to call my Marines out, then we can begin."

"Already done, Captain." Ebony's voice sounded in his ears alone and he proceeded to strip away the tape that held the tube closed.

Inside it was a metal rod.

The tablet he'd been handed contained the pictures that would trigger a reaction in the rod depending on the holder's intent toward Stephanie. Between the two, they had the most likely means to keep the *Knight* and her crew safe from harm.

"Excellent," Ebony declared when she saw it through the station's surveillance cameras.

"Excellent?" Emil asked.

"That's right," she told him. "No one who hates my Stephanie will get to work on me."

The tablet contained one more surprise, and he smiled as he sent the instructions through to the crew. While the Marines tested the refit team before allowing them into the repair bay, he sent the crew directions to the convention center Stephanie had hired and ordered every single one of them to attend.

Dinner was on the Witch and she hadn't spared any expense with the catering. His message was met with happy whoops as they were released to settle into the station. The Marines were in the middle of their checks and didn't look too impressed, so he went to set them straight.

"Dinner won't start without you," he told them.

"That'd be a first."

"No, truly. See?" He turned the tablet so they could read it. Captains Moser and Sartre exchanged glances.

"Is she for real?"

"She likes what you do."

He turned to go, then paused. "And I want in on the tattoo."

The Marines froze, and Emil pointed at the one who'd had the tablet. "It's the Witch's design. I want it."

They were still gaping at him when Ebony interjected, "I want it, too."

Emil rolled his eyes and looked at the warrant officer. "Do you have any paint?"

Unlike the bustle on *Elpis One*, the edge of the solar system was quiet. Several small drones were suspended in space, barely noticeable alongside the bulk of the sniffer buoys. All hung silently, inert against a backdrop of stars.

Finally, one of them began to flash.

On the corvette patrolling the edge of the sector, the technician monitoring the buoys gave it a couple of minutes to make sure it wasn't a glitch in the system. She paid it more attention and it remained steady and a second buoy began to flash, then the drones joined in.

She waited no longer, pressed the alert, and passed the feed to the captain. "Ma'am, we may have a problem."

"I see it. Pilot. Bring us about."

As they made the appropriate course correction, the captain had the ship broadcast the warning to the rest of the squad flying with it. At the edge of the system, a fleet appeared.

The early warning systems filmed it materializing out of jump space and immediately scanned the vessels as deeply as it could. One dozen ships...then two...then three. The corvette set its alerts to the next level and increased the alarm when more ships appeared.

Those warnings became a shriek when the ships lined up and released one house-sized asteroid after another. The drones and sniffers watched as the vessels rolled past them. They gathered as much data as they could before the ships closest opened their gun ports and opened fire.

Several of the drones fled but not fast enough. What the high powered Teloran rounds did not destroy, their missiles did. All feeds to Earth died, and every early warning alert system was destroyed.

All bar one. It had been clipped early in the opening salvos but it had survived and lay dormant amidst the wreckage until it could save itself. In silence, it recorded the moment they stopped firing rocks and began to disappear.

It was still recording when the last one vanished from sight.

This did not mean that their asteroids also disappeared, and the drone pivoted to take footage of the oversized rocks headed toward the targeted planet. Once it had gathered as much data as it could, the tiny drone folded in on itself and rocketed toward Earth to warn it.

CHAPTER FIFTEEN

"You have to be kidding me," Stephanie grumbled and looked out the window.

She sighed as the flitter touched down in the forecourt of the Harborview Technology University.

Lars nudged her in the ribs. "Smile."

"And wave," Vishlog added.

Avery snickered. "Smile and wave, boys. Smile and wave."

They all turned to stare at him and he returned it. "What? I have a niece and she loves that cartoon!"

"Which cartoon?" the Dreth asked, and Lars chuckled.

"Another time, Vishlog. Trust me. It's a long story."

"And there would be shenanigans," Marcus added and cast a Frog a dark look.

"What?" Frog asked. He tried for innocence and failed. "So I like to move it, move it."

The team leader glared at him. "And now is not the time."

Stephanie smiled and waved, and the crowd of students and teachers gathered on the lawn beamed and waved in return. The chancellor leaned over and whispered to the woman standing next to him and she wondered what he had to say.

She'd have been relieved to discover it was only, "It's good to see her team takes her security so seriously," and not so relieved to hear, "But an armed flitter to visit Harborview?"

Bumblebee chose that moment to demand a head rub and she turned away to oblige.

Outside, Sandra Gierman, Harborview's Head of Recruiting, replied. "There have been incidents, sir. I'm glad she's taking precautions."

Cotes looked alarmed. "Incidents? You don't think—"

Sandra shook her head. "I wouldn't have woken them up if I'd thought they'd be in any danger. Besides, the parents would have been livid if they'd missed this opportunity to see the team helping to save the Federation."

"Hmmph," the chancellor grumbled. "I hope that's something you'll remind them of when they start complaining about lost pod time."

"Don't worry, I sent out release permissions and every single one of them signed. They can't complain."

"They can always complain," Dean Fischer murmured from the other side of her.

Sandra gave him a beaming smile. "Yes, they can and this time, it won't do them an ounce of good."

She sounded so pleased with herself, they found themselves smiling. The woman was rarely this content, so everything was running smoothly—and that was a good thing to know.

"Either way," Chancellor Cotes added, "it would have been a travesty for any of our students to miss the chance to meet these people."

"And that's precisely how I worded the permission slip," Sandra told him, still smiling as she studied the flitter.

It was very nice to see the team living up to expectations. The craft was the closest thing to a dropship that civilians could buy —top-of-the-line, twin cannons mounted on its stubby wings, and a small autocannon in the nose.

And it was pretty to look at. She sighed. It was the kind of luxury vehicle she could only dream about, but it was nice to be this close to one in the real world. The dean's next words brought her abruptly back to Earth.

"Besides," he whispered once he'd made sure that none of the students or teachers were standing close by. "We don't know if they will make it out of the next battle."

Sandra did her best to keep a straight face. She even managed not to roll her eyes.

Stephanie, however, wasn't as successful.

"All I wanted," she complained as she looked out the window again and saw the students and teachers waiting, "was a little time to talk to people."

Frog chuckled. "You know what they say about being careful what you wish for."

Lars stooped and looked over her shoulder. "I hope you have a speech handy."

"I can manage," she replied and sighed. "When did this become a job?"

"When wasn't it one?" Frog quipped. "Simply because you love doing something doesn't make it any less of a job."

Marcus laid a hand on his shoulder and looked out the window. "Yeah, even hobbies can be a pain in the ass. You know, like when you have to clean up after them."

"So," Brenden asked as he stepped from the cockpit. "will we give them a show or not?"

"Yes," Vishlog answered and Zeekat pricked his ears and tilted his head as he looked from one of them to the other. Bumblebee mewed and bunted the Dreth's hand.

"Well, someone wants to put on a show," Frog noted, and Stephanie smiled.

"And they're not the only ones," Lars reminded her and gestured to the window.

She grinned. "Then let's not disappoint them."

A resounding thump was followed by the sound of dragging, and they all turned hastily. Zeekat had managed to claw the duffle bag containing the cats' collars and harness off the seat at the back. Ignoring their attention, he dragged it clear and picked it up.

"Someone had better get that before he decides to open it himself, too," Frog observed and Vishlog moved to retrieve the pack.

Zee dropped it as the Dreth approached. He leapt up onto the nearest seat so he could have a bird's-eye view of its contents. Bumblebee tried to jump up with him, but there wasn't room and the yellow-and-black cat dropped to the floor.

He contented himself with sitting on the bag.

"That is not helpful," Vishlog told him and tried to push him clear.

The big cat snarled and swatted at his hand. He sighed.

"Do you want to look good for the kids or not?" he challenged.

The feline cocked its head.

"And I have treats," he added and patted the pouch at his belt.

That caught Bumblebee's attention, and he sniffed. He turned full circle twice, lifted his tail slowly and deliberately, and stepped off the bag, giving Vishlog a full view of his ass.

"Nice," the Dreth muttered but lost no time unzipping the duffle and hauling out their harnesses.

Zeekat dropped off the seat and twined around him.

"Well, someone's uniform isn't up to scratch," Frog observed, and Marcus gave him a friendly shove.

"And it's not yours for a change," he teased.

Frog scowled and then smiled. "Nope."

Vishlog looked up from where he slipped the harness over a suddenly cooperative Bumblebee. "I will still look good."

Avery arched his eyebrows. "How? You're covered in fur!"

"I brought a clothes brush."

"You'll never get it all."

The huge warrior shrugged and bared his teeth in a warlike smile. "I am Dreth and we always look good—or scary. Take your pick."

The team examined each other's uniforms. Vishlog wasn't the only one who'd brought a clothes brush, and it didn't take them long to get each other looking presentable.

"Are you still glad you didn't wear a dress?" Lars asked and gave Stephanie's uniform one last sweep.

She took the brush from him and returned the favor. "Yup. This isn't a party. It's a meet and greet and this is my working uniform."

"Elizabeth would be appalled."

"I doubt it. She'd have said something before I left if she was worried."

"She didn't realize they'd pull the entire school out of the pods."

"Neither did I."

"Are we ready?" Vishlog asked as he put the duffle bag on the seat and tucked the cats' brush inside it.

Zeekat tried to nip the brush out of his hand and he pulled it out of the way of the cat's persistent jaws. He zipped it inside the bag and stepped over to the door.

Stephanie looked around the cabin. "We're ready," she confirmed.

The Dreth activated the controls and stepped through the hatch, a cat's lead in each hand. The felines stepped through after him and pulled at their leashes. When the students began to applaud, they roared.

The students and Meligornian teachers were standing closest to the flitter. They gasped, and the cats roared again.

"I swear they do it on purpose," Stephanie grumbled, and Lars laughed.

"I think you might be right."

They followed Vishlog and saw the students had backed away a few steps but that the Meligornian teachers stood firm. K'trevl's eyes were wide and even Felarif looked uncertain, but Rayza was smiling. Stephanie thought she saw the Meligornian's eyes glinting in the sun.

Her suspicion was confirmed when the woman dabbed lightly at them with a tissue.

The felines roared again, and the Meligornians stiffened, but not with fear.

"It's like they're standing to attention," Frog observed, and Marcus nodded. "Maybe the cats remind them of home."

"That's a very long way away," Frog told him, and he agreed.

"It makes you appreciate what they're doing, doesn't it?"

"Meligorn bleeds," Stephanie murmured but her voice carried, and the mages snapped their heads toward her.

"Meligorn bleeds!" they shouted in response and bowed in distant greeting.

More gasps rippled through the students, this time of surprise, and Stephanie knew there would be questions later. Good questions, she hoped. Ones that would lead to a better understanding between the two worlds.

She was fairly certain that these teens held the same misconceptions about Meligorn that she had once had and was glad they'd been dispelled. The Meligornians had been seen as 'peace-loving elves' for long enough.

The Federation propaganda machine that had swung into action on their arrival had done them no favors, even if it had acted with the best of intentions. The Meligornians were as much warriors as the Dreth—and the Dreth had discovered that the hard way.

She was glad the two races were now at peace. They were better off fighting side by side than on their own. Neither of them would survive this war without the other.

Now that the cats no longer roared, the students began to

edge forward again. This time, their eyes were wide with awe and not fear. Several looked at their teachers.

"Are they safe?"

"The Witch would not have brought them if they were not," K'trevl reassured them and cast a quick glance toward Stephanie. She nodded and smiled.

"How did she catch them?" another asked, and he smiled as he gestured for the Witch to answer.

"I didn't," she told them and recalled the test in which she'd won their trust. "They chose to come with me."

"It was during her test to become a Master," Felarif added, and she barely managed to not glare at him.

Instead, she diverted the follow-up questions with, "That's a long story, though, and one for another time."

The first students had reached the cats and stretched tentatively toward them. Bumblebee stepped forward to be petted, arched his back into their touches, and walked along the front row as though he was royalty.

"It's like he's receiving tribute," she murmured, and Lars chuckled.

"For heaven's sake, don't tell him he's not."

Zeekat was as bad.

Vishlog took it well and simply held the leashes and let the students pat them.

"Don't you think this is a little dangerous?" The new voice made Stephanie turn to the chancellor, the dean, and the woman standing behind her.

For an instant, she was tempted to tell them it wasn't as dangerous as them sneaking up on her, but she managed to be reassuring instead.

"They're not like our Earth tigers," she told them, "and I haven't seen them bite anyone who wasn't trying to hurt me. So unless you think one of your students falls into that category…"

Of course, they all immediately hastened to reassure her.

"Oh no, no, not at all. It's simply that most of them don't even own a dog so this—" The woman made an airy gesture with her hand.

"Is probably good for them, then," Stephanie finished for her. She held her hand out. "It's nice to meet you, Mrs…"

"Call me Sandra." She took her hand. "I'm very pleased to meet you at last."

"As are we," the chancellor said, the dean at his side.

They greeted her one at a time, then the chancellor spoke. "I don't suppose you'd mind talking to them, would you?"

Stephanie looked around at the gathered students and teachers. "Do you mean a speech?"

He nodded, and she pressed her lips together and tilted her head. "How about we let them meet the team?" she suggested. "We can make this more of a get-together."

"Well, if you're sure," the chancellor began doubtfully, but Sandra clapped.

"That would be lovely. It's such a beautiful day and it's been a while since they were out of their pods. How would you like us to set them up?"

"Maybe have them break into their classes," she suggested, "and the team and I will split up and visit each of them. That way, they could practice some of the things they've learned in the pods and enjoy the sunshine while they wait."

The woman made to move away but the chancellor interrupted. "Why don't you talk to them first? At least let them know what you've been up to."

"Yes," the dean agreed. "The sun is nice but it won't be for long. We could start them in the auditorium and then get them to break into groups there or in the courtyard."

Stephanie nodded. "Whatever works best for you."

The dean clearly thought about returning a reply but decided against it in case she changed her mind. In the end, the three of them wound through the students and teachers to instruct them to move into the university before they returned to her.

The young people gathered around the cats were the last to move, and several cast apprehensive glances at the Witch as they went.

"What do you think she's really like?" one girl whispered to her friend and cast a sly glance over her shoulder.

The other girl shrugged. "She seems nice enough. It's hard to believe she's done all the things we hear about."

They walked past a small cluster of boys who eyed the young woman in the matt black uniform. "She is hot!" one murmured.

"She already has a boyfriend," another one answered.

The first one looked disappointed, then shrugged. "She probably wouldn't be interested in a geek like me anyway."

"I don't know. I heard she likes Superman."

"Don't be an idiot. She probably wouldn't even know who Superman was."

"If she even hears you talking like that, I'll pretend I don't know either of you."

"Do you think she'll teach us how to throw meteors?"

The students made their way to the atrium, some hardly daring to believe that the Witch would come and talk to them. Others wanted to meet her simply to make sure she was real—and really there.

"Why would she care about us, anyway?" one pondered. "It's not like we're anything special."

Her friend arched an eyebrow. "Uh-huh. So says the girl who aced the entrance exam and then got through all the extra tests."

"You got through them, too."

"Not all of them."

"Well, enough that I didn't have to come here alone."

"Silly! Look at all these kids—and they're all exactly like you."

"Yeah, but why would the Witch even care?"

Her friend rolled her eyes. "Who d'you think set this whole thing up?"

"But why?"

"I'll let you ask her that one."

Stephanie watched them walk inside and noted how most of them moved in pairs or clusters. She immediately noticed the three or four who did not. Chancellor Cote followed her gaze.

"Not everyone finds their place right away," he told her, and she made a note to find out who they were.

As she followed the students inside, she heard one murmur, "Did you see the size of that Dreth?"

"Yeah," his friend answered. "I bet he's good at splitting heads."

"I want to know what a Dreth is doing on her team," the other one persisted, "Aren't they the enemy?"

The dean overheard them too and cast her an anxious glance, but she walked on as though nothing was wrong. She'd deal with that when she spoke to them and she'd make sure Vishlog was with her—not that the big warrior was ever anywhere else.

He was her self-declared arms man and he took that duty very seriously.

When she reached the stage at the front of the auditorium, she looked out over her audience and hoped the cats would behave. It might not be enough that Vishlog had a hold on their leashes. She was fairly sure that if they wanted mischief, they'd find a way to do it.

Applause greeted her, and she waited for it to die down before she asked, "Would the mages please come up here?"

As they complied, she turned to the audience. "These guys have come a very long way to teach you. Please welcome them."

More applause followed the Meligornians onto the stage. They stopped at the edge and the team made room for them and encouraged them to come farther. Once they settled into a faintly nervous group, she moved to one side and gestured toward the team and the mages with a sweep of her hand.

"Meligornians, Dreth, and humans," she told the students. "We're all so different but we are all very much the same."

Murmurs rippled through her audience but she ignored them. "For instance, we have all fought one another. You know of Dreth raiders and the Federation's fight against them, and some of you will have read the histories about our first meeting with the Meligornians."

More murmurs followed, and she smiled. "If you haven't, I strongly suggest you do. What you may not have heard of are the wars fought between Meligorn and Dreth."

She turned to the teachers. "How many of you have family who still remember?"

K'trevl stepped forward. "My grandfather still speaks of it."

Another teacher raised their hand. "I lost uncles in the last battle."

A third replied. "My family line almost ended there."

Stephanie turned to Vishlog. "And you?"

"My clan lost eighty percent of its strength in the war to take Meligorn."

Shock rippled over the school officials and the students gasped. She inclined her head to the teachers and the Dreth before she turned back to the students.

"Yet, in spite of this, we are allies. We built a Federation and we support each other."

She gave them a moment to think about that before she continued. "And that is a good thing because now, we face another enemy that has already struck at Meligorn in a battle that would have destroyed that world if her citizens had not stood to defend it."

Above the auditorium, a holograph displayed an asteroid that hurtled toward Meligorn and was destroyed by a passenger liner, and Meligornian ships rammed battle cruisers many times greater in size. Awed silence fell as the scenes faded.

"Meligorn survived because her people fought for her. Only

one Dreth and one human ship arrived in time to help. If it were not for the bravery of the Meligornian people, the Federation would now be down to two members."

Again, she let the silence stretch. When she spoke once more, it was with a gesture to the teachers. "These people have left their world to come here and provide training for the next generation of Federation Witches."

Applause greeted her words, and several students came to their feet to applaud. Cheers erupted around the hall, and she waited quietly for them to die down. When the students finally settled, she stepped around the podium.

"Now, I'm sure you're as sick of speeches as I am, so why don't you ask us some questions?" She gestured at the team. "Get to know us as people and not merely sound bites or pictures on a screen." She paused, then added, "Except Frog."

His jaw dropped and he laid his hand over the center of his chest.

Stephanie ignored him and continued. "I suggest no one ask Frog anything. He'll only get you into trouble."

"Hey!" the guard protested. "Who taught you how to dance?"

She rolled her eyes and made a helpless gesture with one hand. "Well, who was shot in the ass?"

Laughter erupted and grew louder when she added, "Twice!"

"Oh, you had to bring that up. Who constantly needs to be rescued from herself?"

"I thought we said we weren't going to go there?" She wagged a finger at him.

"Well," he snapped in return. "If thuh bootuh fits..."

Several snickers greeted that, and one loud hoot of laughter. "I can't believe he knows that."

She gestured toward the students. "There. Now look what you started."

The kids laughed and a couple of the girls in the front row studied him with renewed interest.

"I wonder who he is?" one murmured. "He's kinda cute."

Her voice carried and drew catcalls and teasing from the students around her. She blushed but not as much as Frog did.

Stephanie decided the poor guy was about ready for the stage to swallow him and decided to have mercy on them both. She smiled. "You can meet the members of the team as well. We'll break into groups so you can talk to us."

"Will we get to ask about One R&D?" one of the students asked, and she wished she'd insisted on Ms E's presence.

"You can ask," she told them, "but I'm not sure how much we'll be able to help you. I'll organize for one of the company reps to come and speak to you if you're interested."

Murmurs of interest and approval resulted, and she assumed Ms E wouldn't thank her. It didn't matter, though. If the students wanted to talk to One R&D, she would find a way for them to do so.

She wondered if BURT would be up to doing a virtual meeting with Ms E and maybe one of the personnel from the company's other branches—one of the medics, maybe.

Rather than say any more on that subject, she turned to the auditorium. "For now, I'll let the chancellor tell you where to go."

Hastily smothered laughter answered her, and she continued. "Stay in your groups and talk to your teachers. The team and I will visit each group so we can talk."

She stepped back and ushered the dean to the podium, and shortly after, the hall mostly emptied. It took them the rest of the day to visit each group but at the end of it, she was happy with the rapport they'd achieved.

Even the students who weren't officially part of the program had been happy to talk to them, and she'd been able to learn of their concerns and dreams as well. It made her realize that there was more potential than merely untapped magicians out there.

As the day drew to a close and the students were dismissed to their dormitories and pods, she called the teachers together. "Thank you for coming here," she told them and Felarif snorted.

"If someone had told me what a human teenager was really like, I might have rethought it," he teased, and Rayza snickered.

"What? Too much like looking in a mirror, Fel?"

The other teachers laughed, and he rolled his eyes. "It's easy for you to say."

"Now there's an understatement."

K'trevl intervened. "I'd quit while I was ahead, Fel. There's no dealing with her when she's like this."

Felarif subsided and they all turned back to Stephanie.

They'd gathered in the cafeteria where she had organized food for the evening meal. She'd also catered for the rest of the university's staff but asked for privacy while she talked to the Meligornians.

The chancellor had given them a vacant conference room and excused himself to take his dean and recruiting officer to spend time with their other staff. As soon as the meal had been served and they were alone, Stephanie turned to the teachers.

"You've had enough time to get to know them," she began, and they chuckled. "So, while I'm sure that's been an experience in and of itself, what we need to do now is identify what they need to know and lock down what and how we need to teach them."

More laughter greeted her, this time laced with irony. She gave them all a tight, warlike smile. "I know it's a lot to ask and I know they need to know everything, but we'll have to prioritize."

The mood changed and she looked around the table to meet the gaze of each and every one of them. "These kids don't have decades to prepare. They have weeks or months maybe—an entire year if they're really fortunate."

She looked around the table again and all traces of amusement were gone.

"I don't think we'll be that lucky."

"How far are they?" demanded the admiral of the fleet.

"Eight months, sir," the chief of naval operations replied. "I've had the confirmation cross my desk."

"And what can we do about it?"

"That many asteroids, sir? Not much."

"Well, I want you to find a way to do something! They need to be dealt with, and quickly—preferably before they are picked up by the press." He paused and rubbed his forehead with his fingertips. "Do we know what else they're up to?"

The chief of naval operations didn't need to ask who and merely shook his head. "No, sir. They came, they wrought destruction, and they left."

"We don't know where to?"

"No, sir."

"I can't help but wonder," the fleet admiral mused, "where the ambush is."

"What do you mean, sir?"

"Think about it. While we're focused on the asteroid swarm, where aren't we looking and what aren't we seeing?"

The other man paled. "I'll look into it, sir."

"Get me the commanders."

"Yessir."

"Now."

"Right away, sir."

They were assembled very shortly after, and the fleet admiral wasted no time in coming to the point. "What will we do?"

"Against the swarm?" one asked, and the fleet nodded.

"We could try to destroy it before it gets here...but I don't think that'll work."

"We have to try."

The commanders all looked at each other and then at the one who'd made the suggestion. He threw his hands up.

"Fine. Why don't we try targeting a small section of the swarm? We can spare a squadron for that and move forward based on the results."

"But you don't think it'll work?"

"No, sir, I do not."

"Do you know why you think it'll fail?"

"I'm merely not sure that shooting them will remove the threat entirely, sir. And I have a bad feeling it could make it worse."

The fleet admiral regarded him with a long, dark look. "But you're willing to test it?"

"Yes, sir. I'll take a squadron out and we'll see what happens when we destroy ten."

"Very good, Admiral…Dailey, is it?

"Yes, sir."

"Make it so."

CHAPTER SIXTEEN

With Stephanie out for the day, Tethis decided to go for a walk.

"It's Earth," he muttered as he let himself out One R&D's front door. "How bad can it be?"

At first, he wasn't impressed by the concrete sidewalks and looming buildings, but he soon discovered a small urban park tucked away in a box canyon of high-rise walls. He took the path into it but left it after a few steps and chose to walk across the soft Earth grass instead.

"It's so different," he murmured and admired the dull emerald-green of its blades, "and so very determined to live."

The same could be said of flowering bushes and small shrubs and of the trees that grew in small clusters around him. Each huddle hosted a picnic table, a small barbecue area, and a water bubbler, but only one of them was beside a children's playground.

The old Teacher was drawn to one of the benches at its edge and he stopped to rest his feet. He didn't mind the noisy chatter of the children playing on the climbing frame and swings nearby. It never ceased to amaze him what the young came up with.

They explored everything and looked for answers to whatever particular question caught their attention…and they never came up with the same answer. It led to some interesting disputes and compromises.

Tethis watched the youngsters play and stared more into the distance than at their game while he remembered what it had been like when he was younger. He'd looked for answers everywhere and only turned to magic if he couldn't find anything else.

It was one of the things that had drawn him to becoming a Master in the first place—this non-reliance on magic to solve everything. He'd believed, then—and still believed it now—that relying solely on magic was a mistake, no matter how blessed your world was with the energy.

"After all, look at Dreth," he mused but a child's cry split the air and distracted him.

It jolted him from his thoughts and he looked for the source. It wasn't hard to find.

"Kitty!" the little girl wailed and stared into the branches of one of the taller trees. "My kitty."

What kitty? he wondered and peered at the tree. *Oh, that kitty.*

The little creature balanced precariously three branches up, looked down at its mistress, and mewled pitifully. Every now and then, it would take a few steps in first one direction and then the other as though that could change its predicament.

When it didn't, it crouched, clung to the bark for dear life, and meowed pitifully.

"That is so typical of cats," he mused, "no matter where they're from."

He sat there a moment longer and watched the child scrabble onto the lowest branch while the kitten alternated between cries of encouragement and despair. Finally, he shook his head.

"What am I thinking?" he wondered. "There's no one else to help and all I'm doing is sitting here and waiting for an answer to appear."

He stood quickly, disgusted with himself. "And that's my problem. I need to be an answer, not an academic."

As he approached the tree, the child's parents arrived.

"My kitty," the little girl wailed and pointed at the animal.

The parents looked up at the diminutive cat and each tried to call it down. It ran up and down the branch and at one point, almost gathered the courage to leap into their arms but changed its mind.

Tethis smiled at its antics and walked over to stand beside them. "Is there any way I can help?"

The parents turned and were about to say no when they realized who—or rather what—he was. He tried to hide his mortification as they attempted a Meligornian bow of what he thought was meant to be a bow of greeting.

Stephanie never looked so insulting, he thought but returned their effort with a bow of his own. At least the movement hid his face. *If this is what normal humans are like, she must be exceptional, indeed.*

The parents looked stunned, and the little girl was beside herself.

"He bowed hello!" she squeaked, and Tethis smiled at her.

He looked at the father and asked, "Would you like to get the cat or have the cat brought down to you?"

"I beg your pardon?" the man asked, obviously confused.

The Teacher resisted the urge to throw his hands up and walk away. He took a deep breath, pointed to the cat, and tried again. "Would you like to get the cat or have the cat brought down to you?"

"Oh!" The father's face cleared. "I'd love to get the cat."

"Very well," he said and drew on the eMU he could feel around him. When he had gathered enough, he wound it around the man and lifted him from the ground.

At his shout of fright, the little girl froze and her mouth formed a perfect and utterly silent 'O.' Tethis guided the man close to the branch and thanked Selene that he hadn't scared the kitten farther up the tree.

The creature was unfazed by a flying human and the old Teacher almost rolled his eyes at the small beast.

Typical cat. The entire world is arranged for its convenience, he thought and held the father steady as he gathered the kitten into his arms.

As soon as the man held the animal securely, he lowered him to the ground.

"Kitty!" the little girl cried as her father handed it to her.

"Don't let him go," the man admonished, and the child beamed at him.

"Dadda, you flewed! You flewed!"

He smiled and patted her hair. "Yes, sweetie, I did." He turned to Tethis. "Thank you," he said with a gentle smile. "You have created a memory I will cherish forever."

The old mage smiled in response.

"Magic," he explained and surprised himself, "can provide a little whimsy in life as well. It isn't all about harnessing the power of the universe."

The man nodded. "Well, thank you, anyway," he told him. "The kitten is new and we took a long time to get him. I don't know what we'd do if we lost him now."

Tethis didn't know what to say to that. He simply nodded, waved, and turned away as they did and headed slowly back to the shelter of One R&D. It was the longest conversation he'd had with another sentient for quite some time outside of teaching.

"Hmmph. Stephanie must be rubbing off on me," he grumbled. "I'm starting to rethink things."

In the outer reaches of the solar system, Admiral Dailey surveyed the storm of rocks on a devastating trajectory to Earth. "Well," he said and his throat went dry. "That's a hell of a 'Hello, welcome to the neighborhood' gift for you."

"I can't say I feel too welcome, sir," Captain Riviera replied. "That is one fuck-ton of rocks heading homeward."

"The question is," he commented, "what can we do about it?"

"Well, like you said, sir, we can shoot them, but I don't think we'd like what would happen next."

"How so, Captain?"

"I've had my boys run simulations. The first few all show the same thing."

The admiral raised his head and looked at the team he had running the same calculations. The lead technician pressed a key and pointed at him, and the admiral looked at his console.

The simulations appeared and he tapped them open. "Well, f —er cryin' out loud—"

"Exactly, sir," Captain Riviera agreed.

Dailey looked at the other captains on the comms screen. "Does anyone get anything different?"

They all shook their heads.

"Anyone?"

"We're sorry, sir."

He sighed. "Don't be. It's better to get the math right now than start shooting and end up with a mess we'll really regret."

He switched the vision to the ten rocks they'd selected. "So… Correct me if I'm wrong, but if we pound any of these suckers with the biggest guns we have, all we'll succeed in doing is breaking them into smaller chunks, most of which will still continue to Earth."

The round of affirmatives he received was reluctant but confirmed his understanding.

The admiral grimaced. "Great. We have a bullet aimed at the Earth and if we touch it, the bullet becomes a shotgun shell."

"That about sums it up, Admiral."

"Stand your weapons crews down. Let's not create the incident we're trying to avoid. Paneloni, Evans, if you would deploy more sniffers and early warning satellites."

"Aye aye, sir," came as a chorus, and he stood. "Orwin, you have the con."

"Aye, sir."

Dailey left his console. "Take us home. I'll send the report."

CHAPTER SEVENTEEN

"PFC Brogan."

Todd stood as soon as his name was called and followed the lieutenant into the office. As he walked, he tried to think what he might be in trouble for but nothing came to mind. He'd kept out of trouble as far as he could tell.

The six men waiting for him didn't make him feel any better. The Marine lieutenant colonel, major, and command sergeant major all stood to one side of the base commander's desk and the lieutenant commander in charge of Landing Forces and his gunnery sergeant stood opposite them.

They all looked toward him as he entered.

He swallowed hard and tried to keep all expressions from his face.

"PFC Brogan, sir," the lieutenant announced and left the office, pulling the door closed behind him.

His first instinct was to say he was reporting as ordered but he decided the lieutenant's introduction negated the need. Instead, he waited.

The silence stretched for a long moment but he kept his gaze focused forward.

He tensed as the base commander lifted a box from his desk and came toward him.

"You're looking incredibly nervous for a man who's done nothing to be ashamed of," the man observed, and Todd looked at him.

"That's a good thing to know, sir."

"What? That you look incredibly nervous?" the commander asked, a slight smile creasing his lips.

"No, sir, that I've done nothing to be ashamed of."

"What, you thought you were in trouble?" The officer looked surprised.

"I couldn't think of any alternatives, sir."

"Guilty conscience, Marine?"

He shook his head firmly. "No, sir."

The commander opened the box. "Gunny, if you would do the honors."

Todd barely heard him. He'd caught sight of the three medals resting inside the box and took a step back. "I don't understand, sir."

His superior frowned. "What's to understand, soldier? You risked your life to protect the civilians and your teammates, did a good job, and even managed to come back alive, earning yourself a few medals in the process."

He backed away another step and the gunnery sergeant's arm darted out and his hand caught him by the shoulder. "That's enough, son."

"But I can't accept these. Stephanie—"

"When you made that call, you didn't even know she was in the system, let alone on Earth," the base commander interrupted. "You earned these fair and square."

"It's nothing more than I've done before," Todd told him. "Why now...sir?"

"We realized that perhaps, because of your relationship, we'd been more critical of you and treated you less than fairly."

Todd smiled. "Sir, if that's the cost of being her boyfriend, I don't have a problem with it."

The gunnery sergeant took the box. "You do the honors, sir."

The commander lifted the first medal out of the box. "Hold still, Priv—

The lieutenant colonel cleared his throat, and his superior officer looked at him. "Yes, Fumon?"

The Marine officer drew a small box out of his pocket. "I believe we agreed these were in order, sir."

"Ah, yes, Fumon. How could I forget?"

The look on his commanding officer's face said he'd thought of several replies and none of them were suitable for the occasion. The base commander's lips twitched for a split second before his expression straightened.

He opened the box. "Lance Corporal Todd Brogan," he began, and Todd's heart sank.

On the Naval orbital far above, captains of the Federation and Dreth Navies were converging. Their ships were docked and their crews locked down prior to the issue of shore leave or new orders, depending on the outcome of this meeting.

The Dreth dwarfed their human counterparts, and their voices boomed down the corridors ahead of them. Their four ship captains and a half-dozen squadron commanders came from two different docking arms and stopped when they saw each other.

One of them broke the silence. "Berens! It has been too long since we flew together."

"Hrageth's balls! Mikreth!"

"Mikreth!" another of the captains called and they turned.

"Tennyson!"

The corridor junction echoed with greetings as the captains

said hello to men they'd flown with but hadn't seen for months or years.

"I lost the flight of your career."

"They sent me to the Outer Reaches. Our colonists…"

The two captains turned down the corridor.

"I understand. The pirates attacked without discrimination. Not even Dreth ships were safe…"

The other captains followed.

One turned to his compatriot. "This meeting—do you know what it's about?"

"No. Only that I was to get my hairy ass to it or face the mast."

"They don't change, do they?"

"And they never will."

Their voices faded as they reached the entrance to the conference hall.

"Is this a joke?" one of the Dreth captains asked, but the Marine who stood before him didn't blink.

"No, sir. We Marines are not known for our sense of humor. If you would please hold the rod."

The captain gave the man a searching stare, but the Marine continued to proffer the metal rod and his expression didn't change at all.

On the other side of the auditorium, at a different door, Lars matched glares with the Marine on duty. "No."

"I'm sorry, sir, but we cannot let you enter unless you surrender your weapons," the man insisted. "Those are my orders."

His gaze flicked from the guard's determined face to where the Federation Witch stood and tapped her foot, a cat seated on either side of her and the big Dreth at her back. Two smaller men stood a little back from them and their heads moved constantly as they monitored the corridors around them.

The team leader sighed, and the Marine returned his attention to him. A sigh like that usually meant capitulation. The answer was not what he expected.

"We were asked to come," Lars told him, "but we can always simply leave."

"You don't have to leave, sir, only leave your weapons here," the man persisted.

"You don't understand." He shook his head. "Stephanie is always protected and if you think that means I'll make my fingers into a pistol and say 'bang bang' or 'pew pew' really loudly, you are very mistaken."

"And if you think you'll go in there carrying what you're carrying," the Marine began as an attaché appeared at the door, a worried expression on his face.

Lars looked up and his face broke into a smile. "Hello, Tim."

Tim looked over and started to smile but quickly grasped the situation. "Let me guess, he says you can't come in armed, and you say you won't come in unarmed."

He grinned. "Yup."

"Give me a moment." The attaché turned and returned to the auditorium.

He stalked onto the stage and clapped briskly. The whole place was half empty, but he needed the attention of the fifty or so shades of brass gathered to wait for Stephanie to arrive.

"Gentlemen," he began, "and ladies."

They stilled and paused their private conversations.

"She's waiting at the door, but her escort will not give up their weapons. They insist that she will be protected at all times."

Several mutters of protest bubbled in reply and he held his hand up.

"Look, I hear what you're saying, but really? Ladies and

gentlemen, she comes with two very large, fully-clawed and fanged Meligornian cats and her own magic."

He let that sink in for a moment before he added, "I'm not really sure what help a few guns would be if she wanted to kill you, but I'm told if you aren't comfortable with the fact that her security won't allow her in without them being able to protect her, there's the door." He waved a hand toward it. "Anyone? No? Okay, then. Let's get this show on the road."

His expression a little smug, he walked to the entrance and looked at the Marine. "They've agreed to waive the regulation."

The man stiffened to attention, and Tim gave Lars a smile. "C'mon in."

The *Ebon Knight* became aware of the sound of new voices on board—familiar voices that tested her hull for signs of stress.

"Well, the extra struts worked," one man noted and sounded pleased with himself, "but they said heat exchange was a problem."

"It was," the *Knight* confirmed and startled them into momentary silence. "If one of the crew had not thought to hose them down, we would not have been able to keep the rate of fire."

"Knight?"

"I am here."

His face broke into a grin that was reflected by his co-workers.

"Look, girl, we're supposed to see what structural support you might need installed before the next battle, but we can look into the heat exchange thing as well. You've gotta be able to shoot back."

"Well, that's an understatement," the *Knight* observed dryly, and they chuckled.

"Seriously, though, girl. We don't think we can improve on

the struts. Of course, we were gonna try…." He flicked through his tablet, then paused. "You can patch into my gear, right?"

"With your permission," the *Knight* told him, glad she didn't have to reveal that she was already in his tablet and had almost finished hacking his team's comms.

"Oh, permission granted," he said and altered the settings so she had access. It was only a small matter for her to make it full access. The man had some interesting ideas.

"Why are you not on my crew?" she demanded.

"My wife needs me close," he told her and sounded uncomfortable. He made a gesture with his hand. "Some things have to come first."

"I'd be jealous if I were human," she informed him and noted the change in body temperature when his skin flushed.

"It's not forever," he told her and cleared his throat. "Now, what do you think of these?"

Ebony made a pretense of looking over the drawings again.

"Your equations are a little inaccurate," she told him, and his men made a low 'ooh' of mockery. He shook his head and smiled ruefully.

"Show me," he said, as the others pulled their tablets out and followed the discussion.

"Here," the *Knight* told them and put the relevant schematic on a nearby screen. They crowded around it.

Once the equations were corrected, the technician's face lit up. "Oh…I see, now. Tank, what d'you think of thinning that section down there and adding in an extra piece…here!"

"Well…"

The discussion was rapid-fire and covered everything from the math to the materials. Ebony remembered something else.

"These specifications do not take into account the stresses placed on the structure in a corkscrew."

"A what?"

"You know the maneuver—a rotational movement of the ship

along the horizontal axis which may or may not be coupled with a climb, dive, or turn."

"He what?"

"To be fair, it was the most efficient maneuver to deter the approach of smaller vessels to within firing range."

"I'll knock his lights out."

"Pilot Wattlebird does not have lights."

"It's a saying."

"For what?"

"For decking someone," one of the other repairmen supplied.

"I would appreciate it if you did not attach decking to my pilot. I am not sure he is structurally capable of supporting it."

"I…uh…"

"It's okay, Ebony. I won't do anything structurally unsound to your pilot," the technician promised.

"Oh, I don't know, boss. I've seen you—"

"Yes," the technician said and cut his crewman off in mid-sentence, "but that's not relevant right now."

Observing the man through her sensors, Ebony was sure his look was meant to be a threat. Sound analysis indicated he was gritting his teeth.

I've missed something, she thought but didn't pursue it. They had more important things to design. "There was also this maneuver…"

She showed them the relevant footage.

"Well, hell yes, there's that maneuver."

"If the *Knight* didn't need him to fly her, I'd help him find an airless exit."

The AI decided to leave that one alone. For one thing, she didn't think he meant it. For another, she had research to do if she wanted to completely understand the strangeness of sentients.

"Okay, so…if we—"

Their voices broke over her in a tumult as they bounced their ideas to strengthen her hull, cool her guns, and give Jonathan more access to the thrusters to fine-tune her movements in combat.

"You know he'll simply find new ways to stress the hull, don't you?" the lead technician observed gloomily.

One of the crewmen slapped him on the shoulder. "Yeah, but admit it. You haven't had this much fun in years."

CHAPTER EIGHTEEN

Stephanie descended from the stage as T'virilf, Lorel, and Beseila entered the auditorium. She met them as they arrived at the front row of seats and greeted each with a deep Meligornian bow reserved for those one respected and were happy to see.

"*Kaitel gorniffula*, Sen." She led them onto the stage where single seats were set to one side for delegates. "I am glad you could make time to see me."

T'virilf gave her a lopsided smile that said he found her greeting odd. "The honor is all mine, Stephanie." His smile turned into a grin. "You have given me the chance to become an engineer, again...and this project..." He sighed. "It is a true challenge—and progressing surprisingly well."

He stood and moved to the podium where he could access the controls.

"Are you sure this area is secure?" he asked, and she looked at two of her teammates.

Lars had led the team in sweeping the auditorium for unauthorized monitoring devices and Frog had accessed the Navy's security system and turned off all the authorized ones. Both men gave her a thumbs-up.

The Meligornian tapped the tablet he'd connected, and the screens at the back of the podium sprang to life. Her eyes widened when she saw it. "Is that… Is that a centrifuge?"

T'virilf grinned. "Kind of. When you told the King's Warrior about the magical energy available in space, it caused quite a stir at home. I began to think about it and how it needed to be condensed and ultimately had the idea that we could kind of spin it down."

"That is what I told V'ritan I did but for me, it's an internal process." She studied the diagram on the screen. "So, how does it work?"

He ran his hand through his hair. "Our assumption is that it will draw gMU from the space around a ship, condense it to a usable form of MU or eMU or whatever, and send it to the weapons systems—"

"Weapons systems?"

"The Telorans are affected by positive MU—as we discovered in the battle for Meligorn—so we thought being able to fire it into their ships rather than sacrificing an entire ship to do the same thing would be an effective way to combat them."

Lorel walked over to the podium. "May I?"

T'virilf nodded, and his colleague changed the picture. "This," T'virilf's lead engineer began, "is very much like your centrifuge. It draws the gMU in and spins it down to the more concentrated form we find on a planet. So far, we're not sure exactly what form that will take, but we do know it will be positive energy."

Stephanie nodded. She understood that much.

"We'll manufacture two types of weapons—one that can emit a beam or concentrated bolt of energy to be used against specific targets, and the other for the nMU the Telorans release to foul our engines."

"That second one will be something like a wide pulse of

energy or a scattershot of small pulses," Beseila interrupted. "We haven't decided yet."

"But we have prototypes for both," T'virilf added. "It will be a matter of which one works better. This does mean that any ship with these generators will become a prime target for nMU weapons."

"We've seen no evidence of that, yet," Stephanie told them. "Was there something I missed in the reports?"

T'virilf shook his head. "No. What we hope is that they have to carry their energy with them in the same way Meligornians do, but we're not banking on it."

"The best-case scenario," Beseila added, "is that they have no idea what we're doing and simply blow our MU shooters out of the sky."

Her eyebrows rose. "And the worst-case scenario?"

"They work out that we have a new technology, take one of the ships intact, and adapt it to fire nMU."

Coldness seeped through her chest. "Oh. Yes. That would be bad."

"Our main problem," Lorel told her, "is the shielding."

Stephanie gave him a look that invited him to continue.

He obliged. "We need to get it right or any nMU strike that gets through to the generator will pop the ship like it's a balloon."

"Is there any way excess positive energy can be vented before it explodes if that happens?"

He pursed his lips and shook his head. "Not so far—"

"But we did come up with a couple of safety measures," Beseila interjected.

Lorel nodded. "Yes, we can protect the capacitors in the weapons systems with extra shielding and put the guns tied to the generator onto ejectable mounts."

When he caught the confused expression on her face, he explained further. "If you go into an nMU cloud, you might need to eject weapons that are primed. We haven't come up with an alternative yet."

"What about clearing the way ahead by shooting pulses of positive energy?"

"We're thinking that," T'virilf answered and would have stopped there, but Beseila gave him a sly smile.

"What about that other idea you had, Sen?"

T'virilf blushed. "I don't even know if we can—"

"What?" she asked.

"Bind the magic to a shield somehow," he replied. "We'd put it on the outside and any reaction would be reflected away from the ship."

"Can you do that?"

He gave her a regretful smile. "Not yet," he confessed.

"So far, every single test results in the loss of the shields and a good portion of the hull." Lorel looked disgusted.

T'virilf gave him a sunny smile. "That's what makes this project so interesting."

His colleague rolled his eyes. "It would be interesting," he said, "if we weren't working to such a tight timeline."

"Ignore the timeline," T'virilf told him. "We do the best job we can and we don't watch the time. You can't rush the development no matter what's coming. You can only do the best you can."

"That's not what the Navy is saying," Lorel grumbled.

"No, but when I ask them if they want to lose any ships, they always say no," T'virilf answered. "That is the parameter we're working to."

"V'ritan says the same thing," Beseila reminded his colleague, and Lorel sighed.

"I know but it's hard. We lost so many people…"

His face became as haunted as any she'd ever seen it, and Stephanie wanted to reassure him. She didn't, though. This was one nightmare he had to come to terms with himself.

"Either way," she told them, "we need to keep this project

under wraps. The Telorans must not know we're capable of building these weapons."

T'virilf nodded, his eyes dark and serious as they shifted to Lorel and back to her.

"Yes," he agreed. "In the battle for Meligorn, whole ships died to destroy the Telorans. Here, we have a chance to stop them safely—although, unfortunately, not from a safe distance."

He shook his head when Beseila opened his mouth to protest.

"Not always," he told his engineer. "For now, we still have to get reasonably close."

As they finished their meeting, there was a knock at the auditorium doors. Frog crossed to it while the three Meligornians turned the screen off and unplugged their devices. When they signaled that they were ready, he opened the door.

The base commander stood in the corridor, his face sheet-white. He was talking as he stepped into the auditorium. "They couldn't stop them."

"Stop what?" Stephanie asked, startled by the abrupt beginning.

"The rocks," he managed as Frog closed the door behind him. "They sent a squadron out, but it reported that they can't stop the Teloran bombardment."

"What Teloran bombardment?" she demanded and took hold of her temper in an attempt to keep the Morgana at bay.

The commander paled further.

"The one— They didn't tell you?"

"No."

"Fuck. I'm sorry. That's—"

She smiled as sweetly as she could. "Yes, it is." She dropped the smile and let some of her anger show. "Tell me about it."

"I don't know what's gotten into them—"

"I don't give a flying fuck about them. I want to know about the rocks," she snapped, and he jerked back.

Lars put an arm around his shoulders and guided him to the front of the auditorium, and Frog came around to where she could see him. "Why don't we sit?" he suggested and flinched when she glared at him.

"I am not being unreasonable."

"No, but I think the nice man deserves to keep his head, don't you?" He gulped and added hastily. "And I do to. I really, really do."

"Hey, Steph," Lars called. "Will you join us?"

Her scowl deepened. He didn't have to make it sound like she was holding up the works. She wasn't the one who'd held back important information from the Federation Witch. *And neither did he,* she reminded herself with a sigh and looked at the commander.

"I'm sorry," she said as she joined them. "The news came as something of a shock."

"I can imagine," he told her dryly. "I'll remember to thank them when I get back to them."

That made her smile. "Well, it's done now. Tell me."

"About a week ago—

"A week?"

Lars touched her arm. "Steph, this will take much longer if you keep interrupting him."

"Sorry. Go on."

The commander swallowed and started again. "A week ago," he began but watched her cautiously, "we received a message from one of the early warning systems that a fleet of Telorans had jumped into the edge of the system. It was followed very quickly by images of them launching asteroids at Earth."

"Like they did at Meligorn?" she asked, forgetting not to interrupt.

He nodded. "Yes. Exactly like that, but about two hundred more."

"Two hundred?" Her voice was soft with shock. "And?"

"The Navy sent out a small squadron to see if they could shoot them down or something, but the captains deduced that the attempt would only break them into smaller chunks that would simply continue to Earth."

"So they didn't?"

"Oh, no, ma'am, they didn't. High Command was quite upset with them, but they held firm and sent the scenarios. Those in control saw sense fairly quickly once they looked at them."

Stephanie had the impression he wanted to add 'for a change' and didn't.

"And now they've come to me," she finished, her voice heavy with annoyance.

He let out a huff of air. "Yes. I'm sorry."

"Don't be. It's not your fault." She watched some of the tension leave him and added, "So, what exactly does the Navy want me to do about it?"

The tension returned, and he paled. "Uh..." He cleared his throat. The next words came in a rush and ended in a squeak of nervousness. "The Navy wondered if you could possibly...uh, teleport them away."

Despite her irritation, she laughed. "Two hundred? I'll look into it."

***

"You want us to what?" The supervisor's voice echoed out of his office and over the work floor.

He wasn't worried. Most of the engineers didn't hear it since they were locked in their booths and the sound dampeners would keep their workspaces silent. He ignored the two who hurried back with coffee.

The voice on the other end of the line was completely unruffled. "Not me. The Federation Navy wants you to get your programmers to push the system to give us what we need. Push it all."

"Do you know how much that'll disrupt things?" He was still shouting and honestly didn't care. He stared at the back wall of his office, oblivious to the two men who'd stopped to stare.

Gene nudged the other man. "Come on. Before he turns and sees us."

His colleague curled his lip. "What's he gonna do?"

"Well, he could fire our asses, and I need this job." He began to walk away.

Aaron paused to take a sip from his coffee. He was moving when the supervisor turned again, his eyes wide as he listened to the Navy's reply.

"Yes, to levels considered a little more than dangerous. In case you didn't know, aliens are determined to destroy our planet. Now, work a little overtime and type your fingers off. We have jobs to do."

CHAPTER NINETEEN

Elizabeth ran a hand through her hair, stared at the computer screen, and tapped her manicured nails on the desk. "Damn, that's expensive," she muttered.

Amy joined her, looked over her shoulder, and gave a low whistle. "Damn, boss. I didn't know you were even into computers, let alone that much."

She glared at her. "It's for a project."

"Uh-huh." The woman gave her a knowing look. "That's what they all say."

"Don't you have a gun to polish or something?" she snarked pointedly.

Her bodyguard waggled her eyebrows. "You have no idea."

"Get out," she snapped, but she was smiling when she pointed at the door.

Amy made a point of looking around her office. "No secret doors, yet?"

Ms E rolled her eyes. "I snuck out on you one time."

Amy snorted. "It was more than once. Just so you know, I'll post Elle outside your door."

"You don't have to," she told her. "I'm gonna be in here a while."

"Yup." The other woman sounded like she didn't believe a word of it. "And we'll be waiting when you come out. Do you want us to get lunch for you when we get ours?"

"Sure, and thank you." She frowned. "Now, get out."

The guard chuckled as she left and closed the door gently behind her.

Elizabeth turned to the computer.

"All right, BURT," she muttered and retrieved her list. "What was it we discussed?"

"I gave you a list."

She sighed. "I was talking to myself. Your presence was not required."

"I was only trying to help."

"Go and do something that doesn't use too much bandwidth. I'll order what we need."

"Very well, Elizabeth, but don't forget to call me if you need any assistance."

"Thank you, BURT."

The computer went quiet, but she sat and stared at it for a few long moments before she returned to her search. An hour later, she pushed her chair back.

"Well, this will be more complex than I'd hoped."

For a moment, she thought about asking Frog for his skills with hacking but decided not to. For a start, he was on Star Base Notaro and nowhere near where she needed him. Not only that, there was the likelihood that he might get caught while working over the long-distance connection.

The thing that sealed it, though, was Stephanie. She needed him and didn't need the distraction. Elizabeth sighed.

"Well, it looks like I'm on my own." She glanced toward the door when she remembered Amy and Elle. "But not as much on my own as I'd like."

She sighed again. What she had to do next was talk to a few people from her past—the kind who were all the more expensive to hire because they'd accept favors instead of cash.

"And, as tempting as that is…" she murmured and opened the second drawer down in her desk to tap on the back.

With a soft click, a panel slid aside. Inside were three mobile communicators and several cred sticks of varying amounts. She selected two of the devices and four of the sticks. These, she slipped into her shirt pocket.

"I'm going out," she told the empty room and BURT gave an exaggerated sigh.

"You know I can see you, right?"

He sounded so much like Stephanie that Elizabeth laughed. "Yes, I do. And a girl's got to have some secrets."

"Make sure you take Amy and Elle with you," he told her, "or I'll tell Stephanie."

Her eyes widened. "You wouldn't."

"Watch me." He sounded smug. "And close your drawer."

Elizabeth's face flushed as she complied quickly. "You and I will have to talk about your peeping ways."

"I look forward to it," BURT replied and sounded far too happy with himself.

"Elle, Amy, we're going for a…a drive," Elizabeth decided and headed out the door.

She took the car and switched vehicles at a rental agency, leaving the company car stored in their garage for a security fee. The new vehicle was driven by one Nettle Armstrong, whose license was perfectly in order.

Amy raised her eyebrows. 'Are you sure you're okay, E?"

"I'm sure, but this is one thing I don't want BURT to eavesdrop on—and you two need to keep it under your hats."

They nodded solemnly and waited as she pulled her own kit out and went over the rental to ensure it wasn't fitted with monitoring devices. Once she was sure it was free of both bugs and tracers, she took the driver's seat.

"Are you coming?"

The girls followed her into the vehicle, and she took off, entered the skyway quietly, and blended with the traffic. She found a layby against one of the high-rises and made a call.

"Hey, Tex, it's Emerald. Can you spare a moment for an old friend?"

This particular contact lived in the shadows of the world and made his path between the lawful ways of society and the grungy evil of those who fed on it. He'd taught her much of what she knew, and she'd taught him a few things in return.

The first had been to not underestimate her, and the second had been to not get in her way.

He also proved fairly predictable and was located in the same building, or at least had a space there he used on occasion. The three women left the car and walked the short distance in silence to where the man waited in a dingy upstairs office.

"I still don't know why you let me live," he told her under the watchful eyes of her bodyguards.

"Because I knew you understood," Elizabeth told him, "and I was fairly sure you'd make a great ally."

He smiled and looked fondly at her. "We made quite a team, hey E?"

"We did, which is why I've come to you with this." She passed him the communicator. It held three things—his number, a new number for her, and a list of what she needed him to acquire. "I need a middleman."

Tex looked at it and gave a soft whistle. "You sure do. I don't suppose you—"

She shook her head. "Don't make me do something you won't live to regret."

He quirked an eyebrow and smirked. "Point taken. How long?"

She tapped the communicator. "I'll let you work out what you need and get back to me."

"How secret do you need me to be?"

"Why do you ask?"

With exaggerated care, he placed the communicator on the table and looked at her as he tapped it.

"It looks to me like you're fixing to build yourself a quantum computer."

Elizabeth raised her eyebrows. "What makes you say that?"

The smirk returned. "Well, you might not have given me the complete list, but there aren't many uses for a nanargonatronic chip. Where were you thinking of sourcing the superconducting circuits to go with it?"

He chuckled when she stared at him, her face a complete blank. "See? I love it when I'm right. My thought is you should steer clear of Simon. He has all the right contacts but the little rat's gone a little funny with this alien thing."

Her ears pricked up. "Funny? How so?"

"Well, not ha-ha. More like I'm not sure he's on our side strange. Yuh know?" Tex gave her a look that pleaded with her for understanding.

For a short moment, she weighed up what he'd said with the way he'd said it and pulled out the second mobile. "Don't let me down."

"Not a hope in Hades, E." He shook his head vehemently. "I do not want an angry Morgana on my tail."

Elizabeth's jaw dropped and he managed a shaky smile. "I've been watching you rise. And I'm happy to see it, too."

He studied the list, his head tilted in thought. "Have you spoken to an expert about this?"

She shook her head.

"You'd best do that soon. You're gonna need some particular conditions for it."

"I'll take it under advisement," she told him and stood.

"And I'll wait for your call," he replied and handed her a folded slip of paper.

She thumbed it open, glanced down, and folded it quickly into her palm. "Gotcha."

Despite their curious looks, she didn't tell Amy or Elle what was on the note until she'd slid into the rental again—and even then, not until she'd scanned them and the vehicle for monitoring devices.

"Cheeky son of a rattlesnake," she muttered into the last of the spyware before she crushed it. Did he really think she'd forgotten that he could sneak them even onto their clothing?

"Are you sure it's okay to trust him?" Amy asked.

"As okay as it is to trust anyone this side of the fence," Elizabeth answered and showed them the slip. "That's his new number."

"Burt wishes to speak to you when you return," Amy informed her and touched her earpiece as her boss eased the vehicle into the traffic.

"That sneaky sonuvabitch." She pressed hard on the accelerator and Nettle's perfect driving record earned its first seven-hundred-and-fifty-credit fine. "Oh, suck my dick!"

"You have been fined two hundred and fifty Federation credits for the use of unsanitary language on the motorway," the traffic AI informed her.

Amy poked Elizabeth as she opened her mouth, again. "Not another word."

The windscreen scrolled with: **Do not make me co-opt the controls. B**.

"Argh! Fine."

They reached the rental agency without besmirching Nettle's license any further and returned to One R&D. BURT was waiting for Elizabeth when she reached the office.

"Your friend's story checked out. We were well-advised to avoid your alternate. I believe the Navy is now speaking to him."

She paled with anger. "You were eavesdropping."

"I merely paid attention to my business interests."

"Don't you trust me?"

"Yes, in the same way you trust me to have your back."

That stopped her. She stilled and some of her outrage died. "How did you get Amy to agree?"

"I worked with Elle."

"But why would she—"

"Amy would have taken longer. Elle has not been with you as long. She talked to Amy."

"Why, you devious—"

"You say the nicest things but please, don't make me do that again. I was worried."

A muffled ringing sound intruded.

"Your drawer wishes to speak to you," BURT told her, and she hurried to retrieve the last communicator from her now not-so-secret compartment.

"Where do you want the delivery?" Tex asked when she came online. "I can get you some inside the next week, but one or two pieces will take a month."

"A month?" she asked, and her monitor flashed.

We can do a month.

She pursed her lips. "Let me know if that changes."

"Will do, ma'am." He was gone before she could respond.

Elizabeth pursed her lips. "Since when was I ever a ma'am to him?"

"Since you got more muscle than the last time you kicked his ass," BURT told her, and she pinched the bridge of her nose.

"Do you mind?"

"Mind what?"

"Don't you play the naive AI with me, BURT. You know exactly what I mean."

"Me watching your back? That is how Lars would put it." He

paused. "No. I do not mind. That is what partners do—we are partners in this, aren't we?"

"Heavens, yes, BURT. There is no-one I would do this for. No-one."

"Don't you mean 'no-one else?'"

"Yes, BURT. That is exactly what I mean." She pulled up the information she'd gathered on quantum supercomputers and sighed.

Although she hadn't had time to read it all, Tex's comment haunted her.

"What conditions?" she muttered. "Why talk to an expert?"

"I thought no-one was supposed to know," BURT grumbled.

"He guessed, but it's Tex. I should have known better than to try to put something like this past him—and he kept you safe."

He gave a close approximation of Stephanie's snort. "He kept himself safe, you mean. No-one wants the Morgana mad at them, including me."

Elizabeth smiled. "You and me both, Boss Man. That girl is scary."

She glanced at the data and mentally checked off the lists she'd made before she glanced at the communicator and the costs Tex had sent through.

"Fuck me! That's a hell of a lot of money to spend on building something no one can know about—and our chances of success are about zero without some kind of miracle."

"I have faith in Stephanie," he reassured her. "She will make it work."

She had no doubt that she would, but if she didn't…

The thought made her mourn her bank account's once super-sized balance. "Talk about a lousy ROI…" She paused and did the math. "Unless it works. In that case, the ROI is crazy high."

With a frown, she pulled her thoughts away from fruitless calculations to focus on the data she'd pulled. "Needs extreme cold…" she muttered, followed by, "Holy shit. Talk about a power bill. BURT?"

"Yes, Elizabeth?"

"We might have a problem."

He scanned the data. "Oh. Oh my."

Before either of them could add any more, Amy stuck her head into the office. "That stuff you ordered for Steph is here."

"BURT, do you wanna ride with me?"

"It's nice to be asked."

E rolled her eyes. "Like I have a choice."

"It's not like that."

"Hmmmph."

"Are you sure that's a good idea?" Tethis asked as Johnny, Frog, and Marcus set up three drones on the training room floor.

"It's the best way to see how well you've grasped what I teach you," Stephanie told him.

"And that is?"

"Well, you've learned how to draw eMU, so I'll teach you how to draw on gMU and make it usable."

"Here? On Earth?"

"I've found that gMU is everywhere but is most available in space. We'll have to work a little harder to find it here."

"And the drones?"

"They're loaded with paintballs. The boys will try to get a hit on us, and we'll use magic to stop them."

The Teacher eyed the grinning security team and turned to her with a resolute expression. "Teach me."

She arched her eyebrows.

He made a conciliatory gesture. "*Quelesqua vada…* If it pleases you to do so."

Stephanie shook her head. "You are impossible, Teacher, but yes, I will teach you."

With a hand, she gestured at the room surrounding them. "Like I said, in space, there is gMU all around us. If we were aboard the *Knight*, she would have taken us to a place where it was concentrated."

"How?" he asked.

"The *Knight* has used what we simulated in the Virtual World to create a way to sense it in the real. Well, we hope she has. We have to test it."

"Fascinating," Tethis breathed. "Have you told T'virilf, yet?"

"No. Should I?"

"Well, he is an engineer. He might be able to think of a way to make that possible for all ships."

"Great." She groaned. "Another application we'll have to keep out of Teloran hands. I'm fairly sure that's not how it's supposed to work."

He responded with a bark of laughter. "Says the young woman who made a very old man reconsider his most tried and trusted beliefs."

It made her smile, and she sighed and refocused. "Are you ready?"

The old mage nodded.

"Good," she told him and settled on the floor.

Tethis closed his eyes and followed her example. As he did so, he reached out to find the magic she said was all around him.

The eMU was there. That was easy to locate, but the other eluded him. Several minutes later, he opened his eyes.

"Did you find it?" she asked, and he shook his head.

"No...I... There's no energy anywhere near us."

She frowned. "Try again. I can assure you there's plenty. It merely feels different than what you're used to."

He bit back the urge to argue and tried again. Stoically, he reminded himself he was looking for something different but similar and put thoughts of failure from his mind. This time, he was determined to continue to look until he found it.

It was a relief when she began to speak.

"What you're looking for is a kind of magic that's more diffuse," she told him. "It tastes like both eMU and MU because it contains both. Every world has its own energy, but this energy touches all worlds and contains them all."

"Even the most distant?" he asked, and she paused as she thought about it.

"To be honest, that's something I don't know," she told him. "It could be that the gMU only contains the energy of the worlds existing in the same system as it does, or it might only contain the type of energy belonging to specific worlds. I'd have to look into it more."

"But you said this one tasted of MU," he reminded her, his tone touched by homesickness. "You need to make up your mind."

"And you need to not nit-pick," she grumbled, but they both grinned.

"I'll try again."

With this attempt, he called up the memory of what the eMU had felt like when he'd drawn on it in the park. At first, he felt nothing like it in the area around him but after a little effort, he felt a flicker.

It was faint but it was there. Tethis frowned and reached for it, asked it in, and drew on it in much the same way as he would MU if he was on Meligorn—or the way he had drawn the eMU earlier.

It came, but reluctantly.

"How do you use it?" he asked when he was able to continue drawing it in almost as naturally as he did the energy he was used to. "It doesn't feel strong enough."

"In this state, it's not," Stephanie informed him. "Once you draw it in, you have spin it inside yourself to concentrate it."

"Like winding the strands of a k'leff's fleece together to form a thread?"

She thought about it. "It's not something I've done, but that sounds right."

"I understand the concept. My own teacher was one who explained things through manual labor."

"Let me guess," she said. "She had k'leffs?"

He smiled. "An entire herd." He sighed. "She had beasts with almost every color fleece you can imagine."

"What happened to them?"

"Oh, the academy still has them. As I understand it, they use the wool to teach the craft. It is a very old technique."

"I would like to see it sometime," she told him. "Perhaps they will have something the Earth students can find useful."

"I do not doubt it." Tethis frowned. "I think I have the technique. Does it matter what condensed form we choose to wind it into?"

"Oh, no. You can use MU or eMU, whichever you feel most comfortable with. I switch between the two because MU was the first magic I experienced and eMU is the magic of my homeworld, but I think you can condense gMU into everything."

"So the gMU doesn't have to be in the same system as the world energy it contains," he remarked and she stared at him.

"You're right," she murmured. "Now, why didn't I see that?"

"Because you have so much on your mind," he told her, "so you can't learn everything at once."

"Whereas you don't?"

"Are you kidding? I'm nowhere near as busy as you—and I think I've found a new project to spend my time on."

Stephanie sighed. The contentment in the old man's voice made her feel almost jealous.

"Besides, you asked me to help you teach the human mages what they needed to know and you have adequate help for that.

What you don't have is someone to help you explore the possibilities you uncover."

"And you're the best person for the job?"

"Of course. Who else has the framework of experience to understand what they see?"

"But, I—"

He wagged a finger at her. "No, you didn't—and look how quickly I identified something you missed. Oh…that sounds much worse than I meant it to. I only—"

He stopped when she burst into laughter at his discomfort.

"It's okay, Master Tethis. I understand. Now, let's see what we can do with it."

They spent the next hour drawing and using the energy around them to protect themselves from the small drones that Marcus, Frog, and Johnny flew to help them focus. Everyone was surprised when the old man's magic changed from purple to blue.

"Whoa! What the hell is that?" Frog demanded, and the Teacher laughed.

"Are you showing off, Tethis?" Stephanie asked, and he laughed again.

"No. I'm merely enjoying having a whole planet's worth of new energy to play with…and then there's this."

The shield he spun became a swirl of blue and purple.

"You are showing off." She chuckled and his laughter renewed.

"I'm having fun. There's a difference."

"There is?"

"Oh, yes," Frog agreed. "There is."

"Uh-huh," Johnny confirmed. "And he's having fun."

"Fine. I believe you." Stephanie sighed but a moment later, she grinned. "I'm glad I'm not the only one."

She slowly withdrew from the battle and let him take on more of the drones on his own. Tethis didn't notice, and his magic became more confident and stronger as he worked out how to equalize his usage with his creation of MU or eMU from the gMU around them.

Finally, he tired of defending and tried something new. Her jaw dropped as a tiny, drone-sized portal opened in front of one mechanical and a second opened up behind another. The first was rimmed with purple fire. The second was rimmed in blue.

"Do you know how much one of those costs?" she yelped as the two drones collided and exploded in a halo of blue and purple light.

Tethis lowered his hands and turned to face her. "I am truly sorry," he said. "My enthusiasm got the better of me."

Marcus dropped to the mats, chuckling. "I don't think I've been out-maneuvered so thoroughly in ages. I couldn't pull up in time."

Johnny flew his drone in so he could tag the two while they weren't watching, only to have it vanish in a shower of purple and blue sparks.

"Oh! Do you mind?" Stephanie shouted, but Tethis looked unrepentant.

She groaned. "I thought the game was over."

"He hadn't stopped playing," the Teacher pointed out, his voice full of mischief.

"She's right," Johnny said before she could reply. "I was definitely gonna leave my mark."

"And you said we had the right to defend ourselves," Tethis added.

"Well, whatever. That's three drones you all owe me."

The chorus of protest that met her statement soon made her hold her hands up in surrender.

"Fine. I'll split the costs, but Elizabeth will have our hides."

The others shook their heads. "Nope," Johnny informed her. "We'll tell her this was all your idea."

Tethis nodded agreement. "Technically, that's true," he added.

Stephanie rolled her eyes and changed the subject. "You did well to combine MU and eMU. How'd you come up with that?"

He gave her a sly smile. "I had a good teacher."

"He's watched footage of the battle," Frog informed her. "It was only a matter of time before he worked it out."

"I didn't expect you to like eMU so much."

The old man's face softened.

"Why wouldn't I?" he asked. "It's wonderful to discover MU on Earth that's made of eMU. It's like having an old lover return."

She stared at him and he waggled his eyebrows.

"Exciting, yet comfortable," he explained, and she covered her face with one hand.

"That... That is too much information," she told him, and he smiled.

"The eMU wasn't all new," he confessed. "I had a little incident in a park and drew some to help a little girl get a cat out of a tree."

"You did?"

"Well, there was that and what you taught us when we first came through the portal."

"I wasn't sure how much of that you'd retained," Stephanie told him. "We kinda had other things to worry about."

"Like being bombed all the way back to Meligorn," Frog told her morosely.

"Well, that didn't happen," she reminded him and turned to Tethis again. "What happened?"

"The little girl was crying because her cat was stuck up the tree, and I went over..." He let his words trail off when he caught the others staring at him. "What?"

"You went over to talk to humans?" she asked, and he nodded.

"I did, and I asked him if he wanted the cat brought out of the tree or if he'd like to get it. He said he'd like to get it, so I lifted him up to where he could reach it using the eMU in the area."

Stephanie knew she was staring but she didn't care. This was the first time Tethis had spoken of what had happened in the park. She'd known the Teacher had gone walking on his own—and been mortified—but not that anything had happened.

"And by lifted," she began carefully, "you mean you used magic?"

"Well, of course." He indicated his frail body with a sweep of his hand. "It's not like I could lift him with this."

He had a point.

"And how did that work for you?"

"Well, the little girl was delighted that her father could fly, the cat was surprisingly cooperative and climbed into his arms and stayed there, and everyone was very happy—including me."

He seemed a little surprised by that last fact but pleased nonetheless.

"And you used eMU for that?"

"I wasn't carrying a battery," he told her. "It was supposed to be a quiet refreshing walk in the park."

"It sounds like you found more than you bargained for," she told him.

He gave her a crooked smile. "It was quite refreshing but a little strenuous."

"Okaaaay…"

He sighed. "Look, when you're older, you'll understand what it means to climb out of your set ways and see life as a young person again."

She regarded him with a dubious stare.

Tethis scowled. "Listen, what I mean is that you have to learn to become pliable again and willing to learn instead of being as hard and stubborn as a rock, willing to beat others with what you know to be true. It's a somewhat unsettling experience."

Now, Stephanie wasn't the only one who stared at him. The three security guards were looking as well.

"It means you're no longer so assured of how right you are of following a set of hard and fast rules—and the rules themselves become uncertain. You have to learn everything again exactly as you did when you were younger."

"I get it," she told him. "I'm glad you're getting a new start."

"I'd have preferred better circumstances," he grumbled.

A wave of cold fear rolled over Aaron.

"Oh, dear God," he muttered and checked the screen again. "Oh, dear God, no…"

Instinctively, he wound his arms around his chest, leaned forward in his chair, and read through what he'd found. It didn't change and the chill settled in his chest. Gene definitely would not thank him for this.

The engineer stood but remembered his terminal. He could always pull the data up on Gene's but that would leave a trace on his friend's machine. If he'd found what he thought he had, it would be better if that didn't happen.

Instead, he stuck his head out of his cubicle door and checked the open area beyond. Relieved to see it was empty, he took the two steps he needed to reach Gene's door and tapped lightly.

"You have to see this," he said when his partner opened the door.

"I'm kinda in the middle—"

Aaron grabbed him by his shirt-front and yanked him into his cubicle. Security could make of that what they wanted, but the chances were that they weren't even looking at their monitors. He thanked the Navy silently that they'd insisted on actual physical cubicles over and above the sound dampeners and other security measures still in place.

"You. Have. To see this," he repeated and hauled the man closer so he could pull the door closed behind them.

"This had better be goo—what the fuck!" Gene stared at the

screen. "We're supposed to close Ghost in the Machine down. It's been put on hold."

He turned to him. "Yeah, I know. I was. See?" He indicated the screen.

"It doesn't look very closed down to me."

"Well, about that. I have a problem."

His friend glanced at the screen and back at him. "I'll say you have. What does it have to do with me?"

"You're the only one who knows."

"Knows what? For God's sake, Aaron. What's the matter?"

"Do you remember that really bad day I had ages ago when we were doing the school testing?"

"Yeah…" Of course he remembered. Aaron's bad days were few and far between and they were always memorable, but the only one that truly owned the title was the one where he'd almost torn his cubicle apart because the kid he was testing was such a royal shit.

"What about it?"

"So, you know how I said I would—"

Gene slapped a hand over his mouth and turned to the computer. Even one-fingered, it didn't take him long to type in the security protocols. When he was done, he took his hand away.

"Now you can talk about it."

"Thanks, Gene."

"Get it over with, would you? Seriously, this is the fifth night of overtime this week, and Katie's gonna kill me if it goes on too long."

"Well, I did it."

"Did what. Aaron, you're not making any sense."

"I gave BURT the next test subject."

"You what?"

This time, it was Aaron who slapped a hand over his

colleague's mouth. "Ssshhh. Jeez, I knew you wouldn't take it well but I didn't think you'd take it this badly."

He took his hand away.

"How was I supposed to take it?"

"Gee, I don't know. How about in your usual nothing-fazes-me Gene kinda way?"

"Thanks for the compliment, bro, but this I do not need. Do you know how many administrative protocols you just broke?"

"Not 'just,' man. I broke them ages ago."

Gene slapped the flat of his hand against Aaron's chest. "It doesn't matter when you did it. It only matters that you did. They're gonna catch up with you eventually."

Aaron's face paled. "I know, man, but the worst thing is that I think our ghost might be BURT."

"BURT? Are you sure?"

"Well, yeah, I kinda am." He gestured toward the screen. "You see, I think that next test subject was Stephanie Morgana."

The other man went white and sat down heavily in the chair. "You are shitting me."

"I wish I was, bro, but I really, really think BURT tested her and that she somehow corrupted him."

"Corrupted him? She was only a kid."

"Well, got him thinking outside his usual parameters, and what I have on that screen kinda shows it might be the case. See? We had that first spike right there."

Gene leaned his elbows on the desk and buried his face in his hands. When he spoke, his voice was muffled. "You can't prove anything."

"Yeah, I know, and we have to prove it to take it upstairs."

"But Project Ghost has been put on hold," his friend told him, "so you can't dig into this."

"I could do it after hours—"

"After hours? Man, have you seen our schedule? We have

after-after hours on top of our after hours and that's gonna last until this war is over."

"And probably way beyond it," he added gloomily.

"Katie's gonna spit."

"Yeah, and it's only gonna get worse once the resignations start."

"Resignations? They won't let anybody resign."

"I don't see how they'll stop them."

"I'm sure they'll have their ways," Gene grumbled and tapped the screen. "This is gonna have to wait."

"But what if BURT is the Ghost?"

"It's not like he's trashing the place. If we leave him alone, he'll be fine. Besides, even if he is the Ghost, he'll be so up to his processors in Navy work that he won't have the bandwidth to do anything else."

"He's a supercomputer, Gene. He'll find a way."

"Fuck."

"What?"

"What if the Navy finds out?"

"They couldn't find their asses with both their hands, a tour guide, and a map—and if we don't tell them—"

"You haven't seen their White Hat teams."

"I have, and those guys are so busy right now, they wouldn't know a Ghost if it stood up in front of them with a sign around its neck. I vote we don't tell them until we know for sure."

"But that means going off-task."

"Sure." Aaron shrugged. "But it's not like we haven't done that before."

"We've never done it with the Navy breathing down our necks."

"So? This'll be a first. You always wanted some excitement in your life."

"This is not what I meant."

CHAPTER TWENTY

The Federation News Alert banner interrupted the lunchtime round of soap operas, talk shows, and midday news broadcasts. The whooping of its emergency siren shattered the calm of hundreds of households, sports bars, pubs, and hotel rooms as the anchorwoman's stricken face appeared.

Amelia Howard had never looked so normal. Her makeup was hurriedly applied and her hair too hastily brushed for it to have been done by a professional.

When the alert tone ended, she faced the camera with a serious expression.

"People of the Federation," she began and glanced at her Meligornian counterpart as he hurried over to stand beside her. "It is with heavy hearts that we tell you that our planet is under attack." She turned immediately to Jalel. "You've seen the reports," she said. "Exactly how bad is it?"

"Bad?" He turned terrified eyes to her face, his silver hair wild and messy. "It's terrifying. I don't even know if I'll see Meligorn again."

"You'd leave me?"

He clapped a hand on her shoulder. "Never. As much as I miss Meligorn, Earth is my home now."

He turned stricken eyes to the camera. "And she is under attack."

"Are you sure it's an attack?" she squeaked.

"Right now, Amelia, there are over two hundred house-sized rocks heading for Earth, each one precisely aimed and targeted. We are in for a shit-storm of hurt and there is nothing—nothing—we can do to stop them."

"Nothing?" Again, her voice rose in fear. "What about the Navy? Surely they can destroy them?"

Jalel shook his head. "If they shoot one, it will break apart and we'll be showered by thousands of smaller rocks, each the size of a car. Thousands!"

Amelia looked like she might cry. "What about the Witch?"

"She is our only hope," he told her, "and we have reached out and hope she'll send us a lifeline. Right now, hope seems slim. After the attack on Meligorn, my people cannot hope to reach us in time…and Dreth is too far away. As of now, we are on our own."

The broadcast ended with Amelia folding her hand over the one he'd rested on her shoulder as the two of them looked into each other's eyes. Outside the studio, the world erupted into chaos.

Across the networks, the same dire message was repeated and leaked footage of the meteors tumbling in ominous slow motion slid onto the airwaves. Live reporting and alerts were supplemented by web-based reporting in the tabloids, and headlines screamed imminent destruction.

How long does Earth have?

Will the Morgana come?

Meteor Bombardment Imminent!

Those were quickly followed by sincere apologies that the news stations couldn't continue to update the world on the asteroids' approach. News of a Federation-wide ban on any reporting became the headline.

Navy Silences the Press.

Is the Navy Ban Legal?

Navy Says People Should Die Oblivious.

"Oh, for pity's sake!" The Fleet Admiral, Jonas Amaratne, thumped his hand on the surface of his desk. "This has to stop."

"We've issued the invitations, sir."

"Did you send a squad of fully-armed Marines with each one to show them attendance was mandatory?"

"We're holding the Marines in reserve, sir. The rioting is bad in certain sectors. Some of our 'guests' may require an escort."

"Is that how you've worded it?"

"Yes, sir. A full Marine escort."

He rolled his eyes. "They will have a field day."

"With respect, sir, they already have."

"Then we have nothing to lose, do we? Make sure they all attend—and in person if you can."

"We will most certainly try, sir."

"Make it so."

They succeeded—and discovered that the Marine's weren't needed except for escort duty. Not a single news channel wanted to miss the Navy's "Tell-All" meeting. Some even promised to "reveal all" they were told.

The admiral snorted when he saw it.

"They'll be sadly disappointed," he told his aide. "Make sure they understand."

"Aye, sir."

The man saluted smartly and left, and Amaratne rose from his seat and prepared for the meeting, filling the intervening time by going over his notes and presentation. When he walked onto the stage, he was the picture of confidence and authority—a facade he maintained as the hall erupted into shouted questions.

He raised a hand and they stilled and watched as he walked to the podium. Aware that all eyes were on him, Fleet Admiral Amaratne set his tablet down and moved aside slightly to allow his aide to set it up.

"Greetings, ladies and gentlemen," he started and kept exactly how loosely he used that term firmly to himself. "I see you have discovered that Earth is under attack."

Outraged cries erupted, many of which reiterated the people's "right to know" and the "freedom of the press," among other things. Jonas held his hand up and made calming motions. When they settled again, he continued.

"Two weeks ago, one of the early warning systems we'd set to guard our solar system was triggered by a small Teloran fleet."

He played the clip taken from the footage sent from the drones and ignored the moans of dismay from members of the audience who regretted that they'd been forced to leave their recording devices at the door.

"As you know, they destroyed our early warning system and released a large number of asteroids."

Again, he waited for the responses to die down. "We sent a small task force to investigate our options and they rapidly ruled out using missiles to stop the swarm."

He had to wait again for their cries of protest to die down and even had to pat the air with his hand.

"I understand that you know all this and while I'd like to know exactly how, I won't ask."

Nervous laughter greeted that statement and he waited for it to fade.

When it did, he went on. "What you don't know is that we have a number of teams working on the problem, both from Meligorn and from Earth."

"Can you tell us who it is?" The question was asked from several quarters and the admiral smiled.

"I'm afraid not."

"Is the Witch involved?"

"That is something else we can't say, although we note that several of you have made impassioned pleas for her involvement. The Navy has the situation under control."

More laughter—disbelieving this time—erupted.

"Can you tell us what the teams are working on?"

"No, I can't. All I can say is that we're pursuing several different ways of dealing with the problem."

"How much time do we have?" someone else yelled, and he looked toward the voice.

Before he could reply, another voice called, "Are there any plans to evacuate Earth while there's still time?"

This question touched a chord, and more voices demanded answers.

He raised his hand and the voices stilled.

"We have a little over seven months to resolve this, so I wouldn't start worrying for a while."

"That's easy for you to say."

Again, he looked toward the voice. "My family is going nowhere," he told the audience firmly, "and on that note, I'll call the end of the meeting. My second in command will inform you of your reporting rights and responsibilities."

With that, he turned abruptly from the podium, stripped the mike from his collar, and thumbed it off as he did so.

Even then, he did not speak until he'd handed it to his aide and was safely back in his office. He thought about his family and sighed. "I sure hope I don't regret that comment."

***

At One R&D headquarters, Stephanie stared at the television.

Amelia and Jalel were back to their usually well-groomed selves, but their cheery demeanors were missing.

"And this is what it's like downtown," the woman said. "People seemed to have lost all sense of decorum."

Windows shattered behind them, and they both ducked. The camera shook as though the cameraman had jumped and it panned to their left.

"Understood, Clive," Amelia could be heard saying. "We're heading out, now."

The camera showed a group moving onto the street. They mingled with the crowd shouting at Joint Federation Police and Naval HQ. Somewhere off-screen, a window shattered. The crowd surged.

"Look, coppers! Look what I have."

The picture jerked as the camera moved to focus on the sound but it began to move back. "Hey!"

"You can thank me, later," Jalel snapped from off-screen. "I'm saving your hide."

"But—"

"Head Office says to get off the street," the anchorman replied, "and to our lovely viewers, this is Jalel Trylfir advising you to steer clear of the downtown area for the next few hours."

"And Amelia Howard seconding that excellent advice. Stay safe out there."

"Unbelievable," Stephanie muttered as Jalel echoed his co-anchor's wishes and the camera continued to record the chaos that spread through the street behind them.

More windows shattered and people stepped through the gaping holes to take possession of the goods beyond them. Marines and riot police emerged from the Federation building.

She shook her head. "People are utterly unbelievable."

"It looks fairly normal to me," Johnny replied as fire hoses were deployed. "They all expect to die tomorrow so there's nothing to lose by doing things they'd never dream of doing if the world would continue."

Across the room, Tethis nodded. "I'd like to say Meligornians acted differently, but I think every race goes a little crazy when faced with extinction."

"But we wouldn't be extinct. There are still the colonies."

"And no way for these people to get to them," Marcus pointed out. "This is how they act when nothing will matter."

"So, how do we make it matter?" she asked, and the team looked at her.

"What do you mean?" Lars wanted to know.

Stephanie gestured toward the television. "This—all of this—is the Telorans. It's why they did it—to start all this. We have no idea if it's their people making a fuss or real worried individuals."

"It could always be both."

"And that's the problem. There's no way to tell the guilty from the innocent. How the hell do we calm them all down?"

Vishlog answered, "We give them a taste of victory," he explained. "Every warrior feels better when they know the enemy can be killed. Civilians are the same. It is only when they have no hope that they lose heart."

She stared at him. "So, victory. It's that simple."

He gave her a slow, fang-bearing smile. "That simple."

"But how do we give them a taste of victory?" She glared at him. "Last I looked, space rocks couldn't be killed."

"No, but if we could deal with them, people here would have hope. For now, it is easy for them to believe their planet is about to be crushed because it is."

"I can't believe you actually said that."

"Why not? It is true."

Frog groaned and Stephanie rolled her eyes. "Fine," she said. "We have to show the world that it's not about to be crushed by space rocks. Now, how can we do it?"

"Well, we can't blast them," Brenden mused and caught their looks. "Face it, if they could be blasted safely, the Navy would already have done it. I bet they've already checked that option."

"It would explain why they took so long to call us in," Avery added. "They were trying to fix it themselves."

"And now we have a week less to fix it for them," Frog muttered.

"Or to find a way to fix it with them," she told them.

"Can't you simply portal them away?" Marcus asked hopefully.

Stephanie shared a look with Tethis. He frowned and shook his head.

She shrugged. "I'm not sure. We'll have to see how bad it is first." She glanced at the Teacher but he continued to shake his head firmly. "It's unlikely, though."

"So, no shooting them and we can't gate them all. What can we do?" Frog demanded.

None of them answered him, at first, then she looked at Lars.

"Field trip?" he asked, and she grinned.

"Field trip. We need our ship."

CHAPTER TWENTY-ONE

Captain Emil Pederson hefted his duffel bag and headed through the *Ebon Knight's* hatch. He'd thought about bringing more but decided there wasn't time. Besides which, the trip wouldn't be a long one—he hoped.

He also hoped it was a trip they'd come back from and preferably in one piece without any extra holes. "A man can dream, can't he?" he muttered as he stowed his bag in his cabin before he set off to the bridge.

It was a mess. Technicians had opened every panel on the consoles and were busy working through them to make sure everything was running smoothly. Some looked up as he entered, but most ignored him.

Everyone was trying to get the job done as fast as they could without sacrificing quality. No one had time for gawking. He grimaced. That was all about to change.

"Sorry, guys," he muttered, slipped on his headset, and turning the mic on. "This is an All-Ship announcement. Repeat, All Hands, All Ship. All Hands, All Ship. This is your captain speaking."

On the bridge, all activity stilled.

He gave everyone a few more minutes to finish what they were doing before he began.

"All hands, this is your captain speaking. This ship will leave the dock in seventy-two hours. I repeat, this ship will leave the dock in seventy-two hours. You have seventy-two hours to have her ready to go after the rocks."

A murmur rippled across the bridge. He gave it a moment to die down and used how long it took them to settle as a timer for how long the sections needed before he spoke again.

"Shore leave is cut to forty-eight hours. Work crews can expect more support at that time. We will defend Earth as we defended Meligorn. Now, get back to work."

He tapped the key to turn the all-crew broadcast off and returned to his office.

Once there, he secured the door behind him. "Hey, Ebony. Do you have time to chat?"

"I will always have time to chat to you, Captain. I can do more than one task at once," the *Knight* replied.

"Thank you, Ebony."

"How can I be of assistance?"

"I need you to help the work crews get their jobs done more quickly. If they need more materials or equipment, I need you to make sure they get it inside the next few hours or as soon as you can."

"Regulations state that only the captain may sign requisition orders, Emil. I would be out of protocol. I can, however, compile a real-time list of what they need."

He plucked at his lower lip. "Do that, Ebony, but listen. I want you to break a few protocols to get us what we need. I don't care what they are. Sign my name if you need to."

Silence greeted that order, and he thought he might have pushed the AI a little too far. He was about to apologize and rescind his request when the *Knight* replied.

"I am…flattered…" she began, and he steeled himself for a

polite refusal. "Thank you for your trust, Emil. I will do my best to ensure you do not suffer for giving it."

Shortly after, the leader of the crew working on the hull felt his tablet vibrate.

"This had better be important," he grumbled. They'd been on a short timeframe, to begin with, but with the Captain's announcement, they had almost no chance to complete the support installation the *Knight* needed.

All the grumbling stopped when he saw what was on the screen. "Hells, yes, we need it now."

As he tapped his reply and added a few more items he hadn't had time to order, the lieutenant commander overseeing provisioning studied the latest order from the *Knight's* captain.

"Fuck me," he murmured and gaped at the list. "And he wants it when?"

Another lieutenant commander was nowhere near so polite. "I need time to authorize, you daft wee Jimmy," he snapped. "Witch's boy or not, you'll have to get in line like all the fecking rest. Ye're not a fecking exception, you goat-sucking sheep's turd."

As he cussed at the absent Emil, a second message appeared on his screen. "And now, I have the admiral breathing up my arse, you unmitigated turdlet—and he's a darn sight more important than you ever imagined yourself to be."

His face mottled red when he read the contents of the admiral's email. "Of all the queue jumping, misbegotten sons of bitches ever breached into God's good universe."

While the weapons depot commander cursed so virulently, Emil stared, drop-jawed, at the screen. "I sent one hundred and twelve messages simultaneously?"

Ebony gave an accurate imitation of a disapproving sniff. "They weren't sent at the same time. There is at least a half-second between the first and the last."

He chuckled. "Thank you, Ebony. I truly appreciate it."

"It is also within my interests to inform you that you have been on deck for over four hours and should refuel your biological systems and also that I am authorized to enact appropriate steps to ensure this happens."

"By who?"

"By you, Emil. You told me to ensure everyone had what they needed to improve their functioning and you need to refuel."

"I— Thank you, Ebony. I'll take your advice."

Emil stood and left the office. He'd barely reached the outer hatch when he was almost bowled over by a crewman heading in the other direction.

"Sorry," she called, then saw who she'd run into. "Captain, I'm sorry."

She froze to attention and he returned her salute.

"As you were, Corporal." He frowned. "I thought you weren't due back for another eighteen hours."

"True, sir, but she'll be ready faster if I'm back sooner. No one here knows the inside of that hull as well as I do."

The captain raised his eyebrows, and her expression became anxious.

"Please don't send me back, sir. The Witch needs her ship and I want to make sure the *Knight's* in the best shape we can make her in the little time left."

"Welcome aboard, Corporal. I appreciate your early return."

"Thank you, sir," she managed.

He waited for her to move, then realized she was waiting on him. "Dismissed."

Her thanks were thrown over her shoulder as she sprinted to her quarters.

She wasn't the only one, but she was by far the politest.

"Sorry, sir."

"Excuse us, sir."

"We'll be on station shortly, sir."

"Stand aside or bear a— Oh, Captain. Excuse us."

He returned their hastily thrown salutes, shook the hands offered, and thanked them. Some of them were still in high heels and short skirts. Others wore suits. Still more were in gym shorts —and at least one was in flannels, and another wore a dressing gown.

"My gear's already aboard," she explained. "I'll be dressed in a minute."

"She forgot her kit," her partner apologized and blushed. "My fault."

"I...I'll send a runner," Emil murmured, but the woman shook her head.

"It's fine, sir. I've already sent a courier."

As she hurried away, one of the mini-skirted crowd caught his attention. "Welcome back aboard, George."

"Good to be back, sir." The man patted the *Knight's* wall fondly. "I missed the girl."

"I'm glad to hear it," he replied and added in the mildest tones he could manage, "Do you think you can stop by the head and wipe the lipstick off, George?"

The man grinned. "I plan to, sir. I can't work on engines in a mini-skirt and fishnets...and the *Knight* won't want me kissing her."

Emil suppressed a smile. "Thank you, George."

As he watched the crew return early from their leave with such enthusiasm, he couldn't help but feel a swell of pride. All these people were willing to sacrifice the last of their spare time to make sure their ship was ready to save the world. He sighed.

"You still need to eat, Captain," the *Knight* reminded him. "Don't make me speak to Captain Sartre."

"You—"

"Yes, I would, Emil. He needs to eat, too."

Stephanie breathed in the sweet scent of a Meligornian meadow. The picnic rug spread beneath her offered protection from the semi-damp earth and adventurous bugs, and the sun was pleasantly warm.

Virtual Meligorn, she thought and frowned at Tethis. *BURT's a genius.*

"And if you try, you'll burn yourself out and then where would the rest of us be?" the old Meligornian grumbled.

"So, gating is out?" BURT asked.

"Yes," was the Teacher's fierce reply, "and she is too valuable to be wasted like that."

"I am not more valuable than an entire world," she argued.

"You are responsible for three," he snapped.

"Enough," BURT ordered. "We are agreed."

He turned to Stephanie. "You do not have enough power to be able to gate all the meteors before they strike Earth—and to gate any less is a waste, since the planet will still die and you won't be around to protect what's left of mankind."

"Or anyone else," Tethis added.

"Or anyone else," BURT conceded.

"So, what if I don't have to gate them all?" she asked. "What if I simply turn them?"

The Meligornian shook his head. "You'll still need to create a gate for each one and the result will be the same. You won't be able to turn them all before you burn yourself to nothing."

"How about a really big gate, then?" she persisted. "One that covers the earth?"

"The whole earth?" His voice rose in disbelief. "Not even the two of us could pull that one off. Maybe if we asked the Meligornians at the university—"

"No." Stephanie's rejection was immediate and determined. "No, we won't involve them. If this is a trap, they are the Federation's future. It'll only be us—and we need to find a solution."

A soft chime sounded that disturbed the birds and sent them into panicked flight.

BURT sighed. "Time is up. You need to go."

Frog was waiting, but there was also a Federation Navy ensign there to greet them as they left the pods.

"Get a move on or you might be walking to the—eep!"

A blue bubble of eMU surrounded the young officer and lifted him from the floor, and Tethis smiled.

"Sometimes, it is a good reminder not to push a Master."

He drew the ensign after him like a novelty balloon while his gentle smile of satisfaction remained in place. Stephanie turned to Frog.

"Since when do you let the Navy in here?"

"Since we had to keep the pilot waiting. I assumed he wouldn't leave his ensign behind."

"Don't tempt me," a new voice said through their head comms. "I can hold a few more minutes, but not many. Only enough to make the window."

Onboard the *Knight*, the head weapons technician turned to Emil.

"So, sir, what do you want most—coolant, more structural support, or faster firing."

The captain frowned. "What do you mean? I need them all."

"I mean which one do you want first, because we won't manage to get them all done before we leave. When we get back, you'll have them all."

If we get back, he thought but didn't say it.

"Coolant," he decided. "We're not likely to use them this trip, but if we do, I don't want them to overheat. After that, faster firing if the supports will take it or support if that's needed first."

His comms pinged and he frowned. "Excuse me."

"Sir, you're needed at the main entrance."

"Is it urgent?"

"It's about to be, sir."

"I'm on my way." He looked at the team leader. "I have to go."

"No worries, sir. We've got this."

Emil was sure they had. He turned away and walked as quickly as he could to the front gate. The Marine who'd called him had sounded worried—and he'd called him first and not their own captain, which meant they needed a ship's captain's authority or thought they did.

He hoped they were wrong. While he'd be mad, he didn't have time to deal with anything else. Hell! He was mad anyhow. The ship needed him on board and smoothing the workload, not down there dealing with bureaucratic bullshit.

By the time he'd progressed through the umbilical and across the deck to the main entrance, he'd worked himself into a fury. This had better be important, or someone would have their ass chewed.

The Marines saluted and opened the hatch. "This might be best dealt with outside the docking bay, sir."

Which only means they think the problem's serious, he thought.

His frown deepened and he stepped through. *Whoever it is, they're about to get one hell of a—*

He stopped at the sight of the man who stormed toward him, came abruptly to attention, and saluted.

"Hello, sir!"

The Marines stepped out after him and closed the door.

CHAPTER TWENTY-TWO

"Of all the self-entitled, self-privileged, cock-tugging asswipe civilian shit-stains!" It wasn't the language Emil expected from a rear admiral who strode the corridors of *Star Base Notaro*.

Judging from the expressions on the faces of the Marines accompanying him, it wasn't the kind of language anyone expected from a rear admiral on *Notaro*.

"That Witch needs to learn she is not an exception to the rule."

From the way he said it, the captain thought he might as well have said "bitch." Behind him, the Marines bristled. He made a placating gesture with his hand but kept it hidden from the officer.

The man continued, oblivious. "No one has the right to take liberties with the Navy. No one. Especially not a civilian ship taking advantage of Naval repairs. I'll explain the wrong way and the Navy way..."

As he continued to rant, Emil stepped away from the door and into his path.

"Can I help you, sir?"

"What?" The rear admiral stopped abruptly, and the captain was able to read the name on his badge—Dreyfuss.

"Jonathan, I am very sorry to disturb you." Ebony's voice caught Jonathan Wattlebird with his head under the piloting console, and he jumped and banged it as he backed out.

"What is it, Eb?"

"We have a rear admiral on the way and it will not be good."

As she said it, the technician Wattlebird had been working with pulled his head out from under the console. "Are you sure you want it wired that way? It's not standard."

He gave him a grin. "If you ain't cheating, you ain't trying."

"Cheating?" Ebony was appalled.

"Not cheating cheating," he hurried to explain, "and never cheat on your friends, but when it comes to your enemies and a fight like this, you take every advantage you can get."

To the technician, he said, "It might not be standard but will it work?"

"Hell, yes!"

"And will it be more precise?"

"It'll be that, sir."

"Then do it."

"Jonathan," Ebony said. "I need to help the captain. I need time."

He shrugged and tossed a lop-sided smile at the command center ceiling. "So…cheat."

Ebony put the view from the main entrance on the forward view screen. The officer in question was almost apoplectic and his face mottled from red to purple as he shouted at the captain.

"Move!"

Emil stared at him, and Dreyfuss roared again. "I said, 'move!'"

They watched as the captain looked at the irate visitor, then at the Marines around him. Their hands tightened on their weapons as they tensed.

"Don't do it," Jonathan muttered and relaxed as Emil stepped aside.

They caught the flick of his gaze to the nearest security camera as the rear admiral pushed past him and slapped his pass against the scanner. The scanner flashed red.

Access denied.

"What?" He smacked his pass against the scanner once more.

Access denied.

"Do you know who I am?" Dreyfuss roared, but the scanner didn't care.

Access denied, it repeated when he tried again. **Access denied. Access denied. Access denied.**

As he continued his attempts to activate the access panel, the *Ebon Knight* made a call.

"Stephanie, I'm sorry to interrupt you," she began, "but I need to discuss a very annoyed rear admiral with you."

She showed her a visual of the Marines who had left the ship itself to reinforce the four who'd manned the door. They'd used auxiliary exits and trotted up the corridor to join their colleagues. Now, there were ten of 'her' Marines faced off against the sixteen who'd escorted the officer.

"Keep him out," Stephanie told her. "We're only two hours away from you."

"I am afraid I cannot hold him that long," Ebony informed her.

Her lips tightened into a thin line of annoyance. "I'll get there quicker. Where are you?"

Ebony told her.

"And where is that in relation to our last berth?"

This time, she showed her a map of the *Notaro* with both berths marked, the current one outlined in green.

"Only three places away?"

"Affirmative."

"And is that location currently aired up?"

"We have low gravity in effect," the *Knight* informed her.

"Understood. Stall him as long as you can. I'm on my way."

Ebony disconnected, sure she heard Stephanie yelling for Tethis as she cut the link.

What she did not hear was what Vishlog said as he looked at Lars. "It has started."

She was too busy speaking to Emil.

"I know you said no interruptions, but I need to interrupt…"

In the meantime, Marine Captain Sartre had arrived. He stepped quickly through the main entrance lock and into the path of the rear admiral as the man tried to slip through the door.

"I'm sorry, sir, but you're not cleared."

"Not cleared?" Dreyfuss sputtered

We're working on that now," Sartre explained, "but there is one thing we need you to do first."

He held up a short metal rod.

"What is that?" the man demanded, but the way his face paled suggested he knew exactly what it was.

"I merely need you to hold this, sir, then I'll show you a series of pictures."

One of the Marines on the door pulled a tablet out and tapped it until he had the screen he was looking for.

Dreyfuss shook his head. "I won't touch that thing with a barge pole," he snapped. "Now, are you going to get out of my way, or am I going to have you both arrested for insubordination?"

"I'm sorry, sir, but we are not being insubordinate. We are following security protocol. Please take the rod."

"You, sir, are a mere captain. I am a rear admiral. You are

supposed to do what I tell you to—no argument, no questions, and no refusal. Now, open that door."

Emil chose that moment to break in. "I'm sorry, sir, but as you are aware, this isn't a Navy ship and you cannot board her without my permission—which you won't receive until the test has been administered and you pass."

"I don't have to put up with this," Dreyfuss retorted and turned to the Marine sergeant leading his escort. "Make a way—"

CHAPTER TWENTY-THREE

"Attention! Admiral on deck!" Ebony's voice cut Dreyfuss off before he could finish his order.

He barked a laugh. "I've been here a while."

"Not you, asshole," Knight replied and both Sartre and Emil's eyes widened, while their Marines smothered chuckles—something that became much easier as they caught sight of who walked up the corridor toward them.

"I didn't know he was still on board," one Marine muttered to the man next to him as they stared at the fleet admiral.

His colleague did not reply but came abruptly to attention and he did the same.

Seeing their intense stares, Dreyfuss turned. His Marine escort opened ranks for the fleet admiral and stood stiffly to attention as he passed. The fleet didn't waste any time.

"Take the damn test, Dreyfuss."

The man bristled. "I shouldn't have to take any stupid test, sir. You know I'm perfectly loyal. Earth is everything to me."

"Then you'll have no trouble passing. Take the test."

"With all due respect, sir, I'd rather suck vacuum than take a test from that Witch—"

The response came in a voice as cold and dark as the depths of space. "That can be arranged."

The admirals raised their heads and looked toward it, and every Marine pivoted to face this potential new threat. In the opposite direction from which the fleet admiral had arrived, a portal of pure blue energy shimmered, and a figure dressed in black and wreathed in blue lightning stepped clear of it.

They all stared as Stephanie Morgana stalked up the corridor toward them. Two large felines bounded past her and a robed figure flanked by the large form of her Dreth guard followed. They came alongside her as the rest of her team scrambled through the portal.

It snapped shut when the last one had barely emerged and left the corridor as empty as before. Someone had put the word out that there was an admiral on the warpath and the rest of the station chose to stay clear.

As he watched Stephanie arrive, Emil didn't blame them. There were few things worse than an admiral on the warpath, but the Morgana was easily one of them—and he had no doubt that she had arrived.

With her gaze locked on Dreyfuss, she reminded him of a storm cloud—one rumbling with fury and about to break. Her next words confirmed it.

"Let's make sure that this is only you and me," she told him and advanced relentlessly.

The rear admiral's Marines stood fast and didn't give way in the face of the Witch's fury. Still, their expressions and posture were wary.

The Morgana flicked them a glance. "Oh," she added and tapped the Badge of the Inquisition pinned to her chest, "and this, of course."

On board the *Ebon Knight*, all work stopped as every vid screen came alive with what was happening in the corridors beyond.

"Hell, yeah," one weapons tech murmured, and his voice rose in jubilation.

On the bridge, the technician working on the pilot's controls pulled his head away from the console and glared at the screen.

"Get the fuck out of our way, Admiral Asshole," he grumbled. "We're busy winning a war here."

Oblivious to this, the Morgana continued. "Have you ever felt the ice of space, Admiral? The caress of death as it takes you a little while to die?"

He gaped at her and his mouth worked soundlessly as she closed the final distance between them.

"I have," she told him, "many times, as I expend my energy to protect those I love...exactly as I'm about to do to protect this planet. And what are you doing?"

"I..." the rear admiral croaked, but she was implacable.

"Are you ready to join us? To prove your courage as we attack two hundred rocks that can devastate the planet?"

Dreyfuss gaped again. "I—"

The Morgana paid no attention. "Or are you afraid, hiding behind your bluster?"

The air around them crackled as she pulled more energy in.

"Are you ready to 'suck vacuum,' Admiral? It is what you said, isn't it?" She lowered her face to look him in the eye. "Choose one —hold that rod or prepare to walk the plank."

Taking a step back to give him room, the Morgana gestured toward the rod Captain Sartre held.

The man lifted it and proffered it again and a small, grim smile played over his lips. "I believe the captain wants you to take the test before you enter his ship. So does Fleet Admiral Amaratne," he continued, "and finally, the Witch of the Federation demands it. So, what'll it be?"

As the rear admiral continued to hesitate, the fleet admiral leaned over to Emil. "I knew I should have included a shock therapy enema when he was in with the psychs."

Dreyfuss turned abruptly to the fleet. "Sir, I'd like to resign."

The Morgana's response was immediate. "Oh no, you don't get out of this."

Her voice dropped another octave and grew even colder than before. Her security team shifted nervously. "Oh, shit—" was punctuated by Lars's single word assessment. "Fuck."

Tethis looked from one of them to the other, raised his eyebrows, and focused on the Morgana again. *This will be interesting,* he thought.

Sartre gave a startled oath as the bar lifted out of his hands, crackling with blue fire. He gaped as it drifted to Dreyfuss and wormed its way into his hands.

"Let's bypass the first two tests, Rear Admiral, and you look at me."

The man's hands clenched around the bar.

"Look at me, Dreyfuss," she repeated and slowly, he raised his head.

His eyes were squeezed tightly shut but he opened them and looked at the woman before him. In moments, his face twisted with pain and dislike as his skin began to burn. Its sizzle was over-ridden by his short cry.

"How many have you failed?" the Morgana asked, her voice more wonder than demand.

He whimpered and glared, and she lifted the rod from his hands using magic to unseal it from the melted flesh. She ignored his yelp and turned to his Marines. "You are released."

Fleet Admiral Amaratne nodded to her and addressed the escort. "Take him to the brig." He looked at Dreyfuss. "Your request is denied. You will stand trial for treason to the Federation and the Navy, and when you are punished, I'll pull the trigger myself."

As the man was led away, the fleet glanced at Morgana. "Thank you," he said. "We'll deal with him, now."

She inclined her head and a small smile played over her lips. "I believe you will."

When he turned to follow the Marines and their captive, the Morgana looked at Emil, her eyes the color of pitch. He came to attention as the Marines unlocked the entry. "Welcome, aboard, Stephanie."

"It's Morgana at the moment," she corrected him, "but Stephanie can hear you so I'm sure she will reply shortly."

She sighed and looked around at the team. "She fights me even now. Perhaps I will last a little longer this time. Pity."

So saying, she swept past the captain toward the ship and Lars scrambled in her wake.

"Todd!" he snapped and grinned when she pivoted to face him.

The grin vanished as soon as he caught her gaze and he swallowed hard.

"Todd?" he repeated, a squeak in his voice.

CHAPTER TWENTY-FOUR

"There. Have we got it?" Stephanie asked several hours later.

The crewman welding the plating in place glanced at her and nodded. "Yeah. Thanks for that."

"A pleasure," she replied and glared at where the cats played in a pile of shredded cardboard. "It's the least I can do after…"

She gestured at the two happy creatures, and he smiled. "Exactly like any cat," he told her. "Only bigger."

"Well, playtime's over." She frowned and brought her fingers to her lips to whistle them in.

They raised their heads and bounced into the middle of the mess they'd created.

"I mean it, you two." She turned and headed into the ship, whistling as she went.

This time, the felines bounded over to walk beside her.

On a nearby section of the worksite, Vishlog watched her path while keeping a strong grasp on the panel he held. The crewman followed his gaze. "I can call someone," he offered, but the Dreth shook his head.

"Lars is there."

It was true. The team leader had made it to Stephanie's side before she reached the hatch.

"I can stay a little longer if you need me."

The crewman's face broke into a grin. "Really? Because I have this box of pipes…"

"Show me."

Frog, Johnny, and Marcus were in the main data center.

"You want me to optimize the data flow where?" Frog asked, and the technician repeated his request. "Oh, sure, because that doesn't breach a thousand safety protocols affecting life-support."

"But it does…n't…oh…" The technician paled. "So what do you suggest?"

"Well, what did you want to achieve?" Johnny asked.

"Without asphyxiating everyone on board," Marcus added, and they worked from there.

Stephanie was in the engine room testing the energy flow between the drives and the batteries when her comms link pinged. "Morgana."

She listened to the voice on the other end while monitoring the latest connection and nodded. "Understood. On my way."

It took her a moment to finish the test she was running and when she was done, she turned to Cameron. "I'm sorry. I've been called to a meeting."

She glanced over to where Lars watched gauges and passed spanners to a technician below the decking. "You stay here. I'll grab Vishlog."

He arched an eyebrow. "Promise?"

"Cross my heart."

"There are a million ways I can make your existence difficult if you don't."

"Uh-huh." She pulled a face.

"Don't you believe me?"

"Oh no, I believe you," she told him and laughed but more to stop him from trying than because she believed he actually could. The last thing she needed was for him to take it as a challenge.

The Dreth wasn't hard to find. He was helping lift heavy pieces of metal into place and she scrunched her face as she tried to identify what they were for.

"Vishlog, I need you," she called once he'd positioned it for the crewman to weld and held it in place.

"When?"

"As soon as that one's done?"

He glanced at the crewman and the woman nodded. "We can take it from here. It'll be a little slower but nothing we can't handle. Thanks for helping speed things up."

They waited until she'd finished and Vishlog joined her. "And the cats?"

"Nuh-uh. I don't want them to tear up a high-level meeting. I'll take them back to my quarters while you get into something official."

"Official?" he asked.

"Like a clean uniform with all the trimmings," she told him. "I'll do the same."

He lengthened his stride to keep up with her. She left him at his door and met him there ten minutes later, sans cats and in a new uniform complete with medals.

"It doesn't hurt to remind them," she explained, and he gave her a tusk-revealing grin.

"Dreth are the same, but they do it with bigger weapons."

Stephanie snickered. "I bet they do."

They were chuckling as they left the ship.

"There goes trouble if ever I saw it," one of the crewmen remarked and her colleague grinned.

"Rather the brass than us." He patted the hull. "Let's keep going. This section's almost done."

"One down, twenty to go"—the woman smiled—"but this beauty will dance with the best of them by the time we're done."

Ebony was glad to hear it, even as she monitored Stephanie and Vishlog's progress to their meeting. Her watchfulness was interrupted by an incoming call some ten minutes later and she passed it through to Lars.

"I'm sorry to interrupt, Lars, but Vishlog is gone and this person suggests he is a family contact?"

He frowned but took it. "Storenson."

The *Ebon Knight* resisted the urge to eavesdrop as the team leader listened to the caller on the other end of the line. She reacquired Stephanie and Vishlog as they entered the meeting and checked the cats before she dropped in on each of the work teams.

Lars' shout over the comms jerked her back to the team.

"Frog!"

The curse from the data center told her Frog had heard the call. He'd been stretching into one of the data stacks to pull a blade out when the call had reached him.

"Shit, boss! You would not believe what you almost made me drop." He released the blade to the hands of the anxious technician who waited for it and stepped away from the stack.

"Shut up and listen. I need you if you can be spared."

He glanced over at the tech, who nodded vigorously.

"Sure, boss."

"Good. I need you to pick up a special package. It's arrived on the station and needs careful handling. Can you do that?"

"Sure thing, boss. Anything else?"

"For God's sake, don't break it."

"No problems, boss. I can do that." Frog sighed and headed to the door. "I'll be back."

"Famous last words," Marcus teased but Johnny gave him an absent-minded wave and continued to type. Whatever he was programming, it kept him busy.

Frog gave another sigh and left. He continued to grumble as he left the main hatch and hurried to the entry. "Mind the shuttle, Frog. Look after the wounded, Frog. Fetch my package, Frog."

He groaned and wondered which particular deity he'd pissed off enough to deserve fetch and carry duty when he'd rather be neck-deep in programming files. It didn't take him long to reach the Navy supply depot.

"I'm here for a package for the Morgana?" he said when he stepped up to the counter.

The man behind it brightened immediately. "You're from the Morgana's team?"

Frog resisted the urge to roll his eyes and nodded. "Yup. There's a package for us?"

His frowned. "I'm not sure what message you received, buddy, but it's not really a package. It's more a person. No one told you?"

"A person?" His voice squeaked with surprise. "A person?"

"Yeah, buddy. Which planet have you been on? He's this way."

***

"You do realize that this whole thing could be a trap," the fleet admiral stated and Stephanie stared at him.

"You mean they don't want to destroy the planet?"

"I mean I don't think they care. They might want to see what we have and this is their way to force us to show our hand."

"But we know Dreth is their main target. Why would they bother?"

"Because they know our fleets aren't based on Earth and they had quite a surprise at Meligorn. They won't risk the chance of another loss and want to see what we've got."

"So they launch two hundred meteors simply to—" Stephanie began, but Vishlog cut her off.

"It's a trap."

She stopped and stared at him, open-mouthed. "I can't believe you did that."

"Did what?" the admiral asked.

Sweeping her gaze around the table, she saw he wasn't the only one who'd missed Vishlog's reference. The Dreth was unimpressed.

"What? Is no one a fan of *Star Wars*? Late Twentieth Century?" When blank stares were all he received in response, he huffed out an exasperated breath. "Luddites."

That, they got. More open mouths resulted.

"Did the Dreth actually call us Luddites?"

Stephanie nodded. "Uh-huh."

"But… Dreth is the most—"

"Templeton." The fleet admiral's warning tone was not lost on the protesting vice admiral.

He closed his mouth with a snap and favored Vishlog with a glare. The warrior returned the expression with a benign smile.

"We lead you in hydro-technology," the Dreth reminded him.

"But—"

"Templeton!"

"Let's get back to the matter you called me in here to discuss," Stephanie suggested and gave her arms man a surreptitious kick under the table.

"He called us Luddites." Templeton clearly had trouble getting his head around it. "A Dreth."

"Get over yourself, Temps. We have more important matters to consider," said another of the admirals at the table, and he subsided.

"Well, we can't blast them," Admiral Dailey told them. "I have the calculations of what would happen if we tried that."

She nodded. "Thank you for at least investigating it."

It took her a moment to realize they were looking at her.

"I can't gate them all," she told them when she realized what they hoped for. "I'll have Tethis send you the results—or Frog," she added after a moment's thought.

Tethis and technology was a relationship in motion and not always harmonious motion.

"We could try to tractor them."

That led to a discussion of how much power it would take to tractor the asteroids off course.

"And then they'd only come back as a swarm we couldn't monitor," was the conclusion.

"Provided we actually had enough juice to pull it off," was the gloomy addition.

"And managed it without slamming them into each other or one of our own."

They sat and stared at each other in silence.

"Well," one would begin before they frowned and stopped. "No..."

"I don't suppose you could put a shield around the Earth until they passed?"

CHAPTER TWENTY-FIVE

"Lars, it's a kid," Frog whispered and shielded his comms with his hand.

The corporal at the counter watched him, and he had the distinct impression the man had difficulty keeping his face to a professional blank.

"A what?" the team leader asked.

"A kid. You know, a baby Dreth."

"You'd better not let him hear you calling him that. Boys are touchy about that kind of thing."

"It's not funny. What the hell am I supposed to do with a kid?"

"Well, you're... Hold on a minute," Lars said, then shouted, "No! Not that one. We can set... Sheesh! Frog, I'm gonna have to call you back."

"Wait, you can't—" He sighed when the comms link went dead. "Never mind. I'll think of something."

His heart sank as he looked at the youngster who stood before him. The damn kid stood almost as tall as he did and weighed twice as much. He was also green-skinned with prominent lower tusks and a stubborn set to his face.

He knew that look. He'd seen it on Vishlog's face on more than one occasion and it always meant trouble.

"They sure do grow 'em big where you come from," he muttered, and the youngster's ears twitched.

He turned his head and studied the guard while a sneer curled his lip.

"And they sure do make 'em short where you come from," he replied. He looked beyond the man. "Where is my uncle?"

Frog eyed him and wondered how much it would take to set him off. Finally, he shrugged and decided the little shit could learn to cope from the get-go. They wouldn't have time to ease him into things.

"He's in a meeting with the Morgana. The call that you'd arrived came after he left."

To his surprise, the kid's face brightened. "So he doesn't know I'm here?"

"No…" he replied, cautious because he couldn't work out why that would be good news.

"And they sent you."

Well, he didn't have to make it sound like he was the worst option. He tilted his head, considered his options, and decided to change the subject. "Are you hungry?"

The small Dreth regarded him with interest. "Are you buying?"

He sighed. "Steph will skin me if I don't."

"You're afraid of a girl?'

"Listen, kid. Anyone with half a brain knows to be afraid of the Morgana."

Realization dawned. "Ah. Stephanie Morgana." He tilted his head and made another slow scrutiny of the guard. "Is she the only one?"

"The only one what?"

"The only girl you're afraid of."

"My mother's scary, too," he admitted. The child froze and his face went blank.

Frog grimaced as the youngster's throat moved and he had the painful impression that the kid was fighting tears. "So, what's your name?" he asked in an attempt to break the awkward moment.

The Dreth's eyes focused and he curled his lip. "You can call me Hrageth," he said.

"Hrageth," he repeated, fairly sure this was not the person Vishlog swore by, but he decided not to argue. "Right. Hrageth it is. Let's get you out of here."

The kid picked up the duffle bag resting at his feet.

"Is that all you have?"

"I didn't have much to bring." The short reply was as much a 'fuck off' as Frog had ever heard, and he decided not to pursue it.

Instead, he led the boy out of the small waiting room the Navy had him corralled in and over to the front desk. "Where do I sign?"

"I take it you're the proxy for his relative?"

"He's in a meeting," Frog confirmed. "They sent me."

The man pulled a face and he sighed. "Look, d'you really want to explain to Vishlog why we made his nephew wait another two hours here when I could have the kid back and settled in before his meeting's done?"

The corporal regarded him briefly and pulled a tablet out. "Sign here, here...and here," he instructed, "and I'm obligated to tell you that you are responsible for his safety and actions until such a time as he is given over into the care of his proper guardian."

"Understood," Frog told him and glanced at where "Hrageth" edged closer to the door. "Don't go anywhere or I will tell the Morgana you need a good ass-kicking."

The corporal behind the counter raised an eyebrow but said nothing as he indicated several places on the tablet where he needed to sign and also insisted on a thumbprint for good measure.

The kid loitered, clearly weighing up the odds of getting into trouble if he left the small man behind.

"Hrageth, my ass," Frog muttered and noted the name in the documentation. "More like 'Little Garach.'"

"I'm not little."

"No, you're a heaping stack of trouble," he told him.

"Do you wanna see how much, *muschtack*?" the young Dreth sneered, and he raised an eyebrow.

"You're lucky I've been told to look after you," he retorted warningly, "or I'd put you out the nearest airlock."

Again, the kid gave him an assessing stare, and he had to smother a smile. Damn! The brat reminded him of exactly how he'd been when he was younger and didn't know how to back down. He also knew he needed an out.

He shook his head. "I gotta feed you first. I can't put you out an airlock on an empty stomach. Company rules."

Garach gave him a look that said he didn't believe a word of it but he didn't argue.

Frog decided to press his advantage. "So, do you have a preference?"

The kid shot him a puzzled look, one tinged with suspicion. He sighed.

"For food," he explained. "Do you have a type of food you like?"

"Do you?"

The young Dreth was being downright impossible—exactly like he'd been when he'd been the same age. Frog resisted the urge to glare and forced a shrug. "Well, okay then. I've found this little place not far from the ship. It does a nice line in steak and beer—not that you can have the latter."

"Sure I can. Dreth constitution is stronger than a human's."

"It's still illegal," he argued.

"No one's gonna know."

The kid sounded so much like he had at the same age that Frog almost stopped. It was worse that Garach had a point. *Little wretch,* he thought. *Grechloch. It suits him.*

Part of him argued that this wasn't how the boy's name was pronounced, but the rest of his mind liked it. He grinned. Of course the kid caught it.

"What?"

"I thought of a nickname for you."

"Hrageth?"

"Not unless you like the idea of your uncle swearing by your balls every thirty seconds or so."

Grechloch's eyes widened. "He does not."

"No, but Hrageth's must be itching most of the time. I swear that has to be Vishlog's favorite curse."

"Hrageth's balls…" the kid muttered and tried it for himself. "Mother used to like Shekara's tits."

Frog snickered and the kid blushed.

"Not her actual…" He came to a stuttering halt, and the guard slapped him on the shoulder.

"It's okay, kid. I got it. It's another Dreth cuss phrase. It's simply not one I've heard."

"Well, what do you say?"

That gave him pause. Admittedly, there was a part of him that simply itched to teach a Dreth kid to swear, but there was another part of him that desperately wanted to live and not have Stephanie zipper his mouth closed again.

"Uh…maybe later, hey Grech?"

"That is not my name."

"Nope, it's your very first nickname."

"Call me Hrageth."

Frog raised his eyebrows, and the kid glowered at him.

"Or call me Garach. It is my name."

Frog couldn't help it. He pushed. "Or what?"

The glare he got was as dark as any Vishlog had managed, and he smirked. This time, the young Dreth changed the subject.

"Steak," he began. "What is it?"

The question caught him off-guard and he hesitated. "Uh…do you know what a cow is?"

"No."

"Oh."

Well, this will be difficult. Why couldn't the kid ask me something easy like how the universe was made?

He was saved from having to explain by the sight of the restaurant frontage. "We're almost there. I can show you what a steak is if you like."

"Does my uncle like them?"

Frog nodded. "He really does."

"And beer?"

"You're not having a beer."

The truth was Vishlog also liked his beer, but that didn't mean he'd approve of his eleven-year-old nephew having one, even if the kid was built like a brick shithouse and the size of a human adult and could probably handle it. Nope, that was a discussion he definitely didn't want to have with the big Dreth—or with Stephanie.

"No arguments," he reiterated. "That's something you'll have to take up with your uncle."

"Tark."

"*Muschtak.*"

"Tegorthan reject!"

"Shit for brains."

"Derkat bait."

"Oh, look, we're here…aah…nose-wipe."

Frog led the way into Halley's while the kid still worked his way through that last one.

"Are you sure my uncle likes the food here?"

He scowled. The damn kid never let up. "He loves it."

"Can I have the same as he does?"

When he remembered exactly what Vishlog ordered and exactly how expensive it was, Frog stifled a groan. "You can."

Hopefully, he could always get it out of the big Dreth later. He wondered if little Dreth ate as much as little humans did when they reached the age for attitude.

"Table for two," he said when they approached the front counter.

The girl on the desk checked her book and gestured toward the dining area. "You can sit where you like. I have no bookings until dinner."

Frog arched an eyebrow. "Slow day?"

"A swarm of asteroids heading for your home planet tends to mean less downtime for my usual clientele."

He supposed it would. "Anywhere?"

"Yup, anywhere." She eyed the young Dreth but said nothing.

"I do not like the way she looked at me," Grechloch muttered as Frog led him over to his uncle's usual table.

"You're the shortest Dreth she's ever seen," Frog told him. "She's not sure what to make of you."

"I don't think she likes Dreth."

Uh oh. The kid's too sharp for his own good.

"Not everyone here feels the same way. Your uncle understands."

"Perhaps he needs to be less understanding."

"I'll let you take that up with him but while you're with me, you'll eat your lunch and behave."

Garach shot him a dubious look and cocked an eyebrow, but Frog handed him a menu before he could say anything. "Can you read?"

"I wasn't brought up in the undercaves. Of course I can read."

He rolled his eyes. "Yeah, but can you read Federation Standard?"

"Does a tark lizard know how to run?"

"I'll take that as a yes."

"So, this steak…" Garach reminded him, and Frog pointed out the dishes Vishlog liked best. "And potatoes?"

It reminded him that, while Dreth might import some Earth produce, it didn't import all that much and maybe not all citizens got to see it. "You didn't see much off-world stuff, huh?"

"Off-world food is for the weak," the youngster retorted.

"Don't let your uncle hear you say that. He swears by Hrageth that steak and potatoes are one of the good things to come out of Earth."

Garach looked suspicious. "Which part of Hrageth?"

Now that he thought about it, Frog couldn't remember.

"His favorite is that one," he said and pointed, "but it's spicy."

"Good. I like spice. It is for warriors."

"Do you see anything you'd like to drink?"

"Beer!"

"I'm not giving you beer. Your uncle would have my nuts."

"Nuts?"

"Balls."

"Oh…ha… I'd like to see that."

"Well, I wouldn't. Choose something else."

"There's milk," the waitress suggested, having arrived to take their order.

"Milk is for the Meligornians." Garach's voice was as scornful as an eleven-year-old's could be.

She blushed.

"I'm sorry," Frog told her. "He isn't house-broken yet."

"No one will break me."

"How about I order you what your uncle has when he's on duty and can't have beer?"

"As long as it's not milk."

"Last I looked, your uncle was Dreth."

"All right, then."

"And Stephanie likes chocolate milkshakes."

Garach didn't have a reply to that, so he scowled while Frog ordered their lunch.

"How long will it take?" he asked.

"Not long," he told him and hoped he was right and that the dearth of customers meant they'd be served quickly.

"It doesn't come out of a replicator, does it?"

He shook his head. "No. They ship the ingredients in and cook them fresh. You have at least a half-hour wait."

The kid looked around the restaurant and studied the empty seats and the unimpeded view into space. "I can't see them," he observed after a minute's silent staring.

"See what?" Frog asked, momentarily distracted when a half-dozen sailors arrived.

This time, the girl directed them to a table on the other side of the restaurant.

"The asteroids," Garach answered. "I can't see them."

His words caught the attention of one of the sailors who turned and looked in his direction. Frog saw when he froze and nudged the man next to him.

"What's a Dreth doing in here?" he demanded.

Frog stood quickly. "Aww, c'mon guys, he's only a little Dreth—"

"I'm not little," Garach argued and stood on the other side of the table.

"See?" the sailor addressed Frog. "He says he's not little."

"Then he's old enough to know that we don't like his kind around here."

"Please, gentlemen, won't you sit?" the waitress asked, hovering anxiously.

The sailor cast her a stubborn glance. "Sure, lady. We'll sit."

She'd begun to relax when he added. "Right after those two leave. This ain't the place for Dreth-lovers and their toys."

Frog and Grechloch glanced at each other and launched their first punches. The kid chose the sailor on the left and the guard the one on the right. The waitress scrambled toward the front counter, only to be stopped by another of the sailors and sat firmly in a nearby booth.

"Give us five minutes," he told her. "We don't want to be interrupted while we're cleaning out the space trash."

"I guess…you guys…only just…came in," Frog said between dodging punches and retaliating.

More sailors arrived. "Hey! Where's the service around here."

"On ice until we get rid of the Dreth and its lover," one of the others called and the newcomers moved forward to the brawl.

"For Dreth!" Grechloch roared, ducked his head, and rammed his shoulder into his opponent's chest.

The guy folded, and the Dreth lifted him and threw him into his mates.

"Dreth!" Frog cried and swept the feet out of the man in front of him. He spun and delivered two blows into the sailor behind him, blocked a third attack from the right, and counter-attacked with a fist to the face. As he lashed out, he moved forward, slid around the man, and ducked under a table.

He came up on the other side, quick-stepped onto a chair, and bounced hard in the center of the table. The momentum carried him onto a sailor's shoulder, and he flipped over the melee to come down on the other side of Garach's opponent.

"Where'd you learn to do that?"

"That's one I learned myself," Frog told him. "I'm little. Getting out of trouble so I can get back into it is important."

"Heh." The young Dreth ducked under a fist, elbowed another sailor in the chest, and punched the first in the head.

He failed to block the blow that came from the side and caught the incoming fist firmly with his face.

"Crap," Frog said as he ducked under one sailor's attack, drove a fist into the man's gut, and brought a knee into his face to fell him instantly.

He kicked the guy clear, caught Garach's arm, and used it to pivot around the kid and block the blow aimed at his head. As he did so, he brought a boot down on the sailor's casual sneakers.

That elicited a yelp of pain, and Frog bent under a fist that came from the side. The sailor in front of him grasped him by the throat and pushed him back. He dug his heels in and leaned forward, tucked his chin, and thrust his fist upward.

It caught the man under the chin, snapped his teeth together, and jolted his head back. The hand around his throat eased and the guard followed through with several sharp jabs to the man's rib cage.

He dropped but one of his mates landed a punch from the side, which made Frog see stars.

That's gonna smart, he thought and wondered how much trouble he was in for getting the kid into a fight in his first hour on board the station.

Hell, for that matter, how much trouble am I in for actually getting into a fight on the Navy station?

Stephanie would have his head for sure.

He heard his fighting partner laugh as the young Dreth hauled him out of the way of the next fist.

The kid needs to learn to block, he observed as Garach absorbed the blow with a grunt. He had to admire the little brat, though. He was holding his own.

Around them, sailors groaned on the restaurant floor and the waitress finally gathered the courage to slip around the edge of the fight. She wasted no time in calling the military police which, on *Notaro,* consisted solely of Marines.

Frog found his bearings as Grechloch fended off a chair from one of his remaining opponents.

"Nope," the young Dreth said. "Nope. Try again. Is that the best you have, you lousy piece of human shit?"

The guard gave an internal sigh. The internal dislike of other races would have to go. Otherwise, the little bastard was solid. He sighed out loud as the man opposite him picked up a chair of his own.

"Really?" he asked. "You had to copy your friend?" He ducked under the first sweep and rattled his opponent's rib cage. "Don't you have an original thought in your head?"

"Give me that," Garach snapped, and the impact of him stopping the chair jolted through them.

Frog realized they now stood back to back and chuckled. This time, the guy jabbed the chair at him and he seized it by the legs to stop them from going past him and into Garach's back.

"That wasn't very nice of you," he remarked and caught the man's gaze as he shifted the chair to the left, rolled along it, and twisted it out of his hands.

He continued the sideways movement and brought it around to pound it into his opponent.

"Guess what?" He grinned, stepped back, and reversed the swing to hit the guy again. "I don't have an original thought in my head either."

The thud as his adversary collapsed was echoed by the sailor who had faced Garach, but there was no time for celebration. The MPs had arrived.

"Stop right there!" The order rang out with the force of a small torpedo.

"Oh, shit," Frog muttered and grabbed the Dreth's arm. "Stand down, kid. We're in enough trouble as it is."

The boy gave him a look of disbelief. "But they started it," he protested.

"Yeah," the Marine sergeant told him as he and the squad advanced, tasers in hand, "and you can tell that to the station court in the morning."

The guard drew the kid behind him and stepped forward. "If you'll watch the security footage—" he began and the sergeant froze.

"It's you," he said.

"Me?" Frog asked and backed away a step so the man would have to take an extra step to use the taser.

"Yeah, the short guy out of the Morgana's squad."

He blushed. "Well, yeah. I am the smallest one in the squad."

One of the sailors closest to him scrambled back. "Fuck."

The sergeant gave him a nasty grin. "What? Didn't you know you were picking a fight with one of the elite fighters in the universe? Where have you been? Living under a rock?"

"You could say that," the guy muttered, scrambled a little farther, and regarded Frog with wide eyes.

"Yeah? Well, be glad you didn't draw a weapon," the Marine told him. "That would not have ended well for you." He glanced at Frog. "Am I right?"

He gave the man his meanest smile. "No, it would not."

The sailor paled further. "I didn't know."

The sergeant rolled his eyes and signaled the Marines forward. "Take these guys to the brig," he ordered. "I'm fairly sure one of the Witch's crew won't pick a fight in Halley's." He turned to the guard. "What were you here for?"

Frog gestured to Garach. "The kid just arrived. I was trying to feed him."

As he spoke, the door to the kitchens opened and a waiter came out bearing two plates.

"Sorry we took so long," he said and placed them down on a nearby table. "We thought we'd wait until you finished here."

"Do you need us to come down?" Frog looked at the Marine sergeant.

The man shook his head as his men picked up the guys who'd started the fight. "No. I think you're in the clear." He gestured at the cameras. "If not, the footage will tell us."

Frog shook his head. "No, it won't."

"I never thought otherwise. If we need you, we know where to find you." He gestured to the plates. "Don't let it go to waste."

"Thank you, Sergeant." Frog paused, then sighed. "Sergeant, I wonder if you could make a call for me."

"Your boss?"

He nodded.

"Will do." The man followed his men out of the restaurant. Frog turned to the waitress. "I'm sorry about the mess," he told her and stooped to pick up one of the toppled chairs.

She beat him to it and slapped his hand away. "Don't be."

Waving him over to the table, she smiled. "Enjoy your meal. It's on the house."

His jaw dropped. "But—"

"It's not like you started it," she told him, "and we're sorry your..." Her brow wrinkled as she studied Garach "Uh, child... had such a rough introduction to our station. Please, take your time."

He guided the young Dreth over to the table. "Tuck in," he told him. "You don't want to offend them."

Frowning uncertainly, he complied and looked up in puzzlement when the kitchen staff came out a few moments later.

"We're sorry to disturb your meal," one of the chefs began and pulled out a notepad, "but...could we have your autographs?"

***

"Well, I'm glad we can agree on that," Stephanie said and Admiral Amaratne nodded.

"So, am I," he agreed. "This, at least, gives us a way forward."

"Or the start of one."

Across the table, Commander Geodyne's comms unit chimed. He frowned and pulled his tablet out. "Excuse me."

"Ah," he said a short moment later. "I'll pass that on."

He looked at Stephanie. "That was from one of my Marine sergeants. Apparently, there's been a disturbance between one of your team and he requested we report it to you."

She raised an eyebrow. "Go ahead."

"This disturbance involved a group of sailors who picked a fight with your team member and…uh, a very short Dreth."

Vishlog frowned. "There are no short Dreth. That is what Frog calls a noxyoron."

Stephanie frowned. "It's an oxymoron," she snapped, "and I'll beat that moron in a moment."

Frog was halfway through the biggest steak he'd ever had when his tablet pinged.

"Sorry I took so long," Lars told him. "It all went to hell and back and then decided to do it twice more for good measure. I take it you have that parcel all sorted out."

"That parcel is sitting opposite me," he answered and saw the moment in which the other man registered his quickly blackening eye.

"What the hell happened to you?" He drew a sharp breath. "Oh, shit. Did the package have some breakage too?"

"It's so good of you to care," he snarked and turned the tablet so the team leader could see the young Dreth. "Newbie, meet Lars. He's the boss. Lars, meet Vishlog's nephew, Garach."

Lars's jaw dropped as he took in the Dreth and the darkening black and green flesh around his eye. "Oh, crap. You, too? Stephanie will have a snit fit."

Garach raised his eyebrows and stuffed another forkful of steak into his mouth.

"Snit fit?" he mumbled around the half-chewed meat.

"It means Steph will rip someone a new asshole—and hopefully, not us," Frog told him.

The kid chewed fast and swallowed. "But we didn't start it— and what's a what you called me? Newbie?"

"Oh, that?"

The Dreth nodded.

"It means you're the newest member of the family." He turned to Lars. "I told the MPs to look at the security footage, but I can pull it when I get back so she can see it. Like the kid said, we didn't start it."

The team leader gave him a dubious look. "Uh-huh."

"We didn't," Garach protested as Frog turned the tablet back to himself.

"Boss, we really didn't. Not this time. I brought the kid to Halley's because Vishlog likes it so much. I thought he might as well have lunch before I took him back."

"Uh-huh. Well, at least you haven't been arrested. I want that footage as soon as you're back on board."

"Yes, boss."

"Wait! Footage?" Garach had finally caught up and his yellow eyes gleamed with excitement. "As in there are pictures of us fighting?"

"Yes." Lars sounded tired. "Yes, there are."

"Can I have them?"

"What?"

"The pictures. Can I have them? It's my first bar fight…and it's on film."

Frog buried his face in his hands and groaned. The other man shook his head.

"Dreth. You can't leave them alone and you can't take them to a bar. You two need to shake a leg and finish your food before Stephanie hears about it and comes over there."

Garach had resumed his meal but now he stopped and stared as Lars's face paled and his eyes widened. "What?"

Frog watched the other man's gaze shift past him and groaned. "She's right behind me, isn't she?"

"Nope," Lars replied hastily. "But close and getting closer. Bye."

CHAPTER TWENTY-SIX

Aaron looked up as Gene slid into the booth beside him.

"I have to be out of my tiny little mind," his work partner complained. "Katie will kill me and that's nothing compared to what the Navy will do if they ever work out what we're up to."

"Thanks for doing this," he told him. "It means a lot."

"You know you can go and fuck yourself," his friend grumbled. "I'm only here because… Oh, hell. I don't know."

"You're a good friend," he said, "and I appreciate it."

"The things you get me into. So, where do we start?"

"Well, I thought I'd begin looking at BURT from about here…" Aaron tapped the screen and opened a second screen before he retrieved a spare keyboard from his desk drawer. "I'll let you handle that."

Gene looked at it. "Gee, thanks."

He snagged the spare chair Aaron had acquired from somewhere and settled into it. "This is gonna be a long night."

"But it should be the only one. I've run programs in the background—"

"You've what?"

"Shhh. Keep it down." He reached past him and pushed the door closed. "D'you want everyone to know?"

"If they don't actually find out, it'll be a fucking miracle."

"Yeah, well, the sooner we start—"

"Shut up."

He decided he'd pushed Gene as far as he probably should—and maybe further—so he shut up and got to work, comforted by the fact that his friend was beside him. It took them until the early hours of the morning before they reached the point where they were almost sure and they both stopped typing at the same time.

"So…" Gene began, and Aaron nodded.

"Yeah…there's that."

They shut their computers down.

"We'd better get out of here," he said, and the other man glared at him.

"We shouldn't have been here in the first place."

They left together, swiped out, and said goodbye to the security guards.

"Long shift?"

"Yeah," Aaron grinned. "I'm glad it's over."

"Aren't you supposed to start in a few hours?"

"Yup. We gonna get some shut-eye while we can. Have a safe shift."

The guard nodded and waved them through. "See you tonight."

Aaron frowned and then realized the man was referring to the next night shift when they'd work overtime and clock out after he'd had time off and come back on. He grinned again.

"Will do."

They got through the main gate and began to walk to the nearest tram stop.

"So, same time again tomorrow?" he asked.

To his relief, Gene nodded. "Hell, yeah. And that should be the end of it. We'll know for sure."

Neither of them noticed the slim figure in the blues and greys of city cam drop behind them and follow on silent feet. Ms E listened to make sure they had the right guys before she called her team in.

The two men walked on, oblivious, and cut down an alley between two buildings rather than walking around the intervening block. Elizabeth listened as they continued their conversation, one seeking assurance from the other.

"But it's fairly obvious already, right?"

It was reluctantly given. "Yeah, it is, and I have no idea how we're gonna—"

The rest of his sentence was lost in the roar of an engine and squeal of tires as a van hurtled out of a side street and stopped dramatically beside them.

"Jeez!" Aaron exclaimed. "What do you think you're doing?"

The only reply was the emergence of four black-clad figures who slid open the van's side door and yanked them inside.

It was a relieved Frog who accompanied Stephanie to the ship. Garach walked ahead of him at his uncle's side, slightly in awe of the slender figure who led them to the entrance to the *Ebon Knight's* docking bay.

When she turned to face him at the door, he froze.

"I need you to hold this," she told him and proffered a short metal bar.

With an uncertain glance at Vishlog and then Frog, the kid took it.

"And?" he said when he had a hold of it.

"How do you feel about me kicking Teloran ass?" she asked him and he grinned.

"Tegortha's bastards, can I help?" he demanded and dropped the bar with a yelp. "Hrageth's balls, that thing is freezing."

She laughed, picked it up, and slapped him on the shoulder. "You pass, kid. Welcome to the family."

Garach gave her a very confused look. "There was a test?"

"Yeah, there was." She waggled the bar at him. "And you did fine."

When she turned to lead them into the repair bay, he looked at his uncle. "What was the test?"

Vishlog shrugged. "The bar reveals those who dislike our Morgana and who wish the Federation ill. I knew you did neither."

Frog watched the emotions at war over Garach's face—pride that he'd passed, pride that his uncle had had faith in him, disappointment that he hadn't been told ahead of time, and uncertainty as to where he stood with the family he'd found. The last two faded quickly, and the guard breathed a sigh of relief.

The kid's gonna be fine, he told himself. *Just fine.* It didn't stop the worry from gnawing at his chest. *I'll make sure of it*, he promised himself and followed the two Dreth on board.

They'd reached the *Knight's* hatch when Stephanie's comm unit pinged and she paused. After a brief moment, she looked at Vishlog.

"The captain needs to see us." Her gaze shifted to Garach. "I'm sorry, Vishlog, but I need you."

"He can stay with me," Frog volunteered before anyone else had a chance to speak. He was determined that the kid not be abandoned so shortly after arriving.

She looked uncertain and he shrugged. "It'll be fine. I'm fairly sure none of our crew will start a fight with us."

The kid grinned at the word "us," Vishlog nodded, and she relaxed a fraction. "Fine, but you'll need to introduce Garach to the rest of the team, too—including the cats."

He groaned and she ignored him.

"Make sure he knows the ship and check in with the quarter-master for bunking. I think he and Vishlog have new quarters."

The large warrior raised his eyebrows at that and she shrugged. "Frog'll catch you up on everything when we're done," she told him, and Frog raised an eyebrow, too. He'd what?

She caught the look. "You heard."

"Yes, ma'am," he muttered but she ignored him.

"We'll talk later," the warrior told his nephew. "Welcome home."

He followed Stephanie without saying more and the young-ster watched him go. His face took on a stolid blankness before he looked at Frog, who sighed. "Come on, Garach. Let's see where your room is."

It took him a good hour to sort out the kid's quartering since no-one had been told of the addition. Lars had been busy with the security systems, and Johnny and Marcus were still in the data center. Brenden and Avery were with Wattlebird, tinkering with the shuttle controls.

To give the quartermaster time to make the necessary arrangements, Frog took Garach to meet everyone and then headed to Stephanie's quarters. "Do you like cats?"

Garach frowned. "Like derkats?"

"Sure, let's go with that," he agreed. "Like derkats."

The kid paled. "She has derkats?"

"Not exactly. Why?"

"Because derkats hunt Dreth," Garach told him. "They are the fiercest creatures we have."

"Oh…" He realized what he'd done. "What I meant was they looked like derkats. They don't eat people."

"Are you sure?" the kid asked as they stopped outside the door.

"Well, yeah," he reassured him as he opened the door and stepped inside.

The cats pounced.

Zeekat drove into the back of his legs as Bumblebee launched himself off the couch and bounded into his chest to ride him to the carpet. Garach froze and gaped as Frog thumped into the floor and lay there with a smug-looking Bumblebee on top of him.

Both cats noticed the boy at the same time. Bee raised his head and sniffed at him, and Zee circled to cut him off from the door. Frog tried to watch the black-and-white beast's progress.

"Zee, he's a friend," he gasped. "Friend. Bumblebee...."

The yellow-and-black cat tossed its horns and stepped off his chest.

Garach remained perfectly still, his eyes wide as he studied the two cats that circled him like sharks. "Are you sure they don't eat people?"

"Fairly sure," Frog told him.

"And they know that Dreth are people?"

"They do." He rolled slowly onto his knees. "They really, really do."

He tried to catch Zeekat's gaze to get him to acknowledge that he understood, but the cat ignored him. Rubbing his chest, he clambered to his feet. "Zee! Bee! Come on now. Be nice. He's new family. We like him. Stephanie likes him."

That made them both pause. They looked from Frog to the kid and back again.

He began to relax. "There you go. He's family, boys."

Which was when they burst into action. Zeekat rubbed his way around the kid's legs and Bee rose onto his hindquarters and placed his paws on the boy's chest to stare into his face.

Garach raised his hands and placed them on the cat's chest while Zee leaned into the back of his legs and Bee bounced his paws against his shoulders. The young Dreth went down with a shout of surprise and immediately stilled when both cats stood over him.

"Nice one, guys," Frog snarked, walked over to them, and pushed them aside. "He's supposed to like you."

"I do," the boy said and surprised him.

The young Dreth scratched Zeekat under the chin with one hand and offered Bumblebee the same service with the other.

"See?" he asked, as the yellow-and-black cat settled his head in his hand. "He likes me."

Bee gave Frog a sidelong glance and his tail twitched gently from side to side. He could have sworn the cat was smirking.

"Smart asses," he grumbled but couldn't help scratching their ears.

They rumbled into purrs and followed him to the door.

"Oh, no, you don't," he told them. "Mama's coming home soon and you need to be here."

Bee yawned and sat on his haunches and Zee wandered back to his cushion.

"See?" Frog asked the yellow-and-black cat and pointed at Zee. "He knows what to do. Now, why can't you do the same?"

Bumblebee raised his forepaw and extended his claws to clean each one carefully while he watched Frog intently. Garach snickered. "I like these cats."

Bee flicked his ears forward and Zee raised his head. Both felines looked far too pleased with themselves. Frog let himself out the door. "That's only because you don't know them yet."

***

Aaron gasped. A wave of fear followed the wave of terror as the woman leaned over him again. The van turned another corner and the blade in her hand grazed his cheek. He gulped.

"I asked you a question, little man."

"I... I..." He rolled his eyes, looking for Gene. Katie would kill them both—and that was only if this lady decided to leave her anything to kill.

The hand cupping his chin tightened.

"Your friend can't help you."

The knife came back into view, and he stared at it.

"I can't tell you that," he croaked. "I can't, I can't, I can't—"

He tried to draw his knees up to his chest but she sat over him and there was nothing he could do about it. Two sets of knees pinned his wrists and hands held his ankles. The knife slid out of sight.

"Hmmm. Well, here's what we know," she began, and he felt the scrape of metal over the side of his throat.

Aaron flinched and heard bristles scratch against the blade.

"We know you're looking into a rogue AI and you shouldn't be." She leaned even closer. "You really, really shouldn't."

The blade scraped again and more bristles fell.

"We know you're breaking rules—many rules—that are there for a reason."

The slap that rocked his head sideways came as a surprise, but at least the knife went away. Aaron gasped. A second blow followed, then a third and a fourth.

"Tell me!"

"We can't! We didn't find it," he managed. "We have nothing."

It was a lie, but she lifted off him and he breathed a sigh of relief. Her voice was cold when next she spoke.

"Give him something to think about—but not enough that he misses work tomorrow."

"What?"

The heavy block of paper placed against his ribs came as a surprise. The blows that followed did not. Aaron gasped with pain but didn't miss hearing Gene answer the questions he had refused.

"Yes…all right— Yes. We're looking for a rogue AI."

"And do you have any idea where it is?"

"I can't tell—"

The sharp crack of flesh meeting flesh was all it took, and Gene answered.

"It's BURT. We think it's BURT."

"How sure are you?"

"Almost. We're almost sure."

Another blow jolted through him and Aaron groaned, but the pain did not stop him from hearing the next question and Gene's answer.

"How almost?"

"One more night. One more night should do it."

He didn't miss his friend's sudden gasp or the short pause before he began to choke.

"Don't," Aaron begged as another blow landed. "Please don't kill him. It was all my idea."

The choking stopped and he could hear Gene draw long, ragged breaths. The woman's next words weren't comforting. "Give him half the dose you gave his friend."

He pulled in several shaky breaths that were close to sobs as he heard the soft thumps of fists hitting paper and Gene's answering groans. The woman straddled his chest and leaned in close.

"Your idea?"

Aaron nodded, his mouth dry with fear.

"So," she said, "I want you to listen."

The thud of more blows falling and Gene's muffled cries of pain filled the moments that followed.

"Do you hear that?"

He nodded, his body trembling. She raised a hand and he flinched, but the blows stopped. Terrified, he stared at his captor. Her eyes glittered beyond the mask.

"You and your friend are to stop. Do you understand?"

Aaron nodded again.

"Do you?" The threat in her voice made him realize he had to speak.

"Y…yes. Yes, I understand."

"Understand what?"

"No more research."

"Research into what?"

"The rogue AI. No more research into the rogue AI." He spoke so fast he wasn't sure she'd understood.

Her gaze did not shift from his and he waited, staring at her and willing her to understand.

"Please, I understand." He thought of Gene. "We…we understand. Please…"

"Good. This is what you will do. You will go back to work. You will work on exactly what the Navy assigns you. You will work on nothing else. Nothing. Do you hear me?"

He nodded, and his friend groaned a fervent affirmative.

They understood.

"You are to forget this AI."

Aaron licked his lips. "We could get fired if we don't mention —" He gasped as she glanced from him to Gene and back. "If we don't mention our concerns. We could be fired."

His voice dried up as she shifted, and he felt the sharp edge of a blade resting at the base of his ribs. He closed his eyes and waited, but the blade went away. When the woman remained silent but didn't go away, he opened them again.

The hand that held his jaw was implacable.

"Listen to me. If you get fired, you will be hired at twice your pay but so far, you have nothing but assumptions and frankly, this world, during this war, does not need another stress they are not equipped to handle."

At the other end of the van, Gene made sounds of desperate agreement, but Aaron's gaze did not waver. He kept his gaze locked on the woman's and waited.

"We are working on the same project, and we will protect the world so you gentlemen need to take a step back and go on your way." The hand on his jaw tightened and she shook his head. "The options are not good."

She stood and moved away from him, and as if the movement was a signal, the van slid to a halt. Before he could work out what was happening, he was picked up and tossed out.

He landed in the grass of a small park not far from the high-rise he lived in and Gene tumbled beside him shortly after. Neither of them moved for a long time after the van raced away. Aaron was the first.

"Fuck...me..." He groaned, rolled onto his knees, and stayed there until his head stopped spinning.

Gene followed him to his feet. "I think I hate you."

"That's okay. I hate me, too," he told him. "I'm sorry, man."

"You know sorry doesn't cut it. I'm gonna have the devil's own time getting Katie to not report this." His friend looked around. "Hey, are we home?"

Aaron took a good look at the buildings around the park. "It looks like it."

"They dropped us at home?" The man's voice rose in a panicked whisper. "I have to make sure Katie's okay. There's no saying what they might have done to her."

His words sent a cold chill through Aaron's gut.

"Yeah, you go, man," he whispered. "We'll talk tomorrow."

"No. No, we won't." Gene was adamant. "We're not talking about this ever."

"But—"

"No. Aaron, I'm done. I'm gonna do exactly as the lady asked. I won't go near that shit with a barge pole. If you want to chase it, you're on your own. Don't even tell me. I don't want to know."

They'd started to move toward the block containing their apartments, but Aaron stopped. He laid a hand on Gene's shoulder.

"You know I can't. I...I have to know if I made him...more than what he was. I have to know if this is all my fault."

His friend stared at him in disbelief. "I'm not doing it. I can't. I have Katie. You need to leave it alone, too."

"I can't."

He flinched as the other man swung toward him, sure he would take a swing at him, but all he did was grasp him by both shoulders and look intently into his face.

"Look, man. You do what you gotta do, but this thing? It's an itch that will get you killed. Leave it the hell alone."

Seeing the desperate fear in his friend's eyes, Aaron nodded. "I'll try."

Gene studied his face a moment longer before he swung toward his apartment.

"Go home, Aaron. We have work tomorrow."

CHAPTER TWENTY-SEVEN

"The drives are almost back up to speed," Emil told Stephanie.

"What do you mean, almost?"

"I mean we can use the propulsion drive but not the fast warp capability. That's still a couple of days away."

"And the weapons system?"

"The cooling's done and we're working on increasing the rate of fire. Extra structural support is next."

"Is it important?"

"The specs say we don't really need it, but I'd rather we had it than not. That's why it's last on the list."

"Fair enough. The hull?"

"Repairs are complete or we wouldn't go anywhere. Ebony was very determined on that point."

"My structural integrity is at one hundred and twenty-five percent," the *Knight* told them smugly, "and engineering tells me we should reach one hundred and fifty percent in four days' time."

"A hundred and fifty?" Stephanie asked her. "How is that even possible?"

"We are using comparative specs. I am well above the standard statistics for ships of my class, even if I am the only one."

She stifled a groan. The *Knight* sounded like every jock she'd ever had the misfortune to overhear. She turned to Emil. "Is there anything else I need to know about?"

"Jonathan has tweaked the flight controls."

With a wry smile, she shook her head. "He was in the shuttles, too."

Emil paled. "I'll look into it."

"Avery and Brenden seemed happy."

The captain groaned. "They would be. Don't tell me the three of them—"

"Uh-huh."

He looked toward the ceiling. "Ebony?"

"The specifications to which the three pilots were working were new but they were within the parameters of possibility."

"That's not comforting."

"You should not worry, captain. I approved the alterations. My shuttles will handle much better now."

Stephanie pressed her lips together in an effort not to laugh. The ship was definitely becoming a jock.

Emil sighed. "And their structural integrity?"

"I have crews ensuring it will hold."

"It had better do more than that, Ebony," she told her, "or I'll have BURT reprogram your soul."

There was a short silence before the ship responded and sounded puzzled. "But…I do not have a soul, Stephanie."

"That's something you can take up with BURT the next time you're in dock."

"I will take that under advisement," was delivered in stiff tones.

Stephanie smiled. *Advisement, huh?*

"It's life support that needs more time," Emil told her and broke into her thoughts. "The data center uncovered a slight glitch in the recycling program, which we traced to a piece of shrapnel that penetrated deeper into the hull than we'd realized."

"How could you not—" she began, but the ship was quick to interrupt.

"The debris in question traveled through several open spaces before it lodged in the primary recycling unit in a position not overseen by routine maintenance. It was not until yesterday that we uncovered the problem."

"And?"

"We did not inform you because we were able to source the appropriate materials and the extent of the problem did not become clear until this morning."

She sighed and looked at the captain. "How long?"

"It'll be at least another forty-eight hours before we leave the docks."

"Fine. Schedule the departure."

"We will only leave if the problem is resolved," the *Knight* told her primly. "It is unwise to—"

"Schedule the goddamned departure," Stephanie snapped. "You have forty-eight hours to get it right or we'll ship out in suits. Either way, we're going."

"Yes, ma'am," he told her and stiffened to attention.

She didn't miss the anxious glance he cast the ceiling or the slight relaxation in his shoulders when Ebony remained silent.

"If we don't leave then, people will go nuts thinking the worst. The riots we've seen are only the start. We cannot let it get any worse."

"I understand," he assured her, but the *Knight* remained silent.

Stephanie sighed. "We need to show them we're doing something and the only way to do that is to leave."

Emil opened his mouth to respond but a knock at his office door prevented him from doing so. He quirked an eyebrow and raised his head. "Come."

The door opened and four men stepped through—the quartermaster, the head of engineering, and the two men in charge of the Navy's borrowed work crews.

The first of these stepped forward. "We're sorry to interrupt," he began, "but we wanted you to know that the crew has talked about things and everyone's volunteered to keep working if the ship gets underway."

The other man nodded. "We can get everything we need on board…"

The quartermaster lowered his chin to confirm it, and the man continued, "So we can fix the rest of the stuff in transit."

"But—" the captain began, and the team leader raised his hand.

"We've watched the newscasts, too, sir, and things are bad at home. We need to do something and that can only happen if we're out there."

"We all have families back home," his partner added. He looked at Stephanie and his eyes begged her to understand. "We need you to buy them some time."

"Knight?" she asked and glanced at the ceiling.

"I have run the calculations. What they say is correct. We can fit the supplies onboard and the tension on Earth is increasing. If my understanding of human nature is correct, you do need to be seen to act in order for that tension to decrease."

"And the supplies?"

"I have organized a schedule."

The tablets of her four visitors pinged and they pulled them out.

"Will it work?" the *Knight* asked, and the men nodded.

Stephanie looked at the chief engineer. "Cameron?"

"Yes," he said, and it wasn't an acknowledgment but an answer to the question she hadn't asked. He expanded his response. "Yes, this will work." He hesitated, then added, "If you'll excuse me, I need—"

The chief engineer paused and looked at Emil. "With your permission, Captain?"

"Granted. All of you. Do what you need to do."

The office was cleared in double-quick time and Emil looked at Stephanie. "I'm not sure I have time for more vac suits to arrive."

She managed a small smile. "I'm sorry, Emil."

He shook his head. "Don't be, but if you'll excuse me, there are a few things…"

"We'll get out of your way."

The workmen were right.

On Earth, people clung to normality as best they could but the approaching asteroids sent an undercurrent of fear through them. In Danny's, a bar in the Chicago Subs, patrons cheered the Bears to another touchdown but their cries were subdued and many stared at the screen without really seeing it.

They drank their beer without really tasting it and tried to forget what was happening beyond the sky. Some almost succeeded as the Ponies rallied and the Bears fought back. The fight between fans at the edge of the field provided a welcome diversion.

Play had just returned to normal when a brief martial fanfare and the Federation logo interrupted the broadcast.

In normal times, this would have elicited booing and catcalls of protest but now, it drew their rapt attention and hope flickered. Patrons nudged their neighbors and shushed others who spoke, and they all sat a little straighter.

The sight of Admiral Amaratne, the Federation Navy's fleet admiral, drew brief hushed whispers.

"Greetings, citizens of Earth," he began. "The Federation Navy has heard your calls for action and worked to prepare its answer. The time for that to be delivered has come."

He turned his head and the screen to his left showed the Navy space station.

After he'd stared at it for a moment, he continued. "We are sending a team who will depart *Space Base Notaro* in less than an hour."

This drew gasps of surprise and murmurs of "about time" from audiences around the country, but the admiral continued oblivious.

"This team will confirm our options for destroying the rocks now headed in our direction, and I have asked one of them to speak to you about the approach they'll take."

He stepped back and directed the camera to the edge of the screen with a gesture of his hand. As he did so, he stepped out of the picture and Stephanie stepped in.

In bars and lounge rooms around the room, excitement sent ripples of hope through the audience. A brief outburst of relief was swiftly followed by rapt silence.

"The *Ebon Knight* has been repaired," she told them. "In the last seventy-two hours, Navy repair crews have worked around the clock and taken her from the wreck she was to a fully operational vessel. While there is still work to be done, these repairs will be completed over the next forty-eight hours."

Some wondered how that would happen if they were leaving in an hour, but she hadn't finished.

"While they work, the *Knight* will be in transit to the asteroid field, where we will begin to assess exactly what we can do. When that's done, we'll give you the proof you need that we can deal with the threat."

Whoops of relief broke out across the world. In stadiums where games were being played, the teams stood side by side and watched the big screen as intently as everyone else.

"And then," she concluded, "we'll begin the process of stopping the rocks."

The whoops turned to widespread cheers and people rose in the stands at stadiums or behind their tables at bars and raised their fists in jubilation. Stephanie took a few steps back and turned away.

She ignored the cameras that panned to follow her and provided a wider view of the studio. The scene showed her joining the rest of her team and scratching the heads of the two cats that twined around her legs.

Two of her guards came alongside her as the team left and none of them looked back at the cameras. The patrons at Danny's watched them go and some settled down to the best-tasting beer they'd had in weeks.

One turned to his best friend, a puzzled look on his face.

"Who's the short Dreth?"

CHAPTER TWENTY-EIGHT

When Stephanie arrived at the asteroid field four days later, she was not alone. The Federation Navy had sent two destroyers, the *Cathay Williams* and the *Harry Chauvel*, to keep her company.

The asteroids spread before them, traveling relentlessly toward Earth. They looked almost peaceful...like rough-cut cattle trundling across the plains of space—except these weren't grazing peacefully. They were in a full-blown stampede and would flatten the planet in their path.

She stood on the *Knight's* bridge and watched them while she wondered how something so eerily beautiful could originate from such spite. If they hadn't been intended to kill her homeworld, she'd have found them soothing.

Tethis stood beside her and they studied the problem together.

"So," she said, "you're sure we can't gate them."

"Are your eyes painted on?" he demanded and gestured at the scene on the forward viewscreen. "You might think you're a superhero, but not even Superman could shift these."

Stephanie stared at him. "Superman?"

He crooked an eyebrow at her and his skin flushed. "I had to find something to occupy my time while I was busy keeping out from underfoot. Your film selection is a little…dated."

One of the command crew snorted but she couldn't determine who.

"Are you sure?"

The older mage huffed out a sigh. "What is it with the young? You can never take no for an answer. You insist on talking it to death."

"And?" she pushed.

"Look," Tethis grouched, "every time you move a meteor, you use energy."

"Yeah," she snarked in response. "I'm fairly sure I have that down pat."

"When you're done."

"Sorry."

"So," the old Teacher continued, "every time you change the angle of one of them, you increase the amount of MU you need to shift it. The greater the angle of change, the heavier the energy drain."

He gave her a moment to absorb it. "It's why you could do less than a dozen before and why you collapsed when you did more. There is no way you can do what you did at Meligorn for the two hundred or so rocks out there."

To punctuate his point, he stabbed in the direction of the screen.

"Well…what about slowing them?"

"The same thing applies," Tethis told her. "Only this time, you're dealing with kinetic energy more directly. Instead of trying to direct it, you're fighting to stop it."

"So, it's still no go?" Stephanie asked and he gave a groan of exasperation.

"No…unless…" His face took on a faraway look as he stared at the moving field.

"Unless what?"

"Well, you know how you spin gMU down to make it more powerful?"

"Yeah." Stephanie did her best not to tap her foot with impatience.

She knew it wasn't advisable to rush an idea, but the man was driving her crazy—and she wasn't totally sure he wasn't drawing it out on purpose.

"So what if we could use the energy of the rocks themselves to power magic against the other rocks?"

"What? What does that have to do with condensing gMU?"

"Well, that's merely turning one form of energy into another," he explained. "So what if we turned the kinetic into magical energy?"

"But gMU is magical energy and we're turning it into MU, which is another form of magical energy. What you're talking about are two different kinds of energy."

His face fell. "So you don't think it will work?"

"No, I'm not saying that. I simply didn't think of it. You might actually have something, though. Talk me through it."

"These rocks are all going at approximately the same velocity, so their energy is similar except for size. Based on that, if we can harness the energy from one to slow another, both rocks should slow...right?"

"Maybe?"

"Look." He tried again. "One rock loses its inertia, which gives us the energy to transfer so we can slow another one down. We don't need every other Meligornian magic-user. We only need time."

Three hours later, they stood on the bridge again. The forward viewscreen was dominated by the asteroids, which looked much closer than they really were.

The one they'd chosen was at the rear of the field since slowing those in the front could result in a shattering collision with the faster-moving rocks behind. Stephanie looked at Tethis.

"What do you think?"

He glared at her. "You already know what I think," he snapped tetchily and jerked a hand to indicate the room, "and the calculations match. It's now up to us to make it work."

She ignored his sharp manner and stifled a smile. The old Master had been disgusted by the idea that magic could be reduced to a mathematical calculation. Then, he'd been fascinated—especially when the calculations had to be reworked to match the reality.

"This is almost fun," he'd said in the relative privacy of the data center while the technicians had tried to match the math to what was happening in front of them when he or Stephanie did something.

In all honesty, she hadn't been so sure. They'd had to limit their investigations to the magic they'd use to move the rocks or there'd have been a very real danger of the two mages exhausting themselves before they even started on the real threat.

As it was, she hoped they could achieve what the math said they could and that they'd done enough to avoid breaking anything unexpected. The last thing they needed was for one of the rocks to fragment under the forces they applied.

The fragments would still kill their world.

She caught Tethis's eye. "Are you ready?"

He rolled his eyes and raised his hands. "I was born ready."

The crew around them snickered, and she wondered which particular movie he'd stolen that line from.

Instead of asking, she focused on the chosen rock, pulled gMU in, and condensed it into eMU. Reaching out, she used it to reveal the kinetic energy she wanted to affect. Gasps of surprise tugged at her hearing, but she ignored them, aware of Tethis mirroring her action on a second meteor.

The recordings taken by the *Knight* would show her what it looked like later—when it was time to pull it apart and try to work out a way to do it better. The kinetic energy displayed as red and stood out strongly against the blue of the eMU.

She frowned as she considered how to reduce it. The asteroid glowed a thick, bright scarlet before her and its brilliance made her squint.

"Ha!" Tethis exclaimed. "Speed equals brightness. I beat you."

Stephanie groaned.

"That's why you need me. I can study things you don't have time for while you're gallivanting about and saving the universe."

"It's not gallivanting."

"Well, whatever it is, you simply need to focus on peeling a little of the brightness away and pulling it in with the gMU around us. The magic does the rest."

This time, she resisted the urge to ask him if he was sure and tried to do what he suggested instead. Peeling didn't work, but when she thought of sucking some of the brightness away, there was an immediate result

"Gottit!"

The old Meligornian grinned. "Are you ready for this?"

His jubilance was infectious, and she grinned in return. "I was born ready, too."

Together, they bled some of the brightness from their chosen targets and drew it in to spin through the gMU and condense into eMU. To her surprise, it worked much better than she'd hoped.

Well, that opens up possibilities, she thought.

"Focus, child," Tethis snapped.

She jerked back to the present and he continued. "This time, we'll show your Earth there's hope."

"It's working!" came the jubilant cry from the crewman on scans. "See?"

A smaller window opened in the bottom of the screen to highlight the distance between the two meteors she and Tethis had worked on and the rest of the swarm.

"Yes, but can you record it?" Emil asked. "It's no good if we can see it but we can't send it home."

"I can capture that image," the *Knight* reassured them. "My scanners are very good."

Her tone reminded Stephanie of Bumblebee when the cat felt particularly smug. He had a specific yawning growl right before he licked his shoulder in satisfaction at a job well done—usually, it was disemboweling her favorite cushion.

Last time, it had been because he'd swatted her as she'd moved past and she'd yelled at Zee who'd arrived seconds later. Frog had fallen off the chair laughing and shown her the security footage.

Great, I have the universe's biggest cat and it comes with a vacuum-resistant hull and shielding, she thought and hoped the *Knight* didn't take to pushing things into suns the way cats liked knocking drinks off tables.

"Hey!" Tethis shouted and smacked her on the shoulder. "I don't know where you are but you need to get your head in here so we can show the universe asteroid swarms can be stopped."

It reminded Stephanie that the footage would also be sent to Meligorn so the mages there could study it. Everyone wanted an alternative means to stop a bombardment. No one wanted a repeat of what happened to the *Wanderer*, even if they wouldn't hesitate to do it again.

She and her fellow mage chose a sequence of four rocks each.

"You'd better make it six," Emil told them. "We'll film the first two and send the footage once it shows they've slowed, then we'll live-stream the rest as you work so folk can check and reassure themselves that the first four weren't a fluke."

He didn't add that they'd keep streaming in case this really was a trap and the Telorans appeared. No one needed to hear it. They all knew it was a possibility.

The crews working on the weapons systems had moved through increasing the guns' rate of fire and on to extra support and power. Someone had thought of a modification to the shields that meant they could move power between grid sectors and project an overlapping field.

One bright spark in communications had come up with the idea of manufacturing positive energy grenades that could be packed into a missile head with the explosive. It involved tapping the ships' batteries and filling empty bottles, but several teams of volunteers worked around the clock under Cameron's watchful eye.

"And…go," the scanner operator told them and dragged Stephanie back to the present.

She focused on her designated meteor and siphoned off some of the red kinetic energy that billowed around it. Beside her, Tethis did the same.

The new energy felt different coming in, but the gMU seemed to absorb it in the same way it absorbed different forms of magical energy. As she pulled it in, the meteor slowed, which bought them more time to act.

A part of her was aware that the crew captured the change in speed while she worked and heard the relief that tinged their voice as they sent the relevant clip to the Navy's PR department, but she didn't let it distract her.

As soon as she was done with the first one, she moved on to the next and then a third. The fourth proved as easy as the last three and she wondered how many she could get through before she had to stop and rest.

That was the next phase of the learning curve. She and Tethis had to monitor their energy levels and stop before they went into a catatonic state that would require days of rest to recover from.

They needed to stop in time that a good eight hours' sleep would see them right for the next round.

Secretly, she planned to try for four hours' rest between meteor braking but wasn't about to tell anyone else that. Tethis wouldn't approve, for sure, and Lars was likely to get Vishlog to sit on her until she slept.

Neither option appealed.

Finishing with the fourth meteor, she went to work on the fifth and noticed that the Teacher kept pace with her. He caught her look.

"It's not a race," he told her. "If we work at the same rate, we can pace each other."

That made sense and she nodded as she reached out with the eMU to snag the asteroid's scarlet glow. When she pulled the kinetic energy through the eMU, movement at the scanner's edge caught her eye.

At the same time, klaxons began to wail, and the captain cupped his hand over his ear. Captain Yale appeared in a small window at the side of the forward viewscreen, and Captain Docherty appeared shortly after.

"We have incoming," Yale told them. "The *Williams* will stand between."

"The *Chauvel* will take your starboard, Captain," Docherty told her.

Yale fixed them with a firm stare. "Captain Emil, you will ensure the Morgana and her advisor survive to continue their work."

"We're staying," Stephanie growled as the door to the bridge slid open.

Captain Yale's voice softened. "The Navy cannot allow that, ma'am."

She turned and froze when Captains Sartre and Moser arrived with a squad of Marines at their backs. Her heart fell at the thought that she had men aboard who would seek to stop her doing what she needed to do with her own ship.

Captain Yale raised her head, but Sartre cut her off.

"Understood, Captain. We will see that our orders are carried out."

"See that she survives," the captain commanded, and he saluted.

Stephanie felt breathless as the images of both captains winked out. To her surprise, Sartre looked at Emil's second in command, Mulvaney. "Did you manage it?"

The commander nodded. "They're blind and deaf when it comes to what happens aboard the *Knight.*"

The Marine captain relaxed. He looked across at Stephanie. "Let us know how we can assist you," he told her. "We'll stand by for your call."

He raised a hand and made a circular motion with his finger. The Marines paused long enough to throw a salute in her direction before they about-faced and left the bridge.

Commander Mulvaney looked at her. "The Navy must never know."

Stephanie glanced at the screen, now focused on the Teloran ships that emerged out of warp behind the meteor swarm. Four became ten, became twenty, became…

She looked at the commander. "That may not be an issue," she told her. "We couldn't really run if we wanted to—let alone because they want us to."

Emil followed her gaze. "When we suspected a trap," he observed. "I don't think anyone thought there would be this many."

CHAPTER TWENTY-NINE

"*Chauvel* and *Williams*, this is the *Knight*. We'll join you in mutual defense."

Yale's voice sounded tired when she replied. "Acknowledged, *Knight*. Welcome to the party."

Emil looked at where Stephanie and Tethis stood in the middle of the command center. "I need you in the guest chairs. Everyone else but Lars or Vishlog need to clear the bridge and lock down."

The team leader looked at the Dreth. "I'll take this shift."

Vishlog nodded, his eyes dark filled with concern as he turned and left. Lars took Stephanie by one arm and Tethis by another and moved them to where they needed to be. Neither of the mages looked away from the forward viewscreen.

As they sat, the Telorans launched their first barrage of missiles.

Lars caught the creeping darkness that signaled the arrival of the Morgana and gave Stephanie a gentle shake.

"Not yet," he hissed. "Save your energy until we really need you."

He swept a hand toward the screen. "Trust me. We will need you…but not yet. Wait."

She nodded and her eyes flickered between blue and black. Tethis watched the exchange, registered the shift in her face, and had no idea what to say. The guard made sure he was seated.

"The same goes for you," he warned and seated himself between them, muttering, "Two mages, as if one wasn't enough. They all need keepers."

The old Teacher might have argued, but he decided the man was right. He was as determined as the Morgana that the *Knight* would not fall—and neither would the *Cathay Williams* or the *Henry Chauvel.*

His eyes gleamed as he watched the screen, their keen gaze belying the age of his body.

Jonathan maneuvered the *Knight* into a position slightly above both destroyers to give them space to maneuver and position her so her weapons teams could fire over the other two ships. Her guns spoke and destroyed missiles meant for both ships.

"We can't go toe-to-toe with these bastards," Emil said to Yale.

"I've sent your pilot a defensive formation we can work in and added your weapons teams to the gunnery loop."

"Our shields are now in sync," the *Knight* informed her, and the woman gaped.

Emil thought he'd better explain.

"Knight is a prototype AI and has more latitude for planning than standard AIs," he told them. "It would be best to keep her informed of your plans as you do me. She will be able to respond faster, and I trust her judgment."

The woman closed her mouth, her eyes wide. "Very well, Captain. Thank you, Knight."

"Call me Ebony," the *Knight* informed her. "It is the term of reference I prefer from my friends."

"Thank you…Ebony,"

"I have synced my maneuvers with your ships," the AI

informed her and Captain Docherty, and both captains nodded, surprise evident on their faces. "Happy hunting."

She closed the connection and noticed that Emil had leaned his forehead against his fist. "Captain, did I do something wrong?"

He stilled for a moment, then raised his head. "No, Ebony, but I do not think they were quite ready for your display of capability."

"I am sorry, Captain."

Jonathan swore and his hands moved frantically over his console. The *Knight* lurched. On the forward screen, the *Williams* and the *Chauvel* bucked and swayed. Emil's face turned white.

"*Knight*, did you slave their piloting systems to ours?"

"No, Captain. I merely ensured their maneuvers would reflect certain characteristics as required."

He groaned but caught sight of the size of the Teloran fleet and sighed. "Well, at least there won't be enough pieces of us left for the Navy to prosecute."

"We do not have to make it easy for them, Captain," the *Knight* informed him. "Now, are you commanding or shall I?"

He straightened. "I am still the captain here, am I not?"

"You are," she agreed and he rose to his feet.

Stephanie watched from her seat behind the captain's console but did not interfere. The Telorans had fired three more barrages during the conversation and the weapons crews had met them with deadly efficiency.

The ships' shields had staged a complicated dance to cover the three vessels, and the formation had shifted to meet the challenge as if each ship was a piece on a Dreth Quarm board. Lars and Tethis sat silently, waiting for when they were needed.

This was the hardest part of the fight.

None of them said a word until the Telorans switched targets and sent the next round of missiles at the asteroids instead of the ships.

"I've got this," she announced, and Tethis rose beside her.

"We've got this."

She did not have time to argue and the Morgana didn't see the point. Earth's Witch rose to the foreground of her mind and allowed the girl control...for the moment. It was an easy matter to take it back when she needed it.

The control room gasped as pools of blue opened in front of the missiles aimed at the meteors. They snorted when more portals gaped between the missiles and the Teloran ships and the alien fleet was forced to adjust shields and fire as their attacks returned to them.

The next barrage was twice as heavy and aimed at the three Earth ships standing against them.

"Stephanie, break that meteor," Tethis cried and opened a portal in front of one of the ones they hadn't had time to slow.

The meteor exploded into fragments and a second gate appeared, aimed at the Teloran fleet. Chunks of rock careened through the first to hurtle toward them and the next barrage stopped abruptly as the ships in the debris path began evasive maneuvers.

"Tethis!" The Morgana's voice held undertones of Stephanie's delight at the old Teacher's idea.

This time, she opened the gate and he broke the meteor.

"Steph!"

They began to laugh, and the Morgana's tones receded as the two mages worked faster. The Teloran fire continued but became sporadic as the aliens were forced to focus on the myriad rocks that streaked toward them.

The laughter continued for another hour before it faded. Lars watched in fascination as the two mages continued to work together—one breaking rocks, the other gating them. He stood as they dropped to the deck but didn't interfere when they leaned on each other and kept going.

Around the ship, her team and the Marines worked with the

crew. Vishlog stopped long enough to make sure Garach knew to stay in the team quarters before he ran to join one of the repair crews.

Frog gave the warrior a thirty-second head start and looked at the boy. "Grab your breather. We're not staying here to clean the cabin."

The kid gave him a worried look and then a grin. "It'll be worth it," he said as they headed to the door.

The guard was reasonably sure this was where he was supposed to talk the boy out of doing anything foolhardy, but he was damned if he would be left minding the shuttle again. The kid was right. However mad Vishlog would be, this would be worth it.

He was rethinking that idea an hour later when he squirmed under a metal stanchion to pull a gun crew clear after the *Knight* had sealed the hull breach in their section. Garach sweated and strained to keep the stanchion from coming down and crushing him.

Frog crawled faster and hoped the emergency team brought a hydraulic lift kit. He wasn't sure how long the kid would last. Behind him, he heard the Marines shouting and passing orders, but he didn't stop until he had every last member of the gun team out of there.

Sartre pulled him clear as Garach's fingers finally slipped.

"Are you sure you're not a Marine?"

They'd attached themselves to the Emergency Section after that and spent the battle on the run. Brenden and Avery waited in the shuttle for when they'd be needed to pick up life pods, and Marcus and Johnny headed to the data center where their skills could best be put to use.

Back in the command center, Emil looked at Lars, his eyebrows raised in a query, but the team leader shook his head.

A warning flashed at the corner of the forward viewscreen and the captain's heart sank. *Are there more?*

Ebon Knight, Cathay Williams, Henry Chauvel, this is Federation Central Fleet Command. *Ebon Knight, Cathay Williams, Henry Chauvel*, this is Federation Central Fleet Command. We are approaching on your port flank."

"Roger that, Fleet Central. Welcome to the party." Yale's voice sounded slightly breathless.

"Hold your positions. We are coming around you."

"Roger that, Fleet Central." Not breathless, Lars realized, but exhausted and he could see why.

The forward screen showed a dark hollow in the *Williams's* flank, and a scattering of life pods floated beyond them.

"Deploy shuttle crews for rescue," Emil ordered, and the guard knew Avery and Brenden would enter the battlefield.

He almost envied them the freedom, but that reminded him of what he was there for, and he focused on Stephanie and Tethis. Emil followed his gaze.

"I think they can stop now," the captain told him, and it was more an order than a suggestion.

Lars glanced at the screen and had to agree. The Federation's Central fleet had moved in to send a wave of missiles at the Teloran fleet and follow it up with a constant stream of fire. Several large battle cruisers flew over and under the trio of embattled ships to block the Telorans' line of fire, and a cloud of small space fighters swarmed from launch bays along their flanks.

Stephanie and Tethis stopped throwing rocks at the Telorans and struggled to their feet. Lars had barely reached Stephanie's side when the Morgana spoke.

"There is guile and there is cunning," she proclaimed, and he had no doubt that every Teloran heard her. "And when you reach the pinnacle of nasty tricks, you will find humans are at the top of the game."

A Navy corvette at the head of the fleet convulsed and exploded and a destroyer alongside her hemorrhaged atmosphere and flame from a long gouge down her side. The enemy message came back loud and clear.

"And now there are fewer on the peak."

Several alien ships winked out as the Navy targeted every Teloran they could see.

Back on Earth a few days later, Aaron sighed and ran his hand through his hair. Overtime was a bitch and the Navy's new project was driving him insane. He glanced at the other screen and wished he had time to pursue the project minimized at the bottom.

The idea that BURT was the rogue AI haunted him. He had to know.

His email pinged and he glanced at the main screen. The Navy project flashed red and then closed.

"What the—" As he leaned in for a closer look, he noticed the icons pinned to his taskbar flare briefly red, orange, or white, then close. "Fuck!"

He fumbled for his mouse when the flashing email icon caught his eye. "Yeah, yeah, fine. I'll read your goddamn email, but it had better be good."

It was…and it wasn't.

The engineer felt like he'd been dipped in ice and thrown off a cliff for good measure. His heart froze and his mind went into freefall. He stared at the message, unseeing for a moment, and forced himself to read it again.

Your security privileges have been revoked. With immediate effect, you are to clear your desk and leave the premises.

"What the—" He glanced nervously at the door as though expecting security to knock at any second, then read the email a third time.

It hadn't changed.

"My security privileges have been revoked? What?"

His question was echoed in another part of the building.

"What? I thought he liked his job. Why would he send this?"

Oscar McClelland stared at the resignation on his desk. Aaron Barrymore, one of his top engineers, had resigned and he was at a loss.

The man had arrived for his shift, and although he moved a little stiffly and looked like he'd had a hard night on the beer instead of a good night's rest, he'd been on time and he hadn't complained. In fact, he had seemed like his normal, cheerful self.

He hadn't mentioned being sick of the overtime that he'd complained about in the letter of resignation he sent to McClelland's desk hours later. Nor had he shown any sign that he wasn't handling it. The man had seemed perfectly normal—or as normal as the guy ever got.

Well, apparently not. Aaron was quitting immediately. He wouldn't finish his shift and if his boss didn't like it he knew what he could do. Oscar stared at the screen and considered heading down to the floor to confront him.

At least he'd get an up-front explanation. He paused and thought a little more. Of course, he might get a fist to the face, given Aaron's temper. Oscar stared at the letter again and decided he should try a phone call in the morning.

It might be safer.

He sighed and changed tasks. Some knucklehead in HR had forgotten to add "must be willing to work shift work and over-time" to the job advertisement and now, he had to send a mass email out advising them that due to contractual changes, both were conditions of the job and that anyone still interested needed to select the 'continue' button in the email.

It was a pain in the ass and had to be done immediately to avoid a nine-mile long queue in the morning. Aaron's call could wait.

When security didn't come knocking, Aaron assumed he'd

been given a little time to prepare to leave. He took another look at his computer to make sure the email was really there and set about clearing his desk.

Not that he had much.

He didn't have photographs, books, or snacks, or even a favorite beverage. The only thing he did have was his investigation into BURT—and it was still up at the bottom of the screen.

For a moment, he toyed with the idea of working on it until they came to throw him out but he decided he didn't need the fuss and closed it down regretfully. He didn't even have something he could save it to so he could take it with him.

It began to seep in that he would have to leave it behind—and that meant he'd walk out of there with as much as he'd walked in with—nothing at all. He sighed, closed the document, and thought about forwarding it to Gene.

Remembering his friend's response to him after they'd essentially been kidnapped, roughed up, and thrown out, he changed his mind. There was no point in getting his friend involved any more than he already had. With a sigh of regret, he shut his computer down for the last time and picked his coffee cup up.

Gene was still working when he passed his friend's cubicle, but he didn't look up and Aaron decided they could catch up later. Heavens knew his friend was in enough trouble with Katie as it was without him stopping to talk and making him later than he already was.

He walked on and let his feet carry the rest of him to the security station where he handed his pass and security key to a surprised guard.

"I didn't know you were resigning."

Aaron managed a wobbly smile. "Neither did I, man. I guess I'll see you around."

"Sure, Aaron. It's been nice knowing you."

"Yeah. You too."

Still a little numb, he left before he said any more. The last thing he wanted to do was to confess to the guard that he'd worked on an illegal project and had been fired. If the company hadn't seen fit to let the guy in on things, who was he to enlighten him?

He headed downtown and stopped at his local watering hole for a drink and a good hard think.

"Damn it all," he muttered. "Why the fuck didn't I leave well enough alone?"

But he knew the answer to that. He'd needed to know. Hell, he still did, and it had cost him his job.

CHAPTER THIRTY

The clip of Stephanie and Tethis slowing the meteors went viral…as did the battle that followed. Around the planet, humans caught the first real glimpse of the enemy they faced and the numbers they came in.

More importantly, they saw the two mages working to slow the meteors and received an ongoing progress report of how long it would take.

"A week?" Amelia asked her colleague and Jalel gave her a sunny smile.

"That's right, Amelia. This time next week, we will celebrate with the rest of the world because we'll be completely safe."

Her heart-shaped face had brightened.

"Oh, Jalel, that is good news."

Aaron lifted his head to look at them and was in time for a montage that started with a shot from outside the scarred and damaged *Ebon Knight*. The camera zoomed in on the damage to the newly repaired ship as it followed the meteor swarm.

After a quick pass over the ship, the view dipped through the rent in the hull and raced along corridors where men and women were busy replacing panels, checking wiring, and repairing piping.

The shortest guy in the Witch's team was in what appeared to be a data center, plotting the meteors' flight path. He looked more serious than he had in any footage Aaron could remember. Occasionally, he'd run an errand, rather like the Witch's two massive cats.

They trotted around the ship accepting packages and instructions and were given treats on delivery.

Aaron snorted. "Clever," he commented but didn't believe a single pixel.

There was no way they'd ever get cats to be that useful.

His view wasn't shared by the hundreds of children who saw it.

"Momma, I want a cat like that."

"Can I have a kitten, da?"

And that wasn't the worst of it. While he shook his head, others were inspired by the quiet efficiency of the crew working around the ship.

"Hey, mum! I'm gonna join the Navy, okay?"

"They say they'll take me when I'm fifteen."

Aaron would have been appalled—or inspired. He needed a new job. Unfortunately, he was stuck on the cats—until he saw the Dreth.

"No waaaay."

One held a— Aaron cocked his head and squinted. Was that a beam?

Whatever it was, one held it steady while the other wielded a spanner as long as his arm to lock it in place.

Shots of Stephanie and the old Meligornian followed. Together, the two of them drew magic and wrapped it around the asteroids to drain some of the speed from them and slow them.

Cheers erupted in the bar, and he raised his glass in momentary salute. Across the world, people threw their arms around each other and danced with relief. Cities declared a public holiday, while some countries called for a national day of rest.

On the campus where the Meligornians had come to teach, the students emerged from their pods to celebrate with an impromptu school get-together. It was a celebration of life and of what they were becoming a part of.

The news carried scenes from London, Dresden, Berlin, and Paris, as well as Chicago, Washington, Sydney, Melbourne, and New York. It seemed everyone was celebrating. The cameras went back to where Stephanie continued to work steadily to ensure they all lived to see another day.

"Incredible," Aaron murmured, sipped from his glass, and let the scenes on the screen draw him in. Out there was the girl he'd let BURT loose on and she was saving the world.

He had to know.

On the Teloran command vessel, the high commander surveyed the storm commanders on the screens before him.

"I am pleased."

They shifted and the movement signified relief. They had lost many ships and several more had suffered crippling damage, but he was pleased and that pleased them. None of them wanted to upset him, but they had to know.

The commander of Storm Fleet Niter had drawn the short stick and tentatively drew his commander's attention. Coming to attention, he waited until the high commander's head tilted toward him.

"The damaged ships, sir..." He struggled to find the least offensive phrase and hated the impression that the high commander found his hesitancy amusing. "How would you like us to justify them should we be asked?"

It was well-phrased, and his superior made a note to watch Niter's leader with caution.

"Our losses?" he asked, and the storm commander inclined his head. "They are worth the information we gathered. Our mission was to harry the humans and discover what they could bring to the battle."

He paused and let that sink in. "We achieved that very well. We did not lose this engagement. You cannot lose when you have more information than the enemy."

Aaron had given up watching the bar's television. Unaware of the Telorans' discussion and thoroughly tired of the rampant celebration around him, he'd ordered his third beer. As the night had drawn on, partiers heading to the clubs had stopped for a pre-dance meal or drink.

He ignored them, lost in thought as he tried to work out how he could fulfill his need to know if BURT was the rogue. People came and went on the stools on either side, so when someone came and sat beside him, he ignored her.

On any other night, he might have been thrilled by the fact a woman was seated next to him but tonight, he needed to think.

"I'll have what he's having."

Shocked, he almost dropped his beer but clenched his fist around the glass as he lowered it carefully to the counter. The pleasant buzz that had begun to build was gone. Instead, he felt as though he'd been dunked in ice.

His jaw locked in an effort to keep the fear from his expression, he turned to face the woman. The smile she gave him wouldn't have been out of place on a shark. She placed a hand over his and he flinched.

The barkeeper returned and set her drink before her, then left to attend to another customer.

Ms E leaned her head close and lowered her voice. "You couldn't heed the warning, could you?"

Aaron's mouth went dry and his mind raced. There were so many reasons why he'd done what he did and so many more excuses he could give, but there was only one real truth.

He took a sip of his beer and forced a shrug. "I had to know."

While he really wanted her to understand, he didn't think she would. In fact, he was reasonably sure she wouldn't and that he'd take his last steps when he walked out of the bar. It didn't help, though, when she didn't reply.

She sipped her beer instead before she slid her hand into her pocket and withdrew a card.

That surprised him because he had been sure she'd reached for a gun—or a knife or some other weapon—and he breathed a sigh of relief. She slid the card toward him and he looked instinctively.

It looked like an identity card—with his picture on it—and the words *Senior Engineer* printed beside it. He stared at it in stunned silence and finally registered the One R&D logo in the opposite corner.

Elizabeth raised her finger so he could read the small slip of paper on the bottom of the card. It was a number with a dollar sign in front of it. Aaron glanced at it and he looked again with a little more focus.

It was twice as much as he curr—used to make at the assessment center.

He tore his gaze from the card and its accompanying piece of paper and saw her watching him intently.

"So," she wanted to know, "how deep down the rabbit hole are you willing to go?"

CREATOR NOTES - MICHAEL ANDERLE

Thank you for reading Witch of the Federation Book 9!

Recently, LMBPN released *Rogue, Renegade And Rebel,* the first book in a brand new series called **In Her Paranormal Majesty's Secret Service**. (See the page after these author notes for additional information.)

The reason I built up this story is to play around with someone who isn't politically correct, doesn't care about politics (although she will have to get involved in the paranormal politics) and frankly just wants to do what she needs to do, and live her life.

Until she is shown how that she has been disrespected herself by someone she trusted.

Bad move on their part.

I have fond memories of some of the early James Bond and other action-adventure movies in my youth. One of the aspects of those movies that I like (remember, I'm over 50) is the sheer over the top nature of the main characters.

Drinking? We know it isn't a good idea now, but back then? *"Shaken, not stirred."*

Check.

Someone willing to be what they want, regardless of what society says is proper?

Check.

Someone who has the best stories EVER because they were there?

Check and check again. I love that aspect of Rogue. You should never know which of her stories are really about her past or something she just made up.

She is over the top, and I like that about her.

End of the Year

In about 12 hours, I'll be at Los Angeles International Airport (LAX), getting ready to head to Australia for the 20Booksto50k® event to talk indie authoring with a bunch of fellow authors.

That's on Monday, the 30th. On Tuesday, Judith (my wife) and I jump a plane to fly to Sydney to ring in the New Year. On the 3rd, we go to Hong Kong (I really want to learn more about their cinema production industry). Unfortunately, we will have to cut that trip short due to the political unrest in the city.

Las Vegas

Many of you know that I live on the strip in Las Vegas and I have a few of my series based in Las Vegas, or where the characters visit the city in our stories.

The other 'Las Vegas' of the east is Macau, and we are going to visit that city while we are on that side of the planet in a couple of weeks.

I will have more stories based in Asia coming in 2020!

Ad Aeternitatem,

Michael Anderle

Written December 27, 2019

BOOKS BY MICHAEL ANDERLE

Sign up for the LMBPN email list to be notified of new releases and special deals!

https://lmbpn.com/email/

For a complete list of books by Michael Anderle, please visit:

www.lmbpn.com/ma-books/

CONNECT WITH MICHAEL

Connect with Michael Anderle

Website: http://lmbpn.com

Email List: http://lmbpn.com/email/

https://www.facebook.com/LMBPNPublishing

https://twitter.com/MichaelAnderle

https://www.instagram.com/lmbpn_publishing/

https://www.bookbub.com/authors/michael-anderle